DAL RIADA
Craeg Phadrig
PICTLAND
Oceanus Germanicus
Dun Etin
STRATHA CLUITH
EILEAN ARAINN
BRYNEICH
Eta
Rheamhars
Dun Phris
Uxelodunum
Deas
Vedra
Hadrian's Wall
Banna
Coria
Pons Aelii
Luguvalium
UI NEILL
ULAID
YNYS VANIN
RHEGED
ELMET
Leodus
Aire
Ure
Abus
LEINSTER
YNYS MON
Caernarfon
Plas Coch
GWYNEDD
POWYS
Lindum
Trisantona
Oceanus Hibernius
CORNOVII
GWENT
Afon
CEREDEGION
LINDSEY
Caerwent
Tamares
REGNENSES
DUMNONII
KERNOW
YNYS WIHT
Oceanus Britanicus

PLACES

Banna	Birdoswald Roman Fort, Cumbria
Caernarfon	Caernarfon, Gwynedd
Caerwent	Caerwent, Monmouthshire
Cathures	Glasgow, Lanarkshire
Coria	Corbridge, Northumberland
Craeg Phadrig	Inverness, Scottish Highlands
Dun Etin	Edinburgh, Midlothian
Dun Phris	Dumfries, Galloway
Eilean Arainn	Isle of Arran
Eta	Etal, Northumberland
Leodus	Leeds, Yorkshire
Lindum	Lincoln, Lincolnshire
Luguvalium	Carlisle, Cumbria
Plas Coch	Wrexham, North Wales
Pons Aelli	Newcastle upon Tyne, Northumberland
Rheamhar	Stranraer, Galloway
Uxelodunum	Stanwix, Cumbria
Ynys Mon	Anglesey, Northwest coast of Wales
Ynys Vanin	Isle of Man, North Irish Sea
Ynys Wiht	Isle of Wight, Hampshire Coast

RIVERS AND SEAS

Abus	Humber Estuary
Afon	Avon (Wales)
Aire	Aire
Aodach	Tees
Auvona	Avon (Bristol)
Bourn	Bourne
Cluaidh	Clyde
Deas Vedra	South Tyne
Dubh	Forth
Eden	Eden
Hafren	Severn
Metaris	The Wash
Nyn	Nene
Spe	Spey
Tamares	Thames
Thuaidh	Tweed
Trisantona	Trent
Tuath Vedra	North Tyne
Ure	Ouse
Vedra	Tyne
Oceanus Britanicus	English Channel
Oceanus Germinicus	North Sea
Oceanus Hibernius	Irish Sea

CHARACTERS

Acair	Ailean the Elder's Wife, Calum's Childhood Sweetheart
Aengus	Eochaid's Brother, Dal Riada Ealdorman
Ailbeart	Soldier of Calum's
Ailean the Elder	Usurper Ealdorman of Dun Phris, Calum's Uncle
Ailean the Younger	Calum's Cousin,
Airson	Soldier of Calum's
Aniel	Drest I's Brother, Pict Ealdorman, later King of Rheged
Bane	Ealdorman of Eta, Bryneich Warlord

Bruce the Elder	Calum's Father, Deceased Ealdorman of Dun Phris
Bruce the Younger	Calum's Deceased Brother
Bwlch	Powys Soldier
Calum	Narrator, Usurped Ealdorman of Dun Phris
Canus	Rheged Commander, former Roman Centurion
Ceretic	King of Stratha Cluith, Scot
Coelhen	King of Rheged, Briton
Constance	King of Dumnonia, High King of the Britons
Constantine II	Deceased King of Dumnonia, former High King of the Britons
Daghda	Pict Druid
Drest I	King of Pictland, Scot
Drest the Younger	Eldest Son and Heir of Drest I
Eochaid	King of Dal Riada, Scot
Eoppa	King of Bryneich, Scot
Erb	Deceased King of Pictland, Drest I's Father

Fert	Cohort Captain in Nechtan's Army, Second Son of Bane
Feris	Captain of Cario Garrison, Gwent Soldier
Filib	Calum's Uncle, Stratha Cluith Soldier
Gazella	Calum's Lover
Grannd	Soldier of Calum's
Iacob	Calum's Uncle, Stratha Cluith Soldier
Lenis	Tavern Keeper in Luguvalium
Leyn	Lord of Rheamhar, Captain in Ailean's Brigade
Lupus	Lord of Leodus, Rheged Warlord
Magnus	Ealdorman of Pons Aelli, Elmet Warlord
Maoidh	Pict Divisional Master, Former Druid
Maol	Former Pict soldier, Tavern Keeper in Banna
Meadhan	Ailbeart's Sister,
Muir	Soldier of Calum's
Murdoch	Ceretic's Royal Guard Captain, later Lord of Luguvalium

Neadh	Soldier of Calum's
Nechtan	Drest I's Brother, Pict Ealdorman
Oengus	Deceased king of Bryneich, Eoppa's Father
Pefen	Dun Phris Administrator
Roinn	Pict Divisional Master
Ruadh	Soldier of Calum's
Seorsachadh	Ailbeart's Brother, Deceased Lord of Rheamhar
Sliabh	Ealdorman of Craeg Phadrig, Dal Riadan Warlord
Sti	Soldier of Calum's, Twin of Tamhas
Talorc	Son of Aniel, Pict Brigade Commander, later King of Rheged
Tamhas	Soldier of Calum's, Twin of Sti
Viopprimes	Lord of Lindum in Cornovii, Briton
Vortigern	Prince of Powys
Yaalon	Christian Priest in Luguvalium

ONE

I lay face down in the mud. Thick mud that ran warm with the blood of men - my men. I could hardly breathe but knew if I even flinched then it would be my last breath. The enemy warriors walked amongst the dead, stripping us of our armour, weapons and anything else valuable that anyone was stupid enough to carry into enemy territory. The agonising screams of wounded men in too much pain to act dead, followed by the all too familiar sound of steel slicing through flesh filled the metallic air. An eerie silence fell on that small corner of the graveyard this once lush green meadow became.

Dusk approached quickly. Should I wait until dark and then try to crawl out of this Gods forsaken place? Or wait until dawn? Our ambush was unexpected by the Britons large hunting party. The small skirmish was over quickly but they would not be able to return to Pons Aelli before the sun disappeared behind the rolling green hills. They would wait until first light, for fear of meeting a larger Scot force in the dark. The best plan of action was to wait until they had started their journey home. Then attempt to make my way toward the wall of Hadrian and out of the Brit kingdom of Elmet to avoid detection from sentries and the scavengers still plundering the dead. I was young, foolish, and overcome with a misplaced loyalty to return to the King. Someone had to report the massacre my reckless, and now dead, older brother had caused. The small raiding party lead by my father, Bruce, Ealdorman of Dun Phris were to scout the Britons, discover if the rumours of a large force at Pons Aelli were true, then return to our border taking any livestock we came across.

The rancid smell of congealed blood, urine, faeces, sweat and vomit overpowered my senses as I lay with my face still buried deep in the mud. I was surprised to find a metallic taste resting on my tongue. Today was the first experience of combat or conflict of any kind. The gory massacre was a sign from the Gods. I should have run from the life that now awaited me. Instead, as the setting sun disappeared behind the distant hills, sending the ironically warming blood-red sunset light into our history, I began my suicidal crawl back towards Stratha Cluith.

The pitch black that fell upon the horrific cemetery the field had become was a darkness I had never known before. The ground beneath me squelched as the blood-sodden mud seeped through the sleeves of my leather jerkin as I slowly slunk back toward home. I was thankful for the darkness that night. I could hear Brit soldiers or local scavengers just a few paces from where I had managed to crawl. I could hear the scuffling as they rifled through one of my dead kinsman's personal effects. I could feel the anger of such an act begin to rise deep inside my gut. I heard a deep Brit voice exclaim victory over discovering a religious pendant of silver on a departed clansman. Now was not the time to lose my temper. I vowed I would spend another night somewhere in Briton. Their mouths and nostrils' would fill with the sour soil of this foreign land. My body ached in places I had not known existed until that day. At fifteen summers, I was practically fully-grown, but not even begun to fill in places a warrior needed strength. A bag of skin and bone my father used to call me.

I halted my slow and tedious attempts of crawling through the sodden ground. My father used to... I did not know whether he was dead or alive. I Watched as King Constantine drove his hunting spear through my irresponsible brother's eye. Then the world seemed to collapse and a chaos known only in Formoria descended upon us.

I reached the end of the meadow and the bottom of the small ridge where our sixty men had concealed themselves. The sun was beginning to rise. I had crawled half a league but it had taken me all night, sapping every ounce of strength I had left. The spring dew clung to the refreshingly green blades of grass that spread before me, rising up the gentle incline to where the sun was rising. The first tender rays of dawn would soon reveal my position to the Brit sentries I had somehow evaded all night. My last ditch efforts of escape would be futile. I heard them coming but dare not look behind to see. Wait! The faint but unmistakable sound of hooves was coming from behind the ridge. I thought the untethered horses would have collected by the scavengers throughout the night. Just as I dared to look up, a majestic chestnut brown horse appeared over the ridge and halted directly above me. The commotion that arose far behind me indicated someone had spotted me, be it a sentry, scavenger, or someone who just got up to relieve themselves.

My chest felt like it was going to burst as I took a deep breath and stretched forward, grabbing the horses reins. I used the horse as leverage as I tried to pull myself to my feet. The horse faltered slightly in the sticky, blood-soaked mud, knocking me back to one knee. Get up! I heard myself screaming in my head. I must tell King Ceretic what happened. I pulled on the reins again. This time the horse stood firm and I thrust my legs as high as I could, leaning over the horse's saddle. I landed awkwardly, with my stomach smashing hard against the worn leather. The momentum of my leap carried me forward and I nearly slipped straight off the horse, back into the sodden ground headfirst. I grabbed onto the saddle edge with my left hand to keep me on the saddle. The horse must have realised that every ounce of my strength was drained from the sheer effort to pull myself this far. He slowly but steadily began to trot up the small, lush grass ridge.

So there I was, legs dangling down one side of the horse and my head dangling over the horse's shoulder. My stomach rested on my hands that still gripped the edge of the saddle, somehow keeping me awkwardly balanced. I stared at the strikingly green grass, praying I would not fall. The men who climbed that little ridge must have seen me as a pitiful sight. I was a few hundred paces away, steadily being carried to safety by this unlikely saviour, and could have easily been caught. I faced rearward and could see the small gathering of Brits on the top of the ridge, watching as I slowly trotted away. I do not know if they thought I was dead, dying or just felt that this pathetic excuse of a man was not worth the trouble. They just stood and watched as I disappeared into the distant sunrise. If only they knew who I was to become, maybe they would have ended it all. I turned my head to face forward, closed my eyes, and somehow slowly drifted to sleep, whilst my majestic saviour carried me home.

TWO

My eyelids were heavy as the world reawakened in my mind. It took me a moment to work out why I was moving and how uncomfortable I was. The sharp light from the midday sun stung my eyes as I slowly opened them. I blinked a few times until they adjusted. I swung my legs around into the saddle and sat up properly. My entire body ached, but with an uncomfortable stiffness, rather than genuine pain.

I was unwounded in the fight with the Brits. The hilt of a sword struck me knocking me to the ground. The beast of a man I charged was nearly two paces in height. My father towered over most men, standing tall at over a pace and a half, but this man dwarfed him. He fought a kinsman with his back turned from me. I foolishly charged expecting to take him by surprise.

I never charged anyone before. I knew I possessed superior sword skill for someone my age, but I was still a boy and guileless. I attempted burying the crippling fear taking a hold of my mind, telling me to run and hide, by screaming a deep and terrifying war cry. It failed. A feeble wail that sounded like a whimpering puppy trickled from my throat.

The alert giant moved fluently as I advanced upon him. He instinctively lifted his arm into a defensive position whilst turning toward the misplaced sounds direction. He caught me under the chin with the bottom of his longsword launching me backwards.

The momentum carried me along as I rolled several times before landing face down in the blood-sodden mud. That is where I stayed. The blow knocked me out of the giant Britons striking distance. He turned to face another foolish kinsman trying to ambush the seasoned warrior from behind. I did not see the result of that clash but hold little hope for the Scot. The calm Brit stood self-assured in heart of the battlefield, with his head held high as if he knew of his invincibility.

I looked ahead and saw the reassuring sight of the wall of Hadrian. How long had I been asleep? The closest Stratha Cluith sentry point was a full day's hard ride away. The clear blue sky above shimmered with an unknowing innocence. The sun directly above me beamed down a blistering light sent directly from Elada, the roguish Sun God.

The green trees lining the fields were blowing majestically in the spring breeze. There was a deceitful sense of natural peace in the air. A complete contrast to the destruction and devastation I witnessed what felt like a few moments ago. Only Balor the Blighter could descend such chaos upon the world.

I looked around. This beautiful place was not the sentry point we had come through. The horse trekked back to his home but did not belong to Stratha Cluith. I noticed four guardsmen as I approached the wall. They held white shields depicting the great black bear standing on hind legs. Bane, Ealdorman of Eta, was famous for the big black bear fur-coat he wore into battle. The image was his Emblem. The horse had not taken me home to Stratha Cluith. He had gone directly north to Bryneich. I took a deep breath as I approached the sentry point built into the great wall of Hadrian. I sat up tall in the saddle. I never travelled without my father and felt cautiously uneasy. I still ached with stiffness.

A short man, obviously the most superior of the four, stood up as I reached the passageway. He was likely the son of a nobleman, put on the wall for experience fighting the Brit raiding parties. I pulled on my horse's reins and he obediently came to a stop. The nobleman looked at me, evaluating the young boy who confidently approached the wall. He bristled as I spoke, obviously taken back from my confident manner and deep Stratha Cluith accent.

'I am Calum map Bruce Dun Phris,' I said trying to make

my voice sound as commanding as possible. Dun Phris was in Stratha Cluith, not Bryneich. Telling a foreign soldier who I was had not been the best idea, but I was still slightly dazed from my sleep. I could have turned me away. He continued to stare at me, obviously waiting for me to continue. I found myself explaining everything, despite my better judgement. As my father repeatedly stated, information is power, but I did not know what else he was waiting for.

'I was part of a scouting party sent by King Ceretic of Stratha Cluith. I have grave news from Pons Aelli which the King must hear.' He looked me up and down, evaluating the boy wearing a leather jerkin and unkempt hair, looking unlike an esteemed participant of a scouting party, or the son of an Ealdorman. He finally smiled and stepped back, waving his arm casually, as if to usher me through the stone passage.

'King Eoppa will be waiting for news,' he said as I trotted on through the passage, 'To the East.' I went through the passage expecting to see a little border village. The Romans had had many garrisoned forts along the wall. In the past few years since they had abandoned Briton they had become derelict hotspots of treachery and corruption. They were home to Britons and Scots alike. Nothing occurring in these towns escaped the attention of every Lord, Ealdorman and King on both sides of the wall. The Scots have garrisoned passages but they are tiny villages with no real defence.

I expected to see several little houses lining either side of the derelict cobbled street. They were simple single room homes of wattle and daub for the sentry points garrison soldiers. What I saw the other side of those cottages was beyond anything anticipated. This was not just a border force. All I could see was tents. Hundreds of stained and dirty fabric tents that stretched as far as the eye could see, probably further. The filthy stench of sweat, urine and manure clung to the air. It was a stench you could feel invading your nostrils and taste on the tip of your tongue. I had never experienced such a stale aroma before. It was the stench of an army. Standards' flew high on tops of the largest of marquees, showing the positions of significant Lords and Ealdorman. I had never seen so many standards, let alone so many people. A canvas city had sprung from nowhere.

I steered the horse to the east and guided him through the busy cobbled road that ran in between the cottages. I did not know why I was heading in that direction. I did not want to see King Eoppa of Bryneich. I needed to speak to King Ceretic of Stratha Cluith. He was my King.

THREE

The crowded streets got busier as I travelled east. I passed through easily as people stepped aside for my horse, heading for the largest of the marquees in the distance. The disciplined soldiers stood outside wore chainmail hauberks and iron plated Cuirass. Only the most seasoned of warriors or noblemen could afford such lavish armour and it was unusual for soldiers to wear such finery unless battle was imminent. I was looking at a royal house guard. These soldiers swore to protect the King with their lives. They always dressed for combat, ever ready to protect their King. I had found King Eoppa. A weight lifted from my shoulders in relief. I survived and returned to friends and allies.

I failed to notice the unusually high number of Royal Guards that gathered outside the canvas pavilion. There were too many soldiers for one Royal Guard but I failed to notice. Foolishly, I did not look at any of the men or their shield emblems as I leapt from my horse and approached the entrance. One of the men stepped aside and pushed the loose canvas doorway to one side, allowing me to walk through.

'Excuse the disruption Your Majesties,' boomed a familiar voice from behind me. It was Murdoch, former cohort captain of my father's at Dun Phris. He was now Royal Guard Captain to King Ceretic.
'I know you want to hear this young man's report.' He paused as he indicated towards me. The four men who were hunched over the table in the centre of the marquee all turned around to face me. Upon their heads were simple port style helmets with shortened cheek pieces, all with a thin gold band spanning

round the crown. They all wore the grandest of linen tunics and a long silk cloak of deep rich colour, the colours of the different Scottish Kingdoms. I had found myself in the presence of the four Kings of the Scots.

'This is Calum map Bruce Dun Phris,' stated Murdoch, who bowed and walked backwards out of the tent. He pulled the canvas back across the doorway sending the tent into a gloomy darkness. The harsh light emanated from four candles on a table littered with parchment. I had met King Ceretic on many occasions. He was a regular guest of my fathers, but I never spent much time in his company. He held out his hand impatiently.
'Come, boy, give it here!' He snapped. I looked at him in puzzlement. 'Your father's parchment message,' he snapped, 'pass it over.'

I stood still. My father was one of the few noblemen in Stratha Cluith, or indeed all Scot kingdoms, to be able to read and write. That is why the king often used him as a scout. He did not write a message. He was dead. My father never trusted the word of mouth.   Loyalty was too easy to fake, he would tell me. I stood there with my shoulders slouched and mouth wide open. I was in awe of the company I had found myself in, lost in a world I had yet to begin to understand. I ached, I was hungry and I just wanted to go home. King Ceretic realised something was amiss and walked toward me. He put his hand reassuringly on my shoulder and asked what had happened. The show of affection was too much for me. I started crying.

'There was a hunting party,' I started to snivel. King Eoppa walked over and encouraged me to continue. I told them how my brother Bruce the younger had seen the gold and the royal emblems of the men leading the parade. He foresaw honour and glory and leapt over the ridge to attack one of them, despite my father telling everyone to let them pass. My father followed his son and heir out of irrational loyalty, and our men did the same for my father.

The Brits only had simple hunting weapons but three times the number of men. The slaughter was over before it really began. I took a deep breath as I finished stammering and stuttering my explanation. It was by far the worst few days of my life. My world had changed in ways I could not comprehend. The four Kings all crowded around me as I spoke, looking down with no expression showing on their faces.

'So why are you here?' asked King Drest of Pictland disapprovingly. The question and its intensity confused me. 'You were not slaughtered?' He continued with a menacing tone. 'How are you the sole survivor?' The four kings were staring at me with an intensity that I could not cope with. I crumbled to my knees. My tears flooded the muddy ground beneath me.

'You are a coward, a deserter, a traitor to the crown, to your own father,' King Eochaid snarled. He spat the words with pure venom and an unnecessary hatred. As he spoke, he spat all over my face, unintentionally, with pure rage. He thrust both his hands under my shoulders and lifted me up via my armpits. He shoved me back through the canvas and into the harsh light of the pleasant spring sunshine. He snarled at me again, loud enough for the gathered crowd to hear.

'This boy is a lying coward and a treacherous deserter. He is in association with the very Britons we are here to defend against.' I had not expected such a volatile reaction and had landed on my back with my legs flailing in the air. As I tried to sit up King Eochaid slammed his leather shoe into my chest, knocking me back down. The air flew out of my lungs, as if I a mace struck me in the gut.

'I demand a tribunal,' boomed King Eochaid. He looked over at King Ceretic. He stood in the doorway of the tent, with the canvas leaning over his shoulder. 'Trial by King or trial by the sword,' King Eochaid said looking back at me. He covered my face with spittle as he bellowed to the crowd.

'Trial by King,' answered King Ceretic who stepped forward into the harsh spring light. 'I find him ...' the pause was agonising. He only paused whilst taking a deep breath but it seemed to last an eternity. I was unsure what was happening. 'Guilty,' finished King Ceretic. He looked at the ground as he spoke, which was uncharacteristic of a man who liked to give speeches to his people. King Eochaid took his foot from my chest. Two men came from behind and hauled me to my feet, holding my arms tight behind my back. I made a feeble attempt to free them but the men held firm.

'Calum map Bruce Dun Phris, I renounce your allegiance to my Royal House and the kingdom of Stratha Cluith. You claim no land or title. The punishment for dishonourable discharge is exile, after the gauntlet.' King Ceretic was still looking at the ground in the distance when he spoke. He spoke very matter-of-factly with no real conviction.

'Guard, form a gauntlet!' King Eochaid bellowed to the armoured men stood behind him. Eight men stepped forward. They all held circular iron shields displaying the green eagle head emblem over a blue backing, the Dal Riada Royal standard. They lined up in two ranks facing each other. The low blistering sun stung my eyes. They were still sore from the tearful reciting of what had happened to my father and brother, and our men. The sheer magnitude of the event that had taken place was tragic. I was naively unaware that my plight just begun.

I instinctively bought my arms forward as the two men let go of them. I stumbled forward as a heavy hand shoved me in the back, propelling me toward the soldiers who formed a passageway. The first man on the left raised his gauntleted hand, but I naturally stepped to the right to dodge the blow. I failed to notice the soldier on the right swinging a bludgeon.

The pain ripped through my knee as the wood struck but I stayed on my feet. The man on the left landed his metallic punch square on my jaw, swiftly followed by a kick in the middrift by a third man. The force of the strike drove every ounce of breath out of my body. Nausea overwhelmed me. I was falling toward the ground when another bludgeon hurtled me backwards by striking me on the bridge of my nose. I saw wet claret spray before my dazed eyes. I felt my face burst.

A hand thrust me in the back to propel me forward so the other men could have their turn. My left leg faltered and I fell to one knee. A shield slammed into my unprotected lower leg resting on the ground, the fifth strike. The shattering pain felt like the shield rim had sliced straight through my leg leaving my foot behind.

The next bludgeon strike to the back of my head hurled me forward. Once again, I lay face down in the mud. I was struggling to breathe whilst my mouth and nostrils filled with soil, but this time it was with the bitter taste of treachery. My disloyal liege lord served wrongful justice.

Someone pulled me up to my feet and shoved me toward the two awaiting soldiers. I do not recall any immediate pain as two further blows struck my body before I landed back in the dirt. As I lay, my mind adrift from my body, I closed my eyes and let the darkness sweep over me.

FOUR

I was in darkness. I lay awake but was unable to make the slightest of movement. The room, if I was even in a room, was spinning, and I felt nauseous. My mind floated somewhere above me, apart from my numb body. Was I dead? I heard distant voices, mere muffled sounds. The deep commanding voice sounded familiar but I could not place where from. The other was a shrill that pierced through me like a dagger, but the tone was tender.

'His wounds have healed nicely though,' I heard the shrill voice state.

'Good. Will he fully recover?' The deep voice replied.

'He is young and his body possesses a determined strength given only by the Gods.' It took me a moment to realise he was talking about me. I tried to sit up, move my arm, and then open my eyelids. Nothing, I could not move a muscle.

'So he will be able to run soon?'

'The linctus will keep him still for another day or so but has not eaten or moved properly for several days now. You must be patient with him as he gains his strength.' The shrill voice continued.

'Patience I would have,' replied the familiar voice, 'if I had time to be patient. The boy's uncle wants him dead Daghda.'

'Most men would be after that beating'

'Ceretic gave him a chance by sending him through the gauntlet. A trial by the sword was a death sentence. With your magic, he has a chance.' The commanding voice spoke with a sceptical tone.

'It's not magic,' the shrill voice became so high-pitched I

thought my ears were going to start bleeding. 'I am a druid, a messenger of the Gods, not a magician. I use medicine and my influence with the Gods to heal. Not magic. Now get out and let me redress his wounds.'

'Two of my men will be outside,' the familiar voice replied. 'His uncle will come for him when he learns he survived.'

I heard a wooden door slam shut and there was silence. What had I just heard? Were they talking about me? Was one of my uncles coming to take me home? I desperately tried opening my eyes and sit up but was paralysed. More questions appeared in my mind, mixing with the spoken words. They span inside the empty void my head had become, working my brain too hard. The dizziness and nausea became too much as I closed my mind and drifted back into the darkness.

FIVE

Acair was the most beautiful creature I had ever seen. The sun shone twice as strong whenever she was near. Every word she spoke was as sweet as a skylark twittering in the red glow of dawn. My heart skipped like a playful foal frolicking in a lush green meadow. Her eyes were as clear blue as the cursed sea and I often found myself drowning in them. She sat on an upturned bucket in front of me. Her long slender legs crossed to reveal some inviting flesh just above the knee.

I was in love. I had been since we played as children in my father's great hall. She moved to Cathures with her father, Murdoch, when he left to be captain of the Royal Guard. She had been a skinny little girl back then. Now I was somewhere between being a boy and a man, but Acair was a beautiful young woman. Proposed to marry my brother, the future ealdorman of Dun Phris, she found herself betrothed to my uncle.

'He is so old,' Acair giggled as we sat making fun of Ailean. He was not old, yet to approach forty summers, but too young and beautiful Acair he was ancient. She had visited me every day after I had run the gauntlet. She had helped Daghda the druid attend my wounds whilst I lay comatose. Now I was awake we laughed and joked like those lost years had never existed, but she never stayed long. Ailean would wonder where she was. He would not appreciate his betrothed visiting another man, especially the rightful claimant to his land and title. He needed me dead. Acair stood up.

'I have stayed too long,' she glanced at the door as she spoke, as if expecting Ailean to burst through it.

'Stay a little longer,' I pleaded 'It's so boring being laid here on my own.'

'I will return tomorrow.' As she spoke, she walked over to the table that was my makeshift bed and gently kissed me on the forehead. The wooden door to the cottage slammed shut as she left. I looked forward to Acair's visit every day but they always left me tired. She gave me a giddy feeling in the pit of my stomach, although that could have been the effects of Daghda's linctus. I was still very weak. I closed my eyes.

The wooden door slammed shut again. Daghda would not have returned just yet. Acair must have forgotten something. I opened my eyes and swung my legs around so I sat on the edge of the table. I was staring at a muscular bare chest. Not Acair's. It was Leyn of Rheamhar, one of my uncle's most loyal men. I froze. My mind was not as quick as usual and I did not have the physical strength to either fight or flee. So, I froze.

My windpipe felt like it shattered as his strong hand gripped my throat with force. I could do nothing as his giant arms lifted me from the table with ease. A piercing pain ripped up my spine as he slammed me against a wooden palisade in the wall. I could not breathe. I could feel the blood in my head pulsating around my skull, trying to find a way past the suffocating hold Leyn had on my throat. My eyes began to water. I felt like they were going to bulge right out of the sockets. Strangely, I found myself trying to recall the last time I went a few days without a beating. I felt the last morsel of fight left within me begin to drain away.

'Drop him,' the shrill voice had been driving me insane since I woke several days ago, but now it seemed like the sweetest of melodies. The grip on my throat loosened, although Leyn did not let go. I took a gasping breath of repulsive stale air. My lungs stung as they inflated with a rejuvenated life. Leyn still had me pinned against the wall as he turned to face Daghda.

Daghda was a small man, and although not old, stooped over with a crooked back. He leant on a stick to help with his balance. Leyn kicked out with his giant boot and knocked the stick out of Daghda's hand. He fell straight on his face. I had

25

caught my breath now. Gut retching anger surged from the pit of my stomach as I witnessed this cruel act on a man who had probably saved my life. Leyn turned away from the old man, obviously seeing no threat, to face me again.

I heard a wooden creak and saw a glistening short blade appear from over Leyn's shoulder and rest against his throat. Leyn faltered forward slightly. The man wielding the knife had forced himself against his back to stop Leyn being able to turn. Leyn was strong. He stayed upright, keeping a firm grip on me.

'Let go of the boy, and I will remove the blade,' said a familiar voice. The same I heard in my dream. 'When I step back, you take three steps sideways and leave.' The voice had a commanding authority that demanded obedience. Leyn did not say anything and did not move. The blade pushed firmer against his muscular neck. I felt his arm shudder as the sharp edge pierced his skin. His hand released me.

I had little strength in my legs. My feet hit the ground, my knees buckled and I slumped to the wooden floor. I looked up and saw the blade release from Leyn's throat. There was blood dripping down his neck, splattering all over his bare chest, as it ran through his matted chest hair. It had only been a nick to convince him the man was being genuine. It had worked. Leyn slowly stepped back three paces, then darted out of the cottage. The wooden door slammed shut as he fled.

I looked up to see a tall but slender man staring back at me. He had slick black hair and a short well-kept beard that covered most of his face. He had not had the beard the last time I had seen him but I knew who he was from his piercing emerald green eyes. The eyes of the most intelligent man my father said he had ever met. Nechtan map Erb Pictland, my saviour.

His brother, Drest, instigated the accusation of my cowardice and treachery. Nechtan wiped his dagger and placed it in a scabbard that ran down his leather boot before kneeling down to help Daghda back to his feet. When he spoke, he addressed me. My mind raced as i struggled to concentrate but a friendly face saved me, possibly twice. As long as he was close by then I would be safe. His words sliced through me like his razor-sharp blade had Leyn's thick skin. I felt alone again.

'It's time you left boy.'

SIX

He was right. Ailean knew I was alive and needed me dead. He had gained from my demise and would do anything in his power to keep wealth and prestige he thought he would never possess. If he killed me, no one had a better claim to Dun Phris. I found myself, along with Daghda, galloping down the border road heading back toward Stratha Cluith.

It was a few hours after Leyn had attacked me and the sun was beginning to set. A thin blood red line was slowly disappearing on the horizon. I hoped it was not a warning from the Gods. Nechtan had told me to stay on the border road and ride right through the night. Ailean would certainly have men watching the house, with instruction to follow and kill me. Nechtan said quite a lot in the two hours that it took Daghda to pack and ready the horses.

One thing kept creeping back into my mind. The Scots were marching on Pons Aelli. The Kings knew my report was true. The size of the hunting party we ambushed was undeniable proof there was a large force near, if not in, Pons Aelli. Nechtan confirmed the Kings believed my report but his brother was resolute in his desires to take Pons Aelli this summer. He tried to explain to me why I was treated the way I had. My accusations, judgement and punishment were a necessary public display. The Kings wanted to gain land before the Romans returned. Four summers already passed since they inexplicably left. Some Scot Kings and lords would not attack the Britons if they posed no threat. I reported enough evidence to convince the sceptical leaders that action was necessary. Force needed to be met with force. It was only a few seasons ago these men were fighting each other in a bloody and bitter war. They needed unity between the opposing Scot kingdoms and I had allowed myself to become an example. I did not understand. We walked side by side next to the wall of Hadrian. The gentle spring sun beamed down a warming light. I stopped as the sun disappeared behind a spring cloud.

'You are leading those men to their deaths!' I did not mean to sound so angry, but for some reason I was. I turned to face Nechtan, who was taken aback slightly by my harsh tone. He did not reply, just looked down at me with a sly smile on his face. 'Attacking the fortress that is holding all Briton kings and their armies is suicide.' I continued but my tone was not as harsh. Constantine II, High King of the Britons was dead. The mourning armies of all Brit kingdoms likely still resided inside. He looked at me with his emerald green eyes, waiting for me to continue. I paused. Why had he taken me on this stroll, leaving poor Daghda to pack on his own? My aching body still ailed but my wits were returning.

'Luguvalium,' I said matter-of-factly. Nechtan's sly smile turned into a menacing grin.

'Go on,' he urged. He turned around and we slowly strolled back toward the little cottages where Daghda was waiting with the readied horses.

I galloped toward a kingdom that exiled me days before, with a lame druid as my sole companion, undoubtedly chased by murderous rogues. The pace of the horses had slowed to a mild canter as the sun disappeared behind the lush rolling green hills on the horizon. The full moon shone brightly in the clear spring sky. We rode at a steady canter throughout the night and into the next day. I have no doubt Ailean sent scouts to follow us, but we saw no sign of them. If they wanted to catch us then they would have easily been able to.

We remained saddled and on the move, only stopping at passing streams to allow the horses to quench their first, before continuing with a gentle canter. Giving unscrupulous men the opportunity to take advantage whilst we rested may have proven fatal. It would not be hard to slice a blade across a boy's or lame druid's throat whilst they slept. We saw nothing to concern us, despite knowing there presence. We took it in turns to nap whilst riding. Daghda tied our feet together under the horses belly to ensure we stayed in the saddles. He had packed food and water into leather pouches attached to the front of the saddle, so we could reach them on the move.

A wave of pure relief flowed through my exhausted body as the welcoming sight of a town came into view. We had passed many small garrisons and sentry points, not stopping at any of them. Now I was staring at a fortress within the wall, with the warming orange glow of the setting sun as a backdrop.

I wondered if we were entering glorious Mag Mel, home to the gracious Tuatha de Gods. I hoped it was not the inviting gates of malevolent Formoria, where the malicious Formorian Gods plotted the fall of man. Daghda's namesake was the God that fathered us all. He possessed the ability to communicate with the same named God. Either that or he talked to himself a lot. By now, the Scots would have reached Pons Aelli and their fate sealed. I found myself praying to Oghma, the god of heroes and champion of Mag Mel.

I sat up tall as we approached the gates of Banna. My entire body ached and it was a real effort to straighten my back after riding for so long. I kept glancing upwards trying to catch a glimpse of the soldiers on watch. If I saw their shield emblem or standard, I would have a better idea of how to con my way inside. There was no household guard on the tall walls that stretched high above us, nor any guards in the sentry post. Our horses cantered through the dilapidated gates without challenge.

I slowed my horse upon approach, unsure of how to proceed. This was too easy. I knew the Romans had deserted this place but surely, someone still kept control. Daghda kept cantering down the worn stone road into the town without even a glance back at me. I took a deep breath and followed. I could not let him go into Banna alone.

Dawn of Dark Days

Lugh, the God of truth and justice, was not at Banna. The Formorian Gods had taken a firm grip of this place. I noticed Daghda staring far into the distance in the sky, mumbling to himself. I hoped he prayed for our protection, although it filled me with little confidence. My horse stumbled on the loose stones of the neglected path but she kept her balance. The dilapidated buildings reminded me of the small pile of ruins just outside Dun Phris that was now a holy shrine. The Tuatha De gods lived there before they ascended to Mag Mel above. The streets of Banna were crowded with young children in tattered rags, drunken men lying in a puddle of their own filth, soldiers in frayed leather jerkins and no   visible weapon.

We approached a tavern and I read the sign gently swaying in the spring breeze, Oghma's House. This was the place. Nechtan had warned me not to talk to anyone except his man. I knew I had to be very careful in such a treacherous and delinquent town. Loyalties are easily faked, especially in a border town open to everyone.

An old man with a black patch over his right eye leant the other side of the bar as I walked in. An obnoxious red scar ran from his missing right ear and disappeared under his eye patch. His left arm was resting on the bar. The hand was made of wood. I gasped at the hideous man. I had found Maol the mauler.

He looked straight at me when he heard the gasp. I stared back into his good eye. It was deep brown and bloodshot but there was a surprising kindly glare in it. I did not take my eyes from him as I slowly bent down and gripped the hilt of the dagger Nechtan had given me. I stood up straight making sure I held the pommel tip of the hilt with the broadside facing the tavern keeper. The deep brown eye did not blink as he gazed at the strange men who had walked into his tavern and still darkened the doorway.

The hilt housed a glistening green gemstone embedded into the pommel with a small yellow triquetra etched into its shimmering surface. I held the dagger defensively by my side, hoping he could see the emblem that showed I was an ally.

Maol haphazardly stood up straight and placed a finger to his lips. His eye busily perused the tavern as he limped around the side of the bar with an odd clump. He had a wooden stump in place of his left leg. He moved surprisingly quickly through the tavern and up the rickety wooden staircase at the back of the building. Daghda followed him upstairs and through an open doorway. I followed them up the stairs. Something was wrong. Surely, this monster could not be an ally to Nechtan. The man was glaring down the staircase as if expecting someone else to appear. I hesitated at the doorway. The man grabbed me aggressively with his good hand and flung me across the room. I skidded across the floor, colliding with a table leg in the middle of the room. Maol slammed the door shut, dropped an iron bolt barring it closed and turned around wielding a large war hammer. I had not seen the hammer until then. I found myself wondering where he had hid it. He held it with his good right hand angled across his body with surprising ease. He was a big man, with round shoulders and well over a pace and a half in height. His face was showing no expression, nor aggression, but he was not friend I hoped.

His eye darted around the room erratically. I stayed where I was, hunched over on all fours, leaning against the table leg. The exhaustion from the travel and the fatigue my battered body struggled to heal from overwhelmed me. I collapsed on the dank wooden floor and closed my eyes. I did not know what was happening but could not fight the urge to give in. I let the darkness take over and drifted to sleep.

SEVEN

My gaze settled on the ghastly red scar almost an inch thick on the right side of Maol's face. My blurry eyes stung as they adjusted to the harsh daylight, shining through the small barred window. I swung my legs around the bed as I sat up. The kindness in his deep dark brown left eye was a complete contrast to the hideous mark. He was wearing a pleasant smile but it looked more like a snarl. The right side of his mouth could not move. I had slept on and off for four days. Every time my hunger woke me, he was perched on the table edge. He was watching over me with his maul hammer resting menacingly on his lap. Daghda was asleep slumped in the wooden chair across the room, dribble running down his platted brown beard.

I got to my feet and stumbled across the room. I sat at the table and looked down at the meal in front of me. Stale bread, hardened cheese, salted dried pork and a badly bruised apple with a pitcher of water. I hungrily gnawed at the stiff bread, dipping it in the water to soften it. Since the fateful day at springs end, I was beaten, travelled or slept. My life had changed. Weeks had already past but the memories were fresh and raw. I was a vagrant with nowhere to go and no idea of what I should be doing. I am Calum map Bruce Dun Phris. I needed to start training to fight, analysing tactics and battle strategy, learning how to be a just but strong leader. I needed to acquire the knowledge to be a Lord, no, an Ealdorman. I was the rightful Ealdorman of Dun Phris. It was my destiny.

'Today we train,' said Maol in his gruff voice, as if he was reading my mind. I looked up at him as I stuffed a wedge of cheese into my mouth. 'Nechtan said to wait for him for ten days. You have slept for half of that time.' He paused for a moment before leaping from the table. He landed with a clump as his wooden stump struck the wooden floor. 'I am not sending you away to die. Today we train.'

We did. We trained for four days solid. The first three days I stood on a stall holding an old and splintered shield upright from dawn to dusk. My shoulders burned and my chest was numb. On the fourth day when I woke, Maol sat in his usual spot on the table, but held two short swords. He smiled as he placed one on the floor and kicked it toward me. He seemed possessed by one of the warrior Gods as he demonstrated the seven offensive and three defensive strokes of a blade. I knew this but watched in awe of Maol's effortless expertise. Then we sparred, or at least I tried. With one hand, one eye and a wooden leg Maol danced around me like a water nymph gracefully skimming on a lake's surface.

'It is not who wields a weapon the best who wins a fight,' he said for the umpteenth time. 'Nor the quickest,' he paused again, 'nor the most efficient defender.'

'It is the combatant who controls his mind. Allow thoughts and movement to be one. Think instinctively,' I finished the sentence for him. He grunted at my exhaustive tone and the great big grin on my face.

'It is the man who has the grace of the gods,' Daghda's shrill voice shot across the room. He sat in the wooden chair watching the lesson Maol was trying to give.

'I am trying to teach the boy to think and act instinctively Daghda,' Maol turned to face him.

'It was not your thoughts or instincts that saved you that fateful day Maol. It was my influence with the gods. Don't you forget that,' he continued reprovingly. He stood up and took a step towards us. Then he froze. Maol looked concerned too. He lifted his finger to his lips as he had four days before when I showed him Nechtan's dagger. I stood still but relaxed having no idea what was happening. Then I heard it. I slight creak of wood coming from outside, then an almost silent tap as if a leather boot stepped lightly on a wooden floor. I slowly turned on my heels as Maol lifted his mighty maul hammer across his body and rested it on his left shoulder.

EIGHT

The doorframe shuddered as someone struck it forcefully. It began to splinter on the second blow but the iron bolt held firm. Maol stepped in front of me on the third strike. Daghda was beside me with his staff gripped tightly around the bottom. A plank of the wood splintered before the panel knocked free. It flew across the room but not near where we stood.

A hand reached in to lift the iron bar. Maol kicked out with his wooden stump. I heard bones crunch before the hand pulled away. The iron bar fell to the floor with a dull clatter and the door sprung open. The first man through the door ran straight into Maol's hammer. He bought it down smashing him squarely on the right side of his face. The force flung him across the room smashing him against the wall. I heard the crash but I was not looking. I was staring at the other men running through the door.

Maol swiftly moved forward into the doorframe. He bought his hammer back up across his body striking the next man under the chin. The assailant flew off his feet, knocking two more attackers down the staircase. Screaming and clangs resonated from the tavern below where a brawl raged. Maol stepped back next to me as three men advanced into the tiny room.

I gripped the short sword firmly with both hands, angled across my body as Maol had shown me. The youngest man rushed at Daghda expecting him to be an easier opponent. His short sword held out directly in front of him. Daghda, surprisingly skilfully, faded to the left and ran his staff down the dull side of the assailant's blade. He struck his staff in his mid-drift and bought the balled end up swiftly. The blow flung the man's head forward and the staff struck him under his chin. He flew backwards landing in the doorway.

Maol bought his maul hammer across the body, dropping it slightly before contact, to avoid the poor attempt his foe made to parry. The mighty hammer collided into the oncoming man's hip. I heard the bone-shattering clash and the man crumbled to the ground. The third attacker angled his sword toward me but hesitated before his advance.

Dark fear surged through my body. I set my feet into the correct stance as Maol had shown me. I was not ready for this, but it was now or never. The noise from below had subsided slightly but I could still hear a demanding voice bellowing. The man stood in front of me lowered his sword slightly and turned his head.

The bellowing man stepped into view in the doorway. My attacker quickly glanced at me before sliding past the newcomer and rushed down the stairs. The man swiped his hand around the back of the retreating man's head, like a father reprimanding a child. The man looked at the two men lying unconscious on the floor, and then the two dead men struck by Maol's mauler.

'Well that's four fewer Scots to fight the Brits,' Nechtan said with an unusually serious tone. 'At least you are all ok,' Nechtan said, a smile appearing on his face. I dropped my sword and ran to him, flinging my arms around him in an embrace.

A show of affection was unexpected. If he marched on Pons Aelli, he would be dead by now and the relief had taken over me. He was alive and he had saved me, again. He pushed me away gently and walked over to the table. He gently kicked one of the soldiers on the ground in the back as he stepped over him and sat on the table's edge. They did not bear any standards and had a roguish bandit appearance. That did not matter. I knew my uncle Ailean sent them.

Eleven young men walked into the room purposefully

and aligned against the far wall. They formed two ranks. They looked at me with eager eyes, except the largest. He stared straight ahead with an arrogant air. Nechtan had a serious look on his face as he turned back to face me.

'The Kings agree with your plan of action,' he stated matter-of-factly. 'These men will help you take Luguvalium in six days.'

NINE

Luguvalium was roughly six leagues southeast from Banna, half a night's ride. I had five days to convince Nechtan that his idea, not mine, was destined for failure. We discussed the defensive weaknesses and state of disrepair the fortress had been in last summer, when I had visited with my father. I never mentioned a suicidal mission and definitely did not volunteer.

Nechtan marched into the kings' council upon returning from our stroll along the wall. He knew Drest's obsessive desire to capture Pons Aelli. The Romans boasted the stronghold was impenetrable and Drest wanted to prove that theory wrong. Attacking or besieging Pons Aelli right now was lunacy. Numerous Kings and warlords had been part of the hunting party we had ambushed. Their armies would still likely be inside, mourning the death of the High King.

Constantine II was the predestined commander to lead the Britons through the phase of transition. The Romans departure left Briton weak and divided but he bought all the ancestral Kingdoms together. Their hopes lay heavily upon the shoulders of the celebrated general and great consul who known throughout their empire. Now he was dead. Their ambitions of rebuilding a lost culture and creating a future to rival the Romans imploded leaving behind a sense of injustice. A soul occupied with the dark desire of bloody vengeance can empower a soldier. My brother inadvertently gave such desires to a reported twelve thousand men.

Luguvalium on the other hand was derelict. This walled town was in the Kingdom of Rheged. King Coelhen known for his extravagance did not extend his generosity throughout his

...ingdom, concentrating solely on his own amusement. His fortresses were in a dreadful state of disrepair with limited defences. Frugal pay and conditions for his soldiers meant his army diminished in size and capability.

A handful of poorly trained inexperienced boys and senile old men defended Luguvalium, his largest stronghold. The robust stone walls and durable iron portcullis gates still proved formidable obstacles to overcome. Especially for the dishevelled vagrants stood before me.

'The two big guys won't even fit,' I screamed at Nechtan. 'The moronic twins don't stop squabbling like women and the rest behave like scoundrels.' This conversation took place several times during the tiring evenings of meticulous contingency planning.

We went through every stage of the strategy. We filled the days with gruelling training sessions followed by sleepless nights. My exhausted body felt numb and my mind was in a constantly wandering daze.

'They are scoundrels,' he snapped back on the eve of the raid. 'They are dispensable men, thieves, rascals, and vagabonds. Lead by an ealdor-boy with no king or kingdom, let alone land or men.' His tone was harsh. He was getting tired of my doubting and negativity.

'Every Scot Lord, Ealdorman and King leads their men toward Luguvalium. The entire alliance is segmenting through every fort, town and sentry point along Hadrian's wall.' He looked down at me as he stood up. He spoke in a firm reproving manner.

'They are doing this to avoid detection and reach Luguvalium before the twelve dawn.' He put his hands reassuringly on my shoulders and stared into my eyes. 'You told me this plan. You noticed these weaknesses. You know a way inside and the route to the gatehouse. You stopped my brother's obsession with Pons Aelli leading to a pointless massacre.' He was showing no emotion on his face and made me feel like a reprimanded child.

'You are an exiled ealdorman with no men or supporters. Lead these scoundrels to win the kings' some land, or die trying. You don't have a choice.'

He gently cuffed me around the head before he walked away. My men sat in their saddles waiting for me. Nechtan was right. I become a hero by showing my doubters my true capabilities or I die trying. I had four armies marching towards a fortress expecting the gates to be wide open.

I pulled myself up on the horse Ailbeart held for me. As I looked around at my troop, I found myself smiling. Nechtan picked each man for a reason. Suddenly I understood why. Every man had a defined role and a purpose. We were all capable of doing what we needed to do. I clicked my heels into the flank of my horse and she steadily cantered away.

TEN

Incapacitating fear gripped my body. My heart beat too fast. In my mind, I was not a coward. I was young and inexperienced but it was my destiny to be a leader of men. Nagging doubt raced round my head telling me I was out of my depth. I would lead these men to their premature deaths. The setting sun disappeared behind the far wall of the fortress in the distance. The dank grey stone gleamed in front of the sunlit orange backdrop. The journey took less time than expected.

I thought about going over the strategy one more but they all knew it flawlessly. Reaching our muster point before the sun began to set gave us time for a needed respite. Every part of my body ached with a dull throb. I was still healing. How was I going to take the most formidable fortress in Rheged with my battered body and doubting mind and eleven ill-trained men?

I looked around in the rapidly fading dusk light. Four lads were down at the river's edge filling up flasks. Two more, the twins, were the other side of the rickety wooden bridge. They were supposed to be tying our horses to a little cluster of trees fifty paces away. They were too busy squabbling over the best way to tether. They did not stop arguing.

Muir sat at the foot of the only tree this side of the river. He was the youngest but also the biggest. He talked calmly to Ailbeart who stood leant against the trunk with his arms folded. They were the two I was unsure about bringing. They were both bigger than the rest of us despite Muir's tender age of fourteen summers. Their ability to fit through the small opening in the iron grate we planned enter by concerned me.

The Romans designed the iron slits to stop an intrusion

such as this one. The metal grid blocked the gap whilst allowing the river Eden to flow into the garrisoned town. Both men held an air of confidence that bordered on arrogance but in a calming and reassuring way. I was pleased I had been overruled.

I needed them once the fighting began. The other three men all laid down trying to get some sleep. I knew they would not be asleep. How could anyone sleep before such an audacious raid?

The sun set and left behind an eerie gloom. The full moon was shining intensely and each star sparkled with vigour, lighting the bright evening sky. Typical, we needed darkness to help conceal our advance to the wall. I stood tall, arms loosely crossed, staring into the distance.

I tried to swallow the numbing dread by repeatedly gulping, hoping the other soldiers did not notice. Nechtan advised me to appear confident despite being petrified. My warriors confidence would be greater if they believed I held confidence. I did not. This idea was ludicrous. My share of the plotting was inadvertent. I certainly had not foreseen these events unfolding. I cursed myself for mentioning this dilapidated town and the obvious flaws in its defences.

Spontaneous flames sparked the gloomy night into life as they soared through the distant sky. The three fire arrows looked like distant shooting stars. The signal we waited for. I carefully made my way down to the river's edge, leading the way toward Luguvalium and certain death.

ELEVEN

The night sky glistened with ferocious starlight. The dull shine emanating from the moon followed us as we crept toward the towering walls. We slowly slunk along the inside of the steep banks of the river Eden trying to conceal any shadows a sharp-eyed watchman may spot. Every step that took us closer to the fortress seemed to be louder. Every tiny splash as a loose pebble dislodged and fell into the river sounded like a thousand cavalry galloping across a brook. I panted as if I had sprinted a thousand paces.

I finally reached the stonewall. The night air was cool and I wore a loose leather jerkin for movability but could feel the sweat dripping from my forehead. The dread I felt earlier transformed into sheer determination for success. It was a disjointed plan dependant on the grace of the Gods. So far, the luck had been with us.

I slowly slipped into the river trying to make as little noise as possible. The chill of the water sent a shock through my body expelling the air out of my lungs. I sucked in a deep breath, held my nose, and dipped my head under the refreshingly cold water. I felt slat, after slat, after slat as I felt my way down the iron grate. The gap was not this low last summer. They must have fixed the defences.

King Ceretic rejected Constantine's treaty offer. My father met Constantine II, the Brit High King, to discuss his plans of a united land. His low opinion of the gluttonous king of Rheged, Coelhen, lied heavily within my plan. Had I underestimated his ignorance of the state of his defences?

This was the first stage of many that depended on the

Brits being unprepared. My chest tightened as I fought the natural instinct to breathe. My mind was screaming at me to kick up back to the surface. Then my left hand missed the slat and found nothing. I swung my legs around slipping them through the grate.

I kicked my legs hard and reappeared on the riverbank. My men's relief was clear on all their faces as my head sprung out of the river. I put my thumb in the air signalling for them to join me in the water. Muir was first. I wanted to make sure he would fit through the grate. I would immediately follow, then Ailbeart.

I had used my time wisely during the long journey. We galloped away from Banna, being vigilant for followers. After the first league was behind us, we slowed to a trot. Nechtan and I had discussed the plan with each man several times during the five days of training, but I needed to be sure.

Before we reach the small ford where we awaited the signal, every man recited his part back to me, flawlessly. It was important we all executed our roles to the best of our ability, and although young, we were all able competent in our skills. I was genuinely confident this was going to be a great victory. I was so naive. War is unpredictable, ambiguous and malicious.

I allowed Muir a moment to compose himself as I saw the shock of the chilled water cross his face. He smiled as he reached me, nodding confidently. He appeared arrogant but he was not. He had a self-belief in his ability that I have seen in few men. He was destined for greatness and it emanated from within. We took a deep breath together and both slowly sank into the river.

I had shut my eyes the first time. They were now open to make sure Muir got through the grate successfully. They stung with an intensity I had not expected. I could not see him in the murky water anyway. The undercurrent of the river kept us firm against the grate, which aided us. This time I was kicking the grate with my feet. Each strike sent a throbbing pain through my leather boot. My punt went through the grate. I patted Muir on the head three times, pushing him deeper each time. He disappeared through the gap with a graceful ease.

I stayed clinging to the grate waiting for Ailbeart. He was to count to ten when we had disappeared before diving down to meet me. I waited with my eyes stinging, toes throbbing, and a desperate ache in my chest. My lungs demanded air but I fought the natural urge to take a deep breath. I started to feel disorientated.

I kicked my legs to take me back to the surface as I felt a three taps on my head. I could not see Ailbeart but he knew what he was doing. My hip collided against the sharp edge of a broken slat as I slipped my legs through the small gap in the grate. I felt it rip through my jerkin slicing a small gash into my flesh. The ache in my chest and urge to breath made me panic. I pushed myself through, smashing my right shoulder on the top slat. I kicked furiously as I swam up.

I sprang out of the water with desperation instinctively gulping lungful's of air. Muir grabbed both my shoulders to steady me. If detected in this vulnerable situation, it could prove fatal and I was making too much noise. A dull discomfort throbbed in my right   shoulder under Muir's grip though he gently seized me in a calming manner.

These minor injuries might hinder my ability to fight when it began. None of us had ever fought in any hostile conflicts before. I hoped the sentries were as ill trained as my father had observed last summer. My men were between eighteen and twenty summers except Muir who was fourteen. This was my sixteenth.

Still boys really and only half had any genuine swordsmanship training. We were two arsonists, two hawk-eyed archers, a dog-whispering kennel boy, two sneak thieves lucky enough to escape the noose and four squires with a natural skill for swordplay, and me. We were prodigies with natural ability and intuition. Nechtan personally selected each man for his individual role as part of his strategy.

I remained confident despite my struggle to get through the gap. My belief in this desperate plot grew as each man appeared at regular intervals. Every time someone burst from the icy water gasping for air, we calmly and efficiently steadied him. The undercurrent was desperately pulling at our dangling legs. We kicked frantically to stop us from drifting down the river and separating. Ruadh, the last man, sprung out of the calm pool and Sti steadied him.

I stopped desperately flailing my legs allowing the undercurrent to drift me slowly into the centre of Luguvalium, oblivious to the pandemonium that awaited us.

TWELVE

Chilled water sent tingling sparks surging through my limbs as I allowed the ebb of the river to drift me toward the unknown inside the fortress. Stone steps sporadically broke the large limestone walls that stopped the river flooding the town. I drifted toward one of the sets. I struggled to take control of my arms and legs having submitted to the rivers will. I leant forward and battled to regain control of my limbs.

I inelegantly forced myself toward the staircase and gripped the cold edge. A biting chill ripped through my body as I pulled myself out of the water. I shivered uncontrollably. I was already in pain and the night was young. Ailbeart grabbed hold of my arm as he floated by. I held him against the giant stone step whilst he lifted himself free of the water. Ruadh, Muir and the twins joined us.

The other six floated past, swimming to the eastern side of the river. They were to make their way to the household guard's headquarters. The river Eden split Luguvalium into two very distinct suburbs. The affluent eastern side was made of large Roman stone buildings and cobbled roads. I noticed an instant contradiction as we headed down the muddy puddle in the place you would expect a path. I had not visited this side of the river with my father last summer. The little wooden shacks were falling to pieces. Giant patches of thatch lay on the floor leaving gaping voids in the roofs.

The streets were busier than I had expected but no one took any notice of six strangers strolling through the fort. We were visibly wet and had either a short sword or a bow in our hand. Muir carried a wood-axe, not designed for battle, but he still used it well. I did not know if we looked like we belonged or whether the town folk just did not care. I did not care. I needed to focus on what was coming next.

We approached the western gate. I imagined a raised voice challenging us as we took every step. We had to cross a small courtyard to the tower that housed the spiral steps leading to the wall. My father had noticed four guards on the walls above the gates last summer. I hoped there was still only four but even one could spot us bumbling through the courtyard.

We made it to the bottom of the steps. Me, Muir and Ailbeart carefully crept up the spiral stairwell. I froze. A guard sat on the top step looking straight at me. He did not move. Suddenly he made a disturbing guttural sound and I realised he was asleep. I took the dagger Nechtan had given me out of the boot scabbard before slowly making my way to the top step.

I carefully slouched behind the sleeping guard to look along the wall. Another man sat on an upturned bucket. He was visibly dribbling, also asleep. Two more guards stood in the middle of the wall, maybe thirty paces away, facing outward. I put my arm around the sleeping guards head and placed my blade against his throat. I was not pushing but could feel his muscular neck pulsating against the blade as he drew breath.

I took a deep breath before nodding to Ailbeart. Tamhas, one of the twins, stood on the bottom step. Ailbeart gave the signal, Tamhas in turn signalled Ruadh. Ruadh was the son of my father's huntsman and was a natural with a bow. I watched him with awe whilst he practiced over the last few days. He demonstrated his expertise far and above the other archer in my troop. He would calmly and collectively set one arrow on the ground before stringing another and bending one knee.

I heard him whistle and both guards turned around stepping to the near side of the wall to look down. The Guard farthest away suddenly flew back smashing against the turret on the other side of the wall. He landed in a slump with an arrow in his left eye.

The other Guard ducked and turned in our direction. Muir

jumped over the sleeping guard and charged forward. He waved the small wood-axe maliciously but did not use it. The man stood up straight and Muir struck him with his right shoulder in his mid-drift. He leant forward with all his weight. The guard toppled over the wall.

The sleeping guard slipped off the bucket as he woke up startled. He struggled to his knees as Ailbeart charged guilelessly swishing his short sword from side to side. The Guard managed to draw his sword and easily parry Ailbeart's clumsy lunge. Ailbeart stepped back as the guard leapt to his feet rapidly advancing upon him.

Ailbeart tried to fade backwards in retreat but he had not obviously mastered the move and stumbled over. He fell back landing with his arms sprawled above his head. His short sword skittered away clanging on the stones. The guard lifted his sword above his head with both arms ready to drive it straight through his assailant. The sword tip aimed at Ailbeart chest.

An axe flew straight over Ailbeart's head and bounced off the guards left shoulder. He paused and looked up at Muir. He had thrown the axe twenty paces and hit the target. Muir was too far away to stop him from finishing his manoeuvre. Ailbeart may have been able to scurry away or at least make a valid effort to reach his short sword, but he froze.

The dread of imminent death made him unable to move even in life-saving self-defence. The arrow was even more of a surprise than the wood axe and a lot more effective. Ruadh had managed to make a second perfect shot burying the arrowhead deep in the guard's right ear. The guard dropped to the ground landing on Ailbeart who was stuttering and weeping. Muir ran over to help him up but the deadweight of the guard made him surprisingly heavy. I ran to help and we rolled him over.

Suddenly the magnitude of what I had done hit like a catapulted boulder. I slumped to the ground. The sleeping guard was now in an eternal slumber. My men had fought grown trained guards and done well. I had given myself the cowards kill. I pulled my dagger across the guard's throat as Ruadh's first arrow sprung from the calm darkness. He had not moved as the blood spurted from the slit I had made.

The smell that now filled the air took me back to the field near Pons Aelli at the end of spring. The guard had emptied his bowels and made another guttural sound as if he was drowning. I had stayed crouched down to watch what happened on the wall. I launched myself forward to assist Ailbeart and Muir when there was just one man left and we outnumbered him. Ruadh's second arrow had already killed him by the time I got there.

I sat with my back against the stone rampart wallowing in self-pity. Just like at springs end when the Brit hunting party had slaughtered my raiding kinsmen. Like a coward. Muir and Ailbeart ran to the far turret to raise the iron gates. Ruadh joined me on the wall and fired three flaming arrows towards the shimmering moon.

My men had done the deed and performed their roles perfectly. I sat slumped to the ground hugging my knees close to my chest. The dread had engulfed me. We had completed our mission but a cataleptic shockwave gripped my mind. A sudden realisation hit hard. I was a coward.

THIRTEEN

Darkness gripped my soul. The shimmering moon quickly disappeared behind clouds. The sky glistened with stars moments ago. Now, the deep dark night emanated malice. I sat slumped against the wall with my back leant against a turret. I gently swayed back and forth.

Muir joined me as planned but said nothing. Ruadh was on the southern turret and Ailbeart on the northern. Tamhas and Sti sat at the bottom of the spiral staircase entrance watching the mud path leading to the courtyard. The Brit reinforcements would appear from there.

I sat on the ramparts having masterminded a successful overtaking of an impenetrable fortress but my mind was far away. The odour of blood and faeces had intoxicated me. The stench invaded my lungs when I opened up the sleeping guard's throat and taken me into despair. I did not know what I was doing. I needed to pull myself out of this self-loathing.

I suddenly remembered the others I had sent to the eastern side. I hoped that they were also victorious. If not then our night could only get worse. We had taken the wall but at least sixty garrison soldiers would be resting in the guardhouse headquarters. Whilst they were alive, we had not taken the fortress.

If the other attack failed then we had sealed our own fate after taking these warriors lives. The black dread kept creeping back into my mind. Our reinforcement would not appear on the horizon as planned.

I had sent half our troop to their deaths on the Eastern side. Their task was to infiltrate the prosperous side of town to ensure the off duty sentries could not reinforce the soldiers on the gate. Silencing the war dogs had to be the first objective.

Our kennel boy possessed a peculiar ability of calming the most ferocious of beasts. The large sack of chickens soaked in one of Daghda's paralysing elixirs would help. Once the dogs were fast sleep and unable to raise the alarm the two arsonists would set the guardhouse alight.

I had concerns over setting fire to stone but Nechtan ensured me these pyrotechnic experts could set water ablaze. I had watched as they spilt a thick putrid substance on a large slab behind the Oghma House tavern. The flint hardly sparked before the flames roared into life. The fire burned ferociously with a deep blue flame.

After they had soaked the inside and out of the guardhouse, no one stood a chance of escaping. If some of the luckier ones did make it into the street, the archer and two swordsmen would cut them down as they appeared. I was panicking. The guardhouse should be ablaze by now. The beautiful blue and yellow flames should be stretching into the darkened night sky singing the clouds above.

I stared into the distance hoping to see smoke billowing and a warming glow of success. No smoke and no warming glow. I looked through a turret behind me hoping to see our reinforcements galloping towards the gates. All I could see was a black empty plain.

We waited for the guards to realise something was amiss at the western gate after killing the other half of my troop. They would come with vengeance to take revenge upon untrained inexperienced lads who had killed their kinsmen. I sat with my back against the turret. Mere moments passed but it felt like an eternity.

Ruadh sprung to his feet signalling for help. I could not believe my eyes as I stood up and looked over the wall. Muir ran past me to help Ruadh push against the giant winch housed in the southern turret.

I ran to help when I saw them struggling. Slowly the cog began to turn and the winch began to loosen. Muir and Ruadh span the wheel fast enough to raise the portcullis gate ensuring they remained in control.

I ran across the wall and sprang down the steps two at a time heading for the courtyard. The cavalry had arrived. The other half of my troop had likely failed but we would not be lambs to the slaughter. Even if the guards were on their way, we would now outnumber them.

I stood in the middle of the courtyard. The dread and fear I experienced moments before vanished. My self-hatred was already a distant memory. Triumph engulfed me making me feel a pace taller as cavalrymen galloped into the courtyard.

The leading horse galloped toward me with his head down. The triumphant glee was premature. The dread and fear returned with a sobering blow. The men galloping into the courtyard were the Scots sent to assist with this impossible assault. They all wore the familiar yellow crossed swords on a black backing. They were men of Dun Phris. The man charging toward me was my uncle Ailean.

The terror vaporised as quickly as it had appeared and immediately replaced with an intense feeling of obligation. A calm but self-assured state of mind swelled with in me. The man bearing my rightful standard rushed toward me with his longsword raised maliciously.

I stopped thinking. Uncontrollable instinct surged through every muscle. I launched myself out of the way of the horse naturally rolling over my left shoulder and firmly landing on my feet. I straightened up and drew my short sword. Ailean reared his horse round and charged towards me again. I stood strong. I did not move but I was not frozen. I was not a coward and this man, a man I had once loved, would be the first man to discover this and pay with his life.

My lungs stung as cold air filled my chest. Mt heavy breathing was uncontrollable. A bloodcurdling wail erupted across the courtyard as if a hundred experienced warriors charged toward me. Tamhas sprinted past me toward the mud path. It took me a split moment to realise the wail had not been

Ailean or me.

There were more men in the courtyard than us two. The guards we expected had arrived. My uncle's audacious attack on me filled with true belief and an intense anger. My uncle had already wheeled his horse away to lead some of his men against the advancing Britons. The Britons had probably saved my life. Now I would take theirs.

FOURTEEN

Think instinctively. Maol's voice reverberated around my head. Keep your wits and you will be victorious. Maol was right. Even the most experienced warriors lose their head in combat. In the worst of disarrayed melee, the self-disciplined perform the greatest. Keeping calm and effective is not easy when the world around you descends into vicious chaos.

I stepped confidently toward the Brits consciously thinking about what Maol had taught me. The blonde Brit giant sprang into the front of my mind. I charged him on that fateful day at springs end. He appeared in a tranquil daze that day as he cut down a score of Scots single handed.

A Brit rushed toward me hacking and slashing his short sword in the air. His small circular shield strapped to his left arm angled toward the ground. As I stepped forward to meet his challenge, he flicked his blade upwards expecting me to lunge with my sword as I advanced. I did not. Feinting left, I easily slipped around his sword's tip.

He had leant forward expecting the force of my sword to strike his as he parried. I slammed the upper rim of his shield with the heel of my right boot, following through with my body weight. His right foot slipped in the muddy courtyard. As his knee stuck the sodden ground, I bought my blade back across my body. The sharp edge slid across his face slicing open a deep gash in his left cheek as the momentum of his slip carried him forward. He fell backwards with the force of my blow. I saw fear glistening in his eyes as I angled my repositioned my feet and angled my blade down. His sword arm or shield did not move as I buried the blade tip deep into the man's face.

The blade ricocheted off the bone before I yanked my arm back to pull the blade free. A thick wet crimson mist disappeared into steamed in the cool night air. I knew he was dead but thrust my sword tip through his gullet to make sure. The tip drove through his neck and scraped the hard stone courtyard underneath. I yanked the blade up but my blade hardly budged. I gripped the hilt with both hands and pulled straight up with as much force as I could muster. I slipped backwards.

An axe flew towards my head from the left. The stumble had taken me out of striking range but I dropped to one knee to steady myself. The axeman advanced quickly sensing an easy finish. The rancid metallic stench was intoxicating my lungs again but I was in control of my mind. I realised I was consciously trying to control my breathing but it was futile. I was already exhausted. My young body was battered and fatigued. I was down on one knee with my right arm too far from my body, my sword outward, leaving my head and chest wide open.

I dropped my left knee to the floor and slipped Nechtan's dagger from the boot scabbard. The axeman swung his axe toward my head. I ducked and drop my right shoulder as the menacing weapon swashed past narrowly missing. He carried through the momentum of the strike and slammed his heavy axe-head down hard onto my outstretched blade trapping it against the cold stone. He had misread my intentions. My left arm arced round aiming fast and low. The sharp tip easily sliced through his leather boot and buried deep into the flesh just below his ankle. My arm jolted as the blade scraped against bone before.

He stepped back with his left foot but instinctively raised his axe above his head. I bought my right arm up in a long and exaggerated movement hoping the Brit was naive enough to fall for the same ruse. He thrust his axe downward hard easily deflecting the short sword away. The force pushed me off balance slightly but did not stop my attack. I sank my dagger into my assailant's lower leg, below the kneecap, and then in his groin. I sprang to my feet as I kept stabbing and withdrawing the blade with ferocity. His damaged ankle gave way. He fell hard against the dank courtyard smashing his face against the solid stone.

    I continued my frenzied assault driving the small blade into the Brit soldiers back rapidly. His body squelched as his blood soaked leather jerkin mangled with his flesh. I looked up suddenly realising I had lost control of my wits. Another Brit could have been bearing down on me as I hacked my fallen foes body to shreds. Relief flooded through me. I was hurting and breathless but the fighting had diminished. A few small engagements raged on in the courtyard but the horsed riders efficiently dealt with the threats. I stayed laid across the Brits lifeless body taking short deep breaths that filled my lungs with the cold night air. I had not fought elegantly and my sword skill was far from faultless but I had survived.

FIFTEEN

My heart filled with an unexplained dread as I glanced at the entrance to the square. The warriors that charged had been the inexperienced and vengeful Brits. They fell quickly during the small melees that ensued. Their fight was over before it had begun. The disciplined Brits paused in the passageway standing shoulder to shoulder wedged between two derelict wooden shacks. The small circular iron-rimmed shields interlocked creating a daunting barrier of leather, wood and metal.

It was not a blood-curdling shield wall of thousands of well-trained warriors with the pace tall, curved, rectangular long shields, interlocking to stop the wall from breaking. Every warrior dreads that awe-inspiring sight. Yet this formidable obstacle needed to be overcome.

I watched as two Scot cavalrymen galloped toward the barricade. The horses' speckled white with sweat exhausted from the hard ride from Hadrian's Wall. I saw the panic in the chestnut brown horse's eyes as he sharply wheeled around rather than crashing into the barrier of men and shield.

The rider yanked aggressively to steer the horse back on course. The sudden thrust unbalanced the petrified animal causing its front left leg to falter. Horse and soldier crashed hard into the muddy courtyard. The panic-stricken animal anxiously kicked to regain his feet before cantering away from the shield wall.

The rider skittered across the courtyard and crashed hard into the unprotected legs of the soldiers. A brief glint of metal shimmered in the moonlight. A long sword thrust forward toward the man's head easily gliding through his right eye. The sword quickly disappeared back behind the shield wall. These were a formidable foe.

The second horseman stayed in control of his horse. Three Brits faltered just before he crashed into the wall. The cavalryman broke through at a canter. He sliced his sword downward at an expecting foe who simply parried the strike away with the edge of his shield. The three faltering men quickly regained their position as the ranks behind dragged the rider to the ground. It was a clever feint. A commanding voice bellowed over the ear-shattering clash of weapons and cries of men charging towards their death.

'Form line.' Ailean was in the middle of the courtyard. He sat tall on his majestic jet-black horse rallying his men. I had led this raid into Luguvalium and opened the gates. My uncle had now taken command.

'Form line,' Ailean bellowed the confident command again. A small rank of horses formed up beside him. An oversight of using cavalry as reinforcements suddenly became obvious. We had no shields. Horsed riders tended not to carry shields into battle relying on the speed of the horse and intelligence of the rider to evade assaults. We stood no chance fighting the garrison on foot.

The horse that had thrown his rider cantered toward me. His skin shimmered with sweaty lather as the glistening moon reappeared from behind a cloud. I grabbed his reins and pulled myself to my feet swinging myself awkwardly into the saddle. I clicked my heels into the horses flank and the horse slowly trotted toward the line stretching across the small courtyard. I suddenly remembered why this horse was without a rider.

It unassuredly wheeled round to join the rank of horses waiting to charge the formidable Brit shield wall. Ailean lifted his left hand to signal everyone else to stay before slowly trotting forward. The men directly on his flanks quickly began cumbersomely manoeuvring into a rough arrowhead formation.

The garrison numbered roughly sixty men who faced roughly forty horsed riders. They were ingeniously wedged between two derelict buildings and could not be outflanked. They stood twenty men abreast three ranks deep knowing the horses had to charge. I had already witnessed the hardships of forcing a horse towards such perilous danger. Ailean's hand dropped and the tipped formation uniformly galloped forward. I found myself adrift from the formation as the experienced cavalry galloped ahead. I watched them clash against iron, wood and flesh.

Ailean's horse flailed his forelegs shoving a solitary shield man backwards. The two horses tucked in close behind were instinctively guided into the small gaps forcing the next rank back. The cavalrymen pulled inward pushing hard and fast against the weakened fragment of the metal barricade.

The pointed formation pierced through the centre of the wall, punching straight through all three ranks. The first few horsemen galloped behind the wall. The rear ranked soldiers turned to face them. Cavalrymen forced their horses through the breach causing complete disarray amongst the Brits shield wall. The wall broke.

SIXTEEN

Anarchy ensued. The Brits started hacking at the horses' legs leaving them flailing frenziedly in the mass of blood, flesh and iron. Some men closest to the buildings had seen the wall break and fled across the courtyard towards the open gate. I wheeled my horse round and galloped towards the fugitives.

The horse instinctively curved toward the Brit as I approached the nearest deserter. I swung my sword toward the back of his head as I galloped past. I glanced behind to see him fall to the ground. He stayed face down. I clicked my heels into the horses flank as she skilfully wheeled round, aiming for another man who had almost reached the gate. The Brit suddenly paused before turning round to run back toward me.

The thunderous pounding of more horseshoes thudded against the mud-clad stone courtyard as another division of Scots galloped through the gates. A cavalryman dashed past the fleeing Brit with his sword angled at head height. The horse, rider and sword did not falter as the blade effortlessly sliced through the Brits neck. The headless Brit slumped to his knees before slamming to the ground. His head bounced in the opposite direction. I looked behind.

The last determined Brits finally broke scattering into the darkness of Luguvalium desperate to evade the onslaught. Now it had to be over. It had not been a difficult assault. The sheer audacity of sending twelve untrained men barely into adulthood through a small hole in the wall was lunacy but it worked.

Ailean broke free from the melee and darted toward me. He wore a menacing grin on his blood-drenched face. His sword confidently angled ready for a strike. I wheeled the horse round to face him head on but my heels did not kick into his flanks to signal the charge. I had seen my uncle's expertise in cavalry warfare. My body froze awaiting certain death. I watched without blinking wanting to see the blow that sent me to the after-world.

Ailean's sword arm dropped by his side as the horse's pace waned. He stopped a few paces in front of me but his focus was now on something behind me. He stared through me. The menacing grin had become a concerned frown.

'It's about time,' he snapped reproachfully. I looked around and noticed Murdoch sat confidently on his horse with the handle of his two-handed axe leant ominously over is right shoulder. He was about fifteen paces behind me with a reassuringly confident look on his face.

His men galloped by to help chase down the absconding Brits through the dark dilapidated alleys of western Luguvalium. He calmly dismounted from his horse and strolled over to me with his heavy axe held firm by his side. His reassuring confidence abruptly faded into unfathomable concern.

Without saying a word, he walked to the side of my horse and placed his axe head onto the ground. I felt the blood from my head drift down my body. Nausea overwhelmed me. The world span uncontrollably as slipped from the horse.

I fell inelegantly into Murdoch's readied arms. He cradled me like a baby as he walked towards the mud path that led to Eastern Luguvalium. The dizziness was uncontrollable. I felt myself gag slightly as I began to vomit. My battered body was submitting to the overwhelming fatigue I had felt for so long. I knew death was upon me. I closed my eyes allowing my father's friend to carry me into the after-world.

SEVENTEEN

It took eleven days for the four armies to arrive at Luguvalium. The cavalry had all cantered through the Western gate before sunrise the following morning. The filtration through the numerous towns and garrisons to avoid detection was an ingenious manoeuvre.

Any unusual movement of armed men near the wall inevitably reached the ears of various kings and lords either side of the border. By the time the news reached the right authorities, Scot sentries guarded the walls of Luguvalium.

Most cavalrymen are sons or kinsmen of noble lords, chieftains and champions. They rode straight into Western Luguvalium and quickly took residence allowed the Roman Brits to flee. They harried them to leave quickly with a sinister motive. The Scots plundered the stone buildings, dug in the flowerbeds and upturned the mosaic floorings. The ransacked the wealthier parts of town but did it discretely.

If the unscrupulous shield men reinforced me then different scenes would have unfolded over those few days. They are Gods fearing fighters whose daring and deeds hold no bounds as the frivolously throw themselves to the mercy of the gods by charging at shield walls. They are moulded into monsters of destruction and chaos, trained to be aggressive and unforgiving. It is their way of life. They possess a belligerent and antagonistic inclination for rape and pillaging. These vultures and delinquents are the very men I want to stand next to on a battlefield but I do not sanction the aftermath.

Minor discrepancies did occur in the lower parts of western Luguvalium and three men ran the gauntlet as examples.

The poorer citizens of western Luguvalium did not flee and were not harassed. We were not welcomed but we were not disregarded either. They did not seem to care who was in their town as long as we paid our way.

Murdoch and his men stayed in western Luguvalium and encouraged the soldiers to behave admirably when they arrived. This war was not about plunder and nonsensical raids. The civil war stopped three winters earlier for one reason. The Romans officials and armies had left. Defenceless Briton would soon be part of a new Scot empire. This was not war. This was conquest.

Fire burnt through my outstretched arms. The throbbing discomfort in my shoulders subsided after the first four hours to leave an empty numbness as if my arms no longer attached to my torso.

My aloft shield depicted a yellow triquetra on a green backdrop, Nechtan's emblem. My men stood beside me in the second rank of the formation. I always classed my father's men, the men of Dun Phris, as my men. I looked along the line and saw the faces of Ailbeart, Ruadh, Muir and the squabble twins amongst the eleven under my command.

An immense feeling of loyalty I had never experienced before overwhelmed me. It still haunts me that the other six men I sent to assault the guards quarters did not survived that night. Nechtan recruited the remaining survivors placing us in the ranks of their newest commander, Prince Talorc map Aniel Pictland. He was Nechtan's nephew and proven himself capable enough to warrant command.

The early summer sun blazed in the clear midday sky. Sweat poured down my face smarting as it entered my eyes. The young prince stood in front of us holding his glistening shield aloft with a display of ease. He was roughly twenty summers but dwarfed most men standing well over a pace and a half.

He bellowed the command to stand easy with natural authority in his voice. Some men around me groaned as they lowered their shields rubbing numb, aching parts of their bodies. I slowly lowered my shield by regulation and was pleased to see my troop follow the example.

They were young, but had a natural discipline essential to me as I learnt to lead. I beckoned my lads over after the command to fall out. We had stood on that training square from dawn to midday. Although stiff, sore and exhausted we had all stood firm. The six infiltrators of Luguvalium found an instant comradeship that only forms from arduous situations. For the first time in weeks, my body was not healing. I felt strong and able. I felt like I belonged.

I finished my brief by congratulating my men on their discipline. They began rushing back to the tavern we had discovered on the first night. There was not enough room inside the walls for four armies so most infantry brigades were encamped in the plains outside. The tavern keeper, Lenis, welcomed men with money despite the fact we were Scot. I had my first real taste of ale in that tavern and my first real taste of a woman's love.

The portcullis of the eastern gate began to grind open. All the brigades had already arrived except the one I dreaded. King Ceretic's royal brigade elegantly marched through the gates and into the training square.

EIGHTEEN

My heart raced. Doubting dread rose from the pit of my stomach. Most of my men had marched away. Only Muir and Ailbeart stood beside me. I was glad my new followers would not see this, whatever this was going to be. King Ceretic had banished me from his lands and service. Nechtan had arrived just two days after the raid and I sought his advice immediately.

'I need to leave,' I began without any greeting 'before the Stratha soldiers turn up.'

'You will remain here' Nechtan's carried on walking as he spoke. He did not even look at me. The mid-afternoon early summer sun blazed in a clear blue sky. Sweat visibly dripped from Nechtan as he marched with his men dressed in his full leather attire. He determinedly carried on through the busy cobbled streets of western Luguvalium.

'I am banished...' I began making my case but he interrupted immediately

'...From Stratha Cluith.' Nechtan finished my sentence but quickly continued. 'This is not Stratha Cluith and you are now in my service.' He looked at me with a kindly smile but I realised this subject was not up for discussion.

'Report to the main square outside that great white hall at sunrise with your men. Talorc is your new commander. Now, take me to the nearest tavern, I need a drink.' He slapped my gently on the back. I gave no reply.

I practiced my speech about being in danger and needing to run away for hours. For some reason all of my anxiety about being in the same walls as Ceretic vanished after Nechtan's dialogue. I was his man. Nechtan was one of few Ealdormen granted the privilege to raise his own army. The three sons of Erb, who were Drest, Aniel and Nechtan, all had their own loyal men. My father was the only Stratha Cluith Lord to hold the command of more than one brigade.

The final division marched through the gates in a box formation. This indicated a man of importance was approaching the town to the sentries on the walls. The main purpose of the manoeuvre was to protect the dignitary the closing ranks surrounded but threat remained in Luguvalium. Ceretic liked to put on a show. His shining white armour made him easily visible through the mass of silver chainmail his guards wore. He always imposed a majestic figure.

The training square shuddered as the entire brigade turned swiftly on the command to fall out. The soldiers quickly dispersed to find the nearest tavern or brothel. I felt a sudden uneasiness as his heated gaze fell immediately upon me. Ailbeart and Muir stood beside me chatting casually unaware of the terror that engulfed me. I felt alone as King Ceretic began to advance toward me. For an unknown reason I obediently stood to attention awaiting my next reprimand.

I stood in a foreign army wearing an emblem that was not the Dun Phris crossed swords suddenly feeling like a traitor. In truth, I never vowed any allegiance to Ceretic but Dun Phris was my home. I will always retain a certain degree of natural loyalty. Luguvalium was not in Stratha Cluith so my banishment had not been broken.

As a king Ceretic needed no reason to punish or kill me. I was a foreign soldier now and his actions might evoke the wraith of Nechtan, therefore Drest. They led their opposing armies in a bloody and bitter civil war just a few years ago. The fragile truce remained bonded together with a greater opportunity of invading the south. There was no point fighting each other over small territories when they could conquer and divide every kingdom in the land.

Ceretic showed no emotion as he briskly marched toward me. I flinched as he slammed his foot into the stone courtyard that was caped in dry dusty mud. I thought he was going to march straight into me and knock me down but stopped with his face a mere inch from mine. Our noses almost touched. His icy stare was unsettling but I dare not move.

The last time I saw the man he had me beaten. Daghda suggested it was a warped type of kindness and a trial by sword would have undoubtedly been a death sentence. It was not much of a comfort to me. Ceretic sprayed a warm fleck of spittle across my nose as he cleared his throat.

'Well done boy. This was a great victory.' He spoke matter-of-factly but it was not short. The heavy weight in my heart dissipated. I struggled not to smile. The glee I felt showed on my face as he continued. 'Your exile from Stratha Cluith is negated.' He stepped back slightly but continued to look into my eyes with a stern look on his face as he spoke. 'Stay away from Dun Phris. Pictland is a good place as any for a lowly soldier.' He turned and walked away followed by the four guards that remained inches behind him at all times.

Ceretic immediately stripped any glimmer of hope away. My conviction for treachery and desertion was overturned but it changed nothing. He did not intend to reinstate me as the ealdorman of Dun Phris and demonstrated his resolve by calling me a lowly soldier.

The Kings ambitions required experienced and renowned leaders so my uncle would keep Dun Phris. Ceretic knew of Ailean's dark desires and attempts on my life otherwise he would not have warned me away. I had given the kings the greatest fortress in Rheged but my life still meant nothing to them.

NINETEEN

Ailean's men followed me throughout Luguvalium but I ensured I was never alone. The town was bustling with soldiers and citizens. Any ruckus in an overcrowded fortress inevitably bought witnesses. The likelihood of me surviving this conquest was not in my favour and the Brits would probably do Ailean's bidding for him. He still sent men to watch my every move. I knew Acair was in Luguvalium to marry him and I wondered if the surveillance was because of her presence.

Neither Muir nor Ailbeart said a word as we walked down pathed road and over the bridge into western Luguvalium. The dusty dry mud casing the cobbles billowed into filthy mist that caught in your nose and throat. Our heavy breathing eased as we left the filthy stone road behind and entered eastern Luguvalium.

Thousands of Scot soldiers had churned the muddy causeway into a thick slough that rose to your ankles after every difficult step. The majority of infantry warriors slept in encampments situated outside the walls but they spent their days and their money in the filthy streets and alleys.

My entire troop was crammed into a small room above a tavern. It was awkward cramped but a lot better than an encampment. Lenis welcomed us wholeheartedly on the first day after the assault. Tavern keepers regularly let spare rooms out to soldiers especially in times of occupation. Resident soldiers usually meant less trouble caused inside and Lenis could save a fortune in damages and unpaid tabs. His beautiful daughter welcomed me in her own way just a few nights later.

Gazella had taken my hand after I had closed the door behind the last soldiers to leave. She placed the bolt firmly in place before shoving me hard against the door. I tasted salted salmon as she thrust her tongue into my mouth. I had never been with a woman before and I think she realised quickly. She spent considerable effort in guiding as we made love on the hard damp wooden floor. The memory of her gentle touch sent a rush of blood surging through my body. My heart pounded with excitement as I reminisced about every moment we shared. The sign depicting a poorly painted man wearing branches on his head billowed gently in the wind. Gazella told me the tavern was called *Domus Rex*. I laughed as I translated the name, the king's house. '

What sort of king has leaves in his hair and lives in a run-down shack?' I had jested.

'The great Kings of Rome that defeated your ancestors.' She jested back. She was a clever as she was beautiful and was funny with it too.

My stomach swirled and I became light-headed as I walked through the door. Acair sat at a table in the corner with her father, Murdoch. It was unusual for a woman or child to be in a recently occupied fortress, especially so quickly. Some men insisted on their companions keeping them company and Ailean was one of them. His men followed Acair everywhere. He had not been a cautious or controlling man but the unexpected power had obviously made him anxious. I purposefully made my way to the other side of the tavern where the twins sat with two of my newest recruits. There was no point in aggravating Ailean further. He would succeed in killing me or I would grow smarter and stronger and reclaim my birthright. I knew what I believed would happen. Just bide my time.

Gazella wandered over with a spring in her step and placed two jugs of ale heavily upon the table. She smiled modestly before skipping away. A pang of guilt crept into my mind as she went. She was naturally beautiful and her childlike innocence was endearing. Her playful nature meant she went about her day not worrying and stressing. A foreign army occupied the town but she acted as if nothing had changed. I needed some fun and joviality

My heart had longed to Acair for too many years. I cried for days after she moved to Cathures a few summers ago. We were children then. Now I was a man and the woman that possessed my heart was married to a man that wanted me dead. I sat admiring the lady I loved from afar hoping one day she would be mine.

My gaze shot to Murdoch, her father. Why had the Royal Guard Captain led the Stratha Cluith cavalry the night of the assault? He should never leave the kings side. Murdoch was in high spirits these past few days. I thought it was because his eldest daughter with him. Was his joy a ruse to hide his demotion? Something was amiss. Many promotions and movement of titles occurred in those few days. The kings planned for more townships and land so needed trustworthy and capable captains, lords and ealdormen. My thoughts drifted my attention. I looked back over at the table across the tavern but Dal Riadan warriors occupied the table.

'See you later boy,' Murdoch said appearing next to me. 'I've been called to the Kings council.' His smile beamed across his face. He was rocking back and forth dying to tell me something. He did not tell me. He turned and walked away. Acair kept her distance from me but waved meekly from the doorway. She gave a coy smile as she turned to follow her father. My heart ached as I watched her go. The tavern became gloomier the instant she closed the door behind her. A dark shadow cast over us.

TWENTY

A huge fist flew over my shoulder and smashed down on our table knocking everyone's drink flying. My men groaned or shouted as we stood up to confront the culprit. It was Leyn. He slouched over slightly leaning on the table staring across at Ailbeart. It made sense to watch him. Ailbeart was the biggest man and looked the most formidable. Leyn was lord of a Dun Phris small town, Rheamhar. His highborn status suggested he could hold a more authoritative position, but he was loyal to Ailean. The third iron band on his bare arm indicated his loyalty had been rewarded. His reputation as a fierce warrior and lord of Rheamhar far out-weighed his social station.

The two men stood behind Leyn did not look at Ailbeart. Their attention fixed solely on me. Several other Dun Phris warriors had covertly surrounded us and now stood around the table. It dawned on me that I no longer had any loyalties in Stratha Cluith or Dun Phris. Ailean's stare showed mixed emotions. His deep glare filled with anger and frustration did not mask the fondness that we once shared.

Pefen's stare was cold and calculating. The sullen look he always wore on his thin long face made appear to be constantly sulking. His icy gaze showed distaste for me. He had been my father's administrator and had obviously retained the authority under my uncle. His main role was to maintain law and order throughout their lord's lands particularly in his absence. Administrators rarely leave the province of their authority. What was he doing here? Pefen was a scheming vengeful soul. My father said as much. He warned me Pefen's ambition deeply outweighed his abilities. He told me to keep a close eye on his motives and actions. I found myself wondering if he was serving my uncle or the other way round. Pefen spoke first, strengthening my resolve.

'Celebrating your acquittal, boy?' Pefen sneered with derision. 'You may have fooled the Picts but we are no imbeciles, boy.' He started wagging his finger at me like an old maid telling off her subordinates. I had control of my wits. I knew I had to stay calm. My heart raced and my eyes darted round trying to take in everyone's position without moving my head. I felt my hands become clammy and hoped I was not visibly sweating. I thought Ailean was not stupid enough to confront me in public. Especially during the biggest offensive planned against the Brits in centuries. He was trying to goad me so that I became the aggressor.

Pefen puffed out his chest and lifted his head as spoke again. He was talking loud enough for everyone in the tavern to hear but was not shouting. 'You are a cowardly deserter who hid during the raid into Luguvalium. The Ealdorman of Dun Phris intervened to snatch victory from the jaws of defeat. You vagrants should thank him.' He stopped glaring intensely. His devious beady eyes were hastily switching between the seven that stood around the table. None of us spoke or reacted in any way. 'We will be watching you, boy, and your pretty little pups.' He sneered at us as he spat his insult.

My disciplined men held there nerve but remained ready to react. I had confidence they would follow my lead. I watched all the Dun Phris warriors whilst listening intently to Pefen's failed attempts of provocation. The crowded taverns attention turned to the scene   unfolding before them. I had an abundance of witnesses that they initiated this exhibition. Two can play this game. I took a slow deep breath and relaxed my posture. I stared directly at my uncle ready to take the first blow. My men would retaliate if needed.

'Is the Ealdorman going to speak or is he scared to confront me personally?' I paused for a moment hoping I could continue. Ailean was clearly irked but he retained his composure.

'Maybe that's why your wife keeps seeking me out after only five days of marriage.' Ailean's face distorted as he struggled to keep his nerve. His shoulders tensed and his fists clenched. He would have witnessed my flirtatious exchange with Acair a few moments ago. Pefen had not expected the swift retort. He opened and closed his mouth not sure whether to respond for Ailean. 'If you do not mind, we pretty little pups are trying to enjoy a quiet drink.' I calmly pulled the stool behind me to make sure it was still there before sitting back down.

An intense rage ignited by Pefen surged through my veins. My fists clenched and I could feel deep anger bubbling in the pit of my stomach. My uncle had not saved the Luguvalium assault from defeat. He led the cavalry charge against the garrisons shield wall that secured the overtaking of the fortress but my covert infiltration had been a crucial factor in the success. Ailean's facial expression change when his provocation failed. I began to learn a vital technique in controlling my notorious temper. My father tried to teach me restraint throughout my childhood and his words regularly appeared back in my mind. Control aggression and use your wit. Own your rage, twist it and turn it into determination. Ailean took a deep breath and turned away.

'Be careful nephew. A battlefield is no place for children,' he said calmly as he walked away.

'Sleep with one eye open boy,' there was a menacing tone to Pefen's voice. He followed my uncle. Leyn gave a deep guttural grunt as he stood up straight. He glared with intensity at Ailbeart attempting to goad him into action. He snorted in frustration before stomping after them. The Dun Phris soldiers walked out of the tavern slamming the door behind them.

Lenis kept away from the situation not knowing if it would erupt but quickly appeared with a tray of fresh pitchers of ale. Townsfolk never made money during occupation but the orders quickly passed down the chain of command. Invading warriors ate, drank, stole and screwed anything or anybody they wanted but not in Luguvalium. Every man paid their way and the kings' law kept. There was strategy embedded heavily in these new procedures. The local merchants and tavern keepers thrived and welcomed us warmly. They could make a small fortune as long as the clients behaved. Good business could back fire if a brawl broke out between the soldiers in their tavern, causing mass destruction. We watched over the Domus Rex tavern ensuring everyone paid their debts and behaved. In turn, the kindly old man looked after us.

Ailbeart's stare at Leyn could fuel the fires of Formoria for eternity. His eyes were red and sore from the intensity. Did they know each other? He picked up a pitcher and noisily guzzled the ale pouring most of it down his matted beard and splattered it onto his leather jerkin. He swiftly sat down with a thud and slammed the finished pitcher back on the table with controlled rage. I had never seen him irate before. I realised other men had ongoing disputes. I would wait until the dust had settled and then ask him. His shoulders relaxed as he picked up Muir's pitcher.

'Pretty little pups can't handle ale,' he jested as he gulped down Muir's drink. The tension evaporated and laughter erupted around the table. Daghda joined us and we drank the afternoon away putting the world to rights. Unaware that the kings were holding council slowly pulling the threads that held this world together.

TWENTY-ONE

The euphoric ambience of the tavern vanished as the door flung open and crashed against the wall. Several Bryneich troop leaders bustled into the tavern barking orders to any Bryneich warrior or emblem they recognised.

'Form up outside the western gates,' one of the troop leaders snapped as he pulled a soldier known to him up from his stool.

'What? Why?' asked a Bryneich warrior with two arm rings.

'We march home, master,' answered the cohort captain who supervised the evacuation from the doorway. The divisional master who asked the question stood up and began ushering men out of the tavern. Troop leaders dragged drunken soldiers who tried ignoring the command off their stools and outside by their jerkins, limbs and hair. An eerie tension swarmed across the gloomy room. The Cohort Captain who had kicked the door open darkened the doorway scanning the gloomy room for any missed men. I recognised him but could not recall the name. The other Scot soldiers tried to look away pretending nothing was occurring for fear of mistaken identity during the swift frenzy.

The captain, sufficiently satisfied all under his command had left, hastily turned and crossed the road into the next tavern. Men stood up and took a few paces toward the door to discover the cause of this spectacle but dare not approach too close to the door. A flow of soldiers marched through the mud swamp street. Murdoch stomped toward the tavern. The idyllic expression he wore a few hours ago had changed into concern.

'Calum, return to the Eastern side.' This was not a suggestion but an assertive command. He gripped the back of my jerkin and lifted me from the stool. I had been drinking all afternoon and was too intoxicated to register the seriousness of the situation. I fell to the floor as he loosened his grip expecting me to stand. He bent down and picked me up with both arms under my armpits. I felt the panic in his voice and realised he was shaking as he spoke again. I unsteadily found my feet and looked at him unsure I had heard him correctly.

'The truce has broken. Ailean's men are coming to kill you.' Murdoch's words were a sobering blow of bewilderment. I was in a muddled daze as Lenis ushered me toward the back shoving me through a doorway at the rear of the tavern. I stumbled into a gloomy alley almost slipping in the slushy mud. He pointed toward the east and muttered something about reaching the river's edge. We struggled and clambered through the boggy alleyway sloshing through the ankle deep mud hindered by our drunken state.

Shouts arose from behind before we had fled two hundred paces. I did not need to turn to know they were Dun Phris soldier's intent on killing me. Murdoch pushed an intoxicated Tamhas gently in the back urging him to speed up but he slipped in the mud even more. None of us was in a fit state to run or fight for our lives and Ailean knew this. He would use whatever this situation to kill me. Everyone else was more concerned about escaping the murderous men behind us but Murdoch's words had stuck in my mind.

If the alliance had failed then everything was about to get complicated. Men switched allegiances due to promotions and dreams of expansion. My mind flooded with consequences. It was an invigorating but extremely unsettling time to be a Scot warrior. All the Scot kings tussled for control as we extended our territory. The recent war began when King Drest appointed himself High King of the Scots. He was a ruthless warmonger and able strategist but so were Ceretic of Stratha Cluith and Oengus of Bryneich. Oengus was Eoppa's father. He had been

King of Bryneich when Drest had appointed himself as High King in an attempt to rally all Scottish kingdoms together. Constantine II had united all the Brit kingdoms, and possibly some Welsh, by the same method. Drest's attempt to ally the kingdoms and stop the imminent attack from the age-old nemesis failed. Instead, he instigated a bitter and bloody war. Some wounds were fresh. There was vengeful mistrust submerged deep below the surface of the delicate truce.

We reached the river Eden at the end of the alleyway. The clear fresh water shimmered in the glistening sunlight with dishonesty. I knew how dirty the faeces invested water was. We ran down the muddy track adjacent to the river next to the stonewall gazing at the calm deceptive water. It dawned on me. Kings, Ealdorman and lords appeared noble and righteous on the surface. Their expensive armour and baubles glistened in the sun like the river Eden. Underneath dark and devious currents flowed aiding their ambitious and greedy schemes. This game of deception and underhand treachery was a world I had thrust upon me. I had lost wealth, honour, prestige and my identity because I was unwittingly playing the lords game of deceit.

A shimmering light shone intensely in the distance as the town bridge came into view. The warm inviting glow emanated a sign of hope. My stomach rolled as anger boiled up inside me. I had allowed myself to become a fugitive. The inviting glow was one deception too many as my intoxicated mind snapped. The suns glare reflected back from twenty shields interlocked expertly to block our escape. I would kill every Dun Phris warrior stood in the menacing shield wall blocking our path.

TWENTY-TWO

My legs were not working as fast as my mind. I was running behind Murdoch who stopped twenty paces from the shield wall. My sword unleashed a dreadful scraping noise as she slid from the scabbard. Murdoch continued to look straight ahead toward the daunting blockade but swung his right arm out and grabbed me by the front of my jerkin. I jolted to a stop and stood up straight. I held my sword with a firm grip trying to control the rage blazing within. *Fight with your mind.* I found myself repeating in my head. I took a deep breath and relaxed my shoulders. Murdoch ordered me to stay before slowly letting go of my leather top. He bellowed a command to the awaiting foe.

'I am Lord Murdoch of Luguvalium. In the name of King Aniel of Rheged I command you to clear these streets.' He spoke clearly with genuine authority but what he was saying was not true. Aniel was King Drest's brother and was an ealdorman of Pictland. Murdoch was King Ceretic's guard captain. It was rare for a lowborn soldier to reach the heights of captain but a leap to Lordship was unheard of. I now understood the reason for the breakdown of the truce during the Kings council.

The wall began moving towards us a quarter paces at a time in an expertly accomplished manoeuvre. Murdoch quickly glanced behind but immediately turned back to face the advancing shield wall. His sword made that heart-sinking scrape as he withdrew it from his scabbard. I looked behind and saw the men that pursued us had formed a shield wall to block our escape. The buildings to the right and the river Eden to the left trapped us between two advancing shield walls. We numbered twelve but eleven were in no fit state to fight. Murdoch ordered us to stay before slowly walking towards the advancing warriors. I ordered six men to stand back to back with us to give eyes on both shield walls. Murdoch spoke again as he fearlessly stepped toward the oncoming shield wall.

'I am Lord Murdoch of Luguvalium. Clear these streets. Any law breaking will be severely punished. No Scot is to be harmed within these walls.' He spoke with natural authority. He stepped forward at the same pace as the advancing Dun Phris warriors. He was two paces away when he halted. He was going to get himself killed, and only a few moments after becoming a lord. The shield wall took another step and then stopped within striking distance. A Dun Phris soldier could simply slip his longsword out from overlapping shields and cut down the newly appointed Lord without much bravery required. I immediately checked myself as I took a stride forward. It was too late to go to his aid now. I glanced behind quickly to see the rear wall was still advancing toward us but were roughly a hundred paces away. Murdoch was commanding the men to clear the streets again with his sword lowered by his side, angled correctly.

'Our Lord is an Ealdorman,' interrupted a confident reply from somewhere in the left side of the shield wall. It was not bravery or confidence to make that remark in such an imposing situation but possibly foolish. 'You cannot overrule his command. We are here to execute traitors and murderers and kill anyone else who wrongfully defends such men.'

Even from fifteen paces away, I saw Murdoch's shoulders tense as he lifted his sword up vertically and took one pace back. The shield wall received no order to halt, yet every man faltered before reaching Murdoch. No one was brave or stupid enough to take on Murdoch despite the obvious numerical advantage. All of my men were in leather gaiters and leather jerkins or hauberks but Murdoch was dressed for war. He donned his polished brass plate armour to attend the kings' council and was a daunting figure to oppose even for the most seasoned warrior.

'The piss sodden maggot that dare utter such twaddle

will step forward and prove your worth.' I never heard such anger in Murdoch's voice before. 'Defeat me in single man combat and the gods have spoken. You may carry out your orders. If you do not step forth then every man here will die.'

The likelihood of Murdoch being able to carry out that threat was minimal. Even the most skilled swordsman would need the grace of the gods to slay twenty well-armed trained soldiers formed into a shield wall single-handedly. The threat worked, a tall soldier stumbled forward. A man on his flank not wanting to be executed pushed him forward. Loyalty is fickle.

The man straightened quickly and moved toward Murdoch with an air of confidence he would unlikely of felt. Murdoch was an ageing man but a highly skilled swordsman and known throughout Dun Phris. His age would slow him down but his experience more than made up for that. I recognised the approaching soldier as one of my father's troop leaders. The second bracelet on his arm indicated my uncle had promoted him to divisional master. He commanded forty men, which was every man in both shield walls. He spat at the ground as he glanced in my direction with true derision in his eyes before approaching Murdoch. I once considered these men of Dun Phris as my own but they believed I was responsible for my father's death. The Master stepped toward Murdoch with assurance and I realised I may soon be responsible for Murdoch's death.

Both men angled there blade toward the opponent but Murdoch's stance was shorter and wider than usual. He struggled to recover from fleeing from the tavern in his armour. I feared the worst. The blades collided issuing a resonate clang loud enough to be heard throughout the town. The master easily parried Murdoch's first lunge. His reacting strike was low as he followed through with the parry allowing the blade to fall toward Murdoch's hip. Murdoch gracefully sidestepped and struck the man's wrist with the hilt of his sword. The man's wrist bent slightly allowing Murdoch to bring his sword back toward the master's face. He saw the manoeuvre and stepped backwards. Both men bought their swords back angled slightly upwards emanating another clatter as they collided.

'Seize!' The command originated from behind me. The two combatants stared at each other but lowered their swords before both stepped back. I looked around to see the shield wall dispersing about fifteen paces behind us. Riding through them was the new King.

TWENTY-THREE

I cannot explain why the warriors stopped fighting on a single order bellowed from such a distance. The authoritative command resonated against the mud and thatch buildings lining the street on our right flank. Neither wanted the contest but could not show weakness whilst carrying out their duties. A wave of relief crossed both men's faces as the tension diminished. My men stepped aside to allow King Aniel's horse through as he casually trotted towards the two combatants. The horse stopped obediently without any obvious command from the rider. King Aniel's back blocked my view of the Dun Phris divisional master.

I panted heavily and my head was spinning. Last time a king decided my fate I had ended up disgraced and beaten, fighting for my life. I lost my titles, wealth and allegiance through no fault of my own. This spectacle was my fault. These soldiers were following orders to kill me and I had allowed Murdoch to take my place in a spontaneous trial by the sword. I was a coward and a fraud standing at a distance watching the conclusion unfold. King Aniel skilfully turned his horse to be facing Murdoch forcing the divisional master to step a couple of paces back as the horse's rear leg bumped him out of the way. The King was addressing Murdoch and I could tell from Murdoch's facial expression that it was not a casual conversation. He replied to the king but his body language suggested he was pleading his case. This was no time for me to be feeling sorry for myself again and should go to Murdoch's defence. After several deep breaths to dampen the dread rising from the pit of my stomach, I stepped forward towards them.

Murdoch waved his arm to beckon me over anyway. The king turned and glared as I approached. Every stride I took felt like I was trudging through thick bog like mud up to my knees. This man had absolute power of a man's life and death. I rolled my shoulders back and held my head high trying to stand tall and proud. I bought my feet together firmly and looked up at King Aniel as I stopped a pace away from the graceful jet-black horse. He smiled.

'Calum map Bruce, pleasure to finally meet you.' He spoke without affection and I questioned its sincerity. 'This is the last time disturbance you make amongst our coalition. You and your men are to report to the great hall immediately to receive orders whilst I consider this situation.' He pulled the reins to wheel his horse away before stopping to look back at me. 'I am pleased the Luguvalium plot failed. Do not let success go to your head. Remember your place.' He clicked his heels against the horses flank and the beautiful stead gracefully trotted along the road beside the glistening river.

He had given no chance for me to respond but I had nothing to say anyway. The unexpected gentle manner of the reprieve left me speechless. He mentioned orders, we were finally moving on. The eleven day stay in Luguvalium bought more men each day depleting every resource rapidly. Advancing further into Briton was inevitable.

'Did he say my Luguvalium raid failed?' I asked with a perplexed look on my face.

'Don't worry about that bit, Cal. Take heed of what he said about remembering your place.' He was smiling as he spoke but I felt reprimanded. 'Listen, learn and grow. You will one day be back where you belong.' He put a gentle hand on my shoulder. 'If an oaf like me can reach Lordship then anything is possible. Use that God's given wit of yours wisely.' I opened my mouth to reply but took a deep breath not knowing what to say. I hated the feeling of being oblivious to a situation and I had missed something vital.

'What did he say to you?' I finally asked.

'He doesn't understand why I protect you. He thinks Ceretic wanted rid of me, so appointed me Lord,' he replied with a little chuckle.

My men hurried over eager to know what happened. A few Dun Phris soldiers spat insults and taunts as their shield wall disbursed. None of my men took notice or retaliated. I again found myself in awe of their natural discipline. We were young but my gut instinct sensed we were destined for a greater purpose. The Dun Phris soldiers looked like incompetent slouches as they bumbled along the river's edge.

I bellowed a command for my men to fall into marching order, which they did efficiently. Murdoch smiled before strolling back the way we had ran following his new king. We marched elegantly behind the amateurish warriors who failed to kill me when I was drunk. We did not march in step, as the Roman Brits dressed in their matching garments did. We moved at our own pace but as a complete unit in two formed lines. My mind wandered back to Aniel's statement about the Luguvalium plan failing. Another thought that pulled on my quickly developing loyalty to my troop pushed that matter aside. The Dun Phris master's orders were to kill traitors and murderers. He was there to kill men... not man.

TWENTY-FOUR

Something significant was occurring in the training ground. The exercise yard outside the guardhouse was not big enough for a full brigade to train so we used the courtyard by the eastern gate. It stretched roughly three hundred paces from the gatehouse up to the giant steps that lead to the large white stone building the kings used as the great hall. Men filled every square inch crowded shoulder to shoulder. Every cobbled lane or muddy alleyway entering the square was similarly crammed with men. King Eochaid's men already marched back towards Bryneich but seven thousand remaining warriors listened to the briefing.

My men approached from the paved main road that led from the town bridge. Small gaps appeared allowing us to continue toward the large white stone steps still in formation. We elegantly wheeled right along the front of the stairs. Several figures stood on the top step.

I halted my men right in front of the great hall and turned them around to face the magnificent white stone building. I recognised Talorc immediately as he leapt down the large marble steps with anger displayed on his handsome face. That was the first time I saw him without a smile. He looked a lot like his uncle Nechtan when he was not smiling.

'Send your men to find Captain Fert,' he snapped. 'You and Ailbeart stay here.' He looked to the far end of the steps as he spoke avoiding eye contact with me. 'Fall in with the accused,' he said gesturing toward the end of the steps where a small group of men stood. He turned around to head back up the steps but paused to face me again. '…behave,' he said making eye contact with me for the first time. This was serious and I was in deep trouble but the reason for Ailbeart's presence perplexed me. I watched my troop struggle through the mass of bodies squeezed into the square. I worried they would never find one cohort in the overcrowded courtyard. Fert could have been anywhere. I took a deep breath and tried to concentrate on the situation before me.

I recognised several men as we strolled toward the line stood on the bottom step. Most notably Pefen, Ailean and Leyn were there. Yes, this was definitely about the scene in the tavern but nothing came of it. I stood next to two Dal Riadan soldiers I had seen fighting some Picts a few days ago. The Picts outnumbered them three to one and should have easily outfought two men but these Dal Riadan warriors gave as good as they got. The man directly to my left smiled as he recognised me showing the gap in his teeth. The missing ones now lay somewhere on the floor of the Domus Rex tavern. His badly bruised left eye gleamed bright yellow and purple.

I turned my attention to the figures on the top step instantly recognising the three regal figures in front of the majestic building. Several princes and Ealdorman stood directly behind the kings of the Scots. Talorc stood next to Nechtan directly behind Drest. Men in the front rank started pushing back against the packed rank behind to avoid the galloping horse charging into the crowded courtyard. Aniel jumped from the saddle with elegant ease demonstrating his competence as a seasoned cavalryman. He took a few deep breaths at the top of the staircase after bounding up the giant steps two at a time. Ceretic smiled and graciously nodded his head in acknowledgement as Aniel walked by.

Drest handed something over to Aniel and I realised it was a magnificent bronze helmet with a thin gold band along the crown. He placed it on his head before clearing his throat to address the crowd. He bellowed his announcement with a deep authoritative voice that reverberated throughout the heaving courtyard. I knew his voice would not carry to every man present. The message would ripple through the ranks as he spoke.

'I am King Aniel. I claim Rheged as a Scottish domain. Together as one people we will continue our conquest.' He paused whilst his message echoed back through the streets. An exultant roar resonated through Luguvalium. Aniel majestically waited for the cheering to subside but held his left hand aloft to signal he wanted silence.

'Lord Murdoch of Stratha Cluith descent is my first man of Rheged and Lord of Luguvalium.' A section of the courtyard erupted into a commotion as the Dun Phris royal guard cheered the success of their previous captain. Aniel did not pause and continued.

'He has reported several disturbances in our streets and these situations will no longer be tolerated.' He now spoke with aggressive venom. Recently warring kingdoms forced to ally together was inevitably going to see festering feuds boiling over and score settling. Yet the kings' council would not accept it. 'The culprits have been identified and now face a trial by the king.' As he spoke, I heard a raspy voice bark an order to my left. The line marched up the steps but the order had not reached my end of the line and it was not a very successful manoeuvre. We halted three steps below the platform where the Kings stood before being turned round to face the masses of soldiers.

Lines of men snaked through the main roads and back streets of the cobble and stone part of town. The evening sun was setting behind the rolling hills outside the walls. I was trying to keep my wit and concentrate on the situation at hand but could not help trying to figure out how my fate had ended up in the hands of a merciless king again. The last judgement resulted in a gauntlet that nearly took my life. My stomach turned and my head began to spin as if a bludgeon struck me as Aniel's final words sunk home.

'I find all accused guilty.'

TWENTY-FIVE

Uncontrollable fear took over. Nausea and terror swirled within the pit of my stomach. An aching throb thudded above my right eye as a drink-fuelled migraine set in. My intoxicated state intensified the shock of another unjust judgment. I played little part in Ailean's attempts on my life. In Bryneich, Banna and Luguvalium I had done nothing but defend myself trying to avoid altercation the best I could. Then I remembered the public exchange just a few hours ago in the tavern. I goaded Ailean and my provocation fuelling his outlandish and public attempt on my life upon hearing the peace treaty had broken.

Sweat soaked through my leather jerkin dripped from my nose onto the marvellous white steps. The sweltering early summer sun was causing a relentless heatwave but the sun was setting and the air was rapidly cooling. I knew it was panic. I deliberately slowed my breathing, taking in gulps of refreshingly cool stale air. The stench that swirled through Luguvalium stuck in the back of my throat.

Someone else spoke now and the recognition of the voice had an unexpected calming effect. Ceretic addressed the armies now. I faced away from the men of authority stood behind but knew the voice of the man who sent me into exile and made me a fugitive from my own flesh and blood. He addressed the army as a collective although the Bryneich warriors already marched home.

'It stops here. No more disruption will occur within this coalition. The perpetrators of any hostilities or score-settling will feel the full severity of the law.' He spoke in a slow and deliberate manner giving pauses to allow his words to pass through the busy streets. 'Any feud is to be dealt with correctly. King's word is law. Abide by our judgements or face strict discipline,' he calmly continued. 'The punishment for these men is deduction of two months wages.' A wave of relief washed over me as I realised there would be no physical punishment. My young growing body recovered quickly I was still not fully healed from the beatings. I needed both body and mind to be healthy as I proved my worth during this conquest.

Life is like a game of latrones. Superior tactics and strategy was the key to victory and I played blindly for too long. I learnt quickly when I had played latrones with my father and would learn the lord's game rules just as quickly to regain my rightful place. Ceretic's announcement continued after he took a deep breath. We gathered for orders but everyone wanted to know why Eoppa marched his Bryneich soldiers away so early in the campaign.

'Now onto a far greater matter, marching orders. The men of Dal Riada and Pictland march towards Pons Aelli at first light. We came south for land and we will take it together. My men of Stratha Cluith have another purpose with no more or no less important, as does Bryneich.' The pause left an uneasy tension in the air. The armies were splitting up so the truce must be broken. Aniel announced himself as a fifth king. He was Drest's brother and therefore Drest gained immense power. Eoppa's father and Ceretic went to war to stop a similar situation just a few years ago.

'Brit blood will be spilt and enrich the land that we will grow and thrive on. Honour and glory waits. We are different kingdoms...' I was facing forward trying to maintain a disciplined posture as Ceretic spoke but my head whirled and my stomach wretched. Ceretic bellowed these last three words with a true determination in his voice. '...but one people.' I turned around to see him lift his right arm straight in the air with his heavy long sword pointing high into the pinkish sky as the sun set behind the wall.

An immense roar emanated from the one people. The

blood-curdling sound would strike fear into the heart of the most seasoned and disciplined of foes. These men cut their teeth fighting Irish invaders and each other. They knew how to mould the fear that consumes a soldier stood before a shield wall. They had learnt the art of war and now would teach the weak and vulnerable Brits. Briton was ripe for the picking and we would feast over their corpses.

'Fall out,' whoever commanded this rank of disgraced felons bellowed the final order. Every man rushed down the giant white stone steps desperate to leave the humiliation behind. I gestured for Ailbeart to follow then rushed into the chaos of three armies as they tried to disburse. I wanted to report to Fert my cohort captain to make sure my troop found him. I felt an excited anticipation. The awe-inspiring speech from Ceretic filled the air with an excited anticipation. Warriors visualised leading a cohort, captains imagined their own emblem once they were knighted, lords fantasised about ruling a kingdom. We approached midsummer and we were yet to face any real resistance from the Brits.

Our spies reported Constantine's death had ripped a wave of great shock and unrest through their union who were lost without their destined saviour. Constance, Constantine's eldest son, claimed the sovereignty of Dumnonia and held the mantle of high king despite his inexperience. Rumours were rife he trained as a Christian priest and was no warrior. Despite encouraging news flooding into Luguvalium, we had not made much ground. One fort in disrepair was hardly a successful campaign of conquest. You could taste glorious future in the optimistic air that evening. I expected the entire population of Luguvalium to propel into a euphoric frenzy that would carry into the taverns and the village of tents outside the walls. It had not. The positive atmosphere remained but turned into a feeling of relaxed determination. I found Fert and was relieved to see my men too.

'Fetch your kit and return to our encampment.' There was no greeting and though not short I felt a hint of anger in Fert's tone. I lead my men to the tavern to collect our kit. The place was empty. We went straight upstairs and packed our kit bags but Lenis met us at the bottom of the stairwell and politely asked for our payment.

'On my return, I do not have the time now. You will get it, Sir.' I did not sound very convincing as I rudely brushed by him He did not question me further and stepped aside to allow us to leave. He was a kind soul and I could see why he liked resident soldiers to help collect fees. I stood by the door until my troop sauntered out of the room.

'Tell Gazella I will return to her.' This time I tried to sound convincing.

'Gazella will be waiting for my money, son,' he replied. I smiled at the nice old man and left through the back door. I had no intention of returning to Luguvalium or paying him what I owed but I felt a pang in my chest at the thought of not seeing Gazella ever again. She was the first woman I had laid with and knew a small part of my heart would always belong to her.

We found a small space on the edge of Fert's small cramped encampment. We lit a campfire but quickly settled down for the night although I knew I would not sleep well. At first light, we began our gruelling march toward the perils of battle.

TWENTY-SIX

The campfires burnt out during the night and the sun was yet to show on the horizon. The star-filled deep blue night sky fizzled with menace. The full moon shone with an intensity that made it easy to imagine shapes creeping through the encampment. I sat up startled when something firmly struck my foot to discover the dark shape was Fert. He gestured for me to get up then cautiously snuck away toward the next troop.

I wearily stood up to pull on my leather jerkin and leather trousers. Sleeping naked in the open air was probably not advisable but the stifling summer night's heat made it impossible to drift off to sleep leather-clad. I woke my men in the same manner I was startled to movement. A thin glowing line appearing on the horizon was a deep and sinister red. I touched the triquetra marked stone embedded into the hilt of my dagger and prayed it was not a sign from the gods. Foolishly, my young mind still questioned the almighty power both the virtuous gods of Tuatha de and the malicious Formorian gods hold upon this realm.

I shrugged away the thought and relit the fire to warm some water for washing and breakfast. The campfire quickly sprung to life and the noise of a busy army bustled in a gloomy half-light rudely interrupting the calm peaceful night. An eerie tension filled the air and the goose pimples on my arms began to tingle. The voice I heard from behind me was not one I had expected. I froze expecting a sword blow to cut me down. My sword was still in its scabbard leaning against my kit. I turned around as my uncle he repeated his words with a gentle tone.

'Can we talk nephew?' Ailean wore a leather jerkin like

me. It was unfair for his horse to carry the unnecessary weight of his full armour in the height of summer during the hard ride awaiting. He had no sword visible but he would have concealed any weapons he carried amongst another Lord's army. I doubted he was stupid enough to attack me here after yesterday's humiliating public shaming. This was my sixteenth summer and I had grown considerably in the past few months. I realised I was nearly as tall as he was now but he was still the bigger and stronger man. I said nothing but looked at him gesturing him to continue.

He looked around at the inquisitive eyes of my men staring at him menacingly. I began walking toward the river for some privacy. We walked in anxious silence until we reached the water's edge. The sun appeared low in the dawn sky. His face showed no emotion but he seemed calm. Ailean and I took regular strolls throughout my childhood. I spent more time with my uncle and cousin, both called Ailean, than I had my own father and brother. My father travelled a lot during peace and way whilst my brother was a brute. He bullied and belittled me and I preferred the company of my less boisterous cousin.
'I have behaved dishonourably toward you.' he stared out at the shimmering water avoiding eye contact. 'I apologise and hope in time we can be civil again.' We ambled along the embankment as if we had no care in the world but I needed to get back to my troop.

'I believed you capable of treachery and cowardice but I was wrong. I know you better, son.' He stopped and stared at me but expressed no emotion on his face. 'I am glad this has worked out this way and pleased you seem happy with the Picts.' He lifted his right arm and I dodged ducking my head slightly. He gently placed his hand on my shoulder finally displaying a smile on his strong handsome face. I was still a little drowsy from just waking up and his words sank in slower than usual. He paused between his sentences but I was struggling for a retort so he continued.

'Fight hard and think well my dearest nephew. I will see

you when our armies reunite.' He squeezed my shoulder gently before letting go and walked away. I watched a man I had admired saunter away toward the stretching walls of Luguvalium. I spoke no words during the brief exchange. I rushed back to my troop with his words resonating through my mind. I wondered if this talk was genuine or if he wanted me to drop my guard thinking I was safe from another ambush. He not a bitter man and would not have made the effort for that small ruse. Maybe the public embarrassment made him realise he had lost his chance to kill me or he thought the coming battles would rid me of this world anyway.

He apologised for believing ill of me but not for the attempts on my life. My own uncle thought me responsible for the death of his brother, which surely gave the true motivation to murder me. He sought revenge and justice rather than a move to retain power. My mind whirled with uncertainty as I once again struggled to find the answers to questions I could not comprehend. My troop busily prepared for the long march ahead. I started bundling the little kit I had in an old and fraying kit bag Maol gave me. I looked up to see Daghda rushing towards me in a frightful panic.

TWENTY-SEVEN

'Calum, Calum!' Daghda yelled my name as he darted towards me in a troubling state. 'You cannot march today,' he said in a commanding manner. 'The army must protect Luguvalium but no one will listen.' He flailed his arms in distress.

'What are you talking about Daghda?' I tried to place my hand on his shoulder reassuringly to calm him down. He knocked my arm away and continued with his babbling.

'The fox chases after the rabbit and the wolf enters the den to feast on the cubs, Calum.' He stopped flailing his arms and took a deep breath. 'The Gods are giving signs Calum so we must listen. I saw the fall of Luguvalium last night,' he said pleadingly.

'Why have you come to me with this Daghda? What can I do?' I could not stop an army from marching even if I had wanted to, which I did not. I was desperate for battle to prove my worth.

'Nechtan left last night and No one else here will listen to my advice. You have the ear of men of power Calum so use your influence.' I did not understand what he was talking about or why he had sought me out. The men behind me finished dismantling the encampment and began to fall into marching order.

'Did you take any elixir last night?' Daghda always babbled about the gods but I noticed on our trail to Banna that his frantic rants worsened after he had taken linctus.

'Yes of course. That is how I communicate with the gods but what I am saying is true. When we march out the Brits will march in. Please trust me.' He became desperate with his pleas.

'I don't know what you are talking about but even if I did I am just a troop leader and need to fall in. You had a bad dream. If you are sure about this then go after Nechtan or return to Pictland. A battleground is no place for a druid.' I snapped my retort harsher than intended. I disgraced my cohort yesterday with my public reprimand and did not want to make things worse by making them late to march.

'Listen to me young man.' Daghda's tone became serious and bitter. 'I came to you because you have the intelligence to know that we have a greater purpose.' He pointed his finger aggressively at me when he spoke. 'We are pieces in the gods' game of war. From what I hear, you are an exceptional latrones player so take heed. It is placing the pawns correctly, which gives you the upper hand Calum. Do not upset too many pawns on your rise up.' I saw anger in him that I had never seen before and realised I had really upset him.

'I do hope I am wrong. I will take your advice and leave so I am not here when the wolves arrive.' He stomped past me with a surprising pace for a man with a hunched back. Daghda spoke a lot about the powers of the gods and the battles between the virtuous Tuatha de gods and the malevolent and malicious Formorian's. I did not understand their relationship with men but should have listened to Daghda. His bond with them is genuine. I handled that situation wrong and took my frustrations out on the wrong man. The conversation with my uncle confused me and I was angry.

'Daghda wait.' I called after him but he either did not hear or ignored me and continued on his way.

'Cal, we've got to go,' Ailbeart called from the campfire. The rest of my troop started walking toward the muster point to fall in. I abandoned my attempts at calling Daghda back and quickly caught them up.

TWENTY-EIGHT

'It's the Lord of nowhere! How do you feel marching alongside us commoners?' Roinn always spoke with a question even when he was being derogatory. He was another Stratha Cluith soldier who found himself in the Pict brigade lead by Talorc. Most men in Talorc's brigade were from the other three Scot Kingdoms with very few of his men being Pict warriors. I knelt down by the riverbank washing my face to cool down. The relentless summer heat gave no reprieve for men in leather and iron that marched along the wall of Hadrian. I chose to ignore Roinn's belittling teases. Any retort toward the spiteful and vicious divisional master would result in ridicule or discipline. No response irritated him more, having little patience and quick to temper when mocked.

'Are you too noble to respond to your superior Ealdorman?' He strolled closer toward me when the first taunt failed to cause a reaction. I took a sip of water from my cupped hands before standing up whilst shaking off the excess water.

'My apologies master. I did not know you were talking to me. I am a troop leader. You're witty remarks surpass me,' I replied with fake sincerity. 'It has been a fast march today. My legs are not used to it unlike a seasoned soldier as you would be.' Roinn tilted his head slightly like a dog unsure of a given command. His eyes were wide with curiosity as he considered the legitimacy of my retort. Muir and Ruadh stood behind me sniggering as they tried to suppress their laughter. I tried to hide my sarcasm but my men knew me too well. Fortunately, Roinn never did comprehend my wit. He smiled coyly after deciding he won that battle of banter.

'Fert asked me to send a troop forward to the vanguard. He wants someone experienced and capable to set a good pace for the day. Should I send you and your pups instead?' He giggled at his own poor attempt at a jest then walked away followed by his usual entourage. All four soldiers glared at me with distaste as they sauntered by. The rest of our division, in fact, the entire brigade, held my troop with an icy disregard. Now was not the time to dwell upon such trivia. We needed to reach the front of the army before the gruelling hard march through the scorching summer's day resumed.

A few of my men groaned as I ordered them to start moving again because we stopped for a matter of moments but I did not want to be the ones to hold up the brigade. We hurried to the front of the vanguard whilst the rest of the army enjoyed a brief respite and a respectable opportunity to quench their thirst. Fert sat up high on a splendid chestnut horse on the top of a small ridge. The horse speckled white with flecks of sweat that shimmered in the blazing sunlight. Fert smiled when I approached but beckoned to a troop of scouts. He briefed them quickly as we climbed the gentle slope and they galloped away just as we reached the peak.

'I knew he would send you Cal. I'm glad he did. I'm leading the vanguard for the next couple of days and I couldn't cope with his incessant questions and nonsense wisecracks.' Fert smiled and was in good spirit. He clicked his heels into the flanks of his horse and she turned elegantly. 'Off we go then. We've got Brits to kill.' I heard habitual groans behind me from the usual complainers but my men followed Fert's horse to restart the march.

TWENTY-NINE

Ruadh and I led the line. We had not been marching long when Fert rode beside me and dismounted to walk beside me. He led his horse by the reins for the next two days. We spoke freely about many trivial matters. He spent quite a while paying homage to salmon. He did teach me an easier way to fillet and skin them though. He also spoke a lot about the townspeople of Eta although I did not know anybody he mentioned. I did promise if I ran into the butcher's wife I would not tell her about his daily visits to the bakery whilst the baker was out on his deliveries.

'Ignore him Cal.' Fert appeared from behind me sat upon his horse after witnessing another icy exchange between me and Roinn. He rode his horse whenever we rested to check on his division but preferred to march on foot. 'There jealous and suspicious. It's not worth your time to dwell on.' He obviously spotted it bothered me. Every day we spent on the march my troop got increasingly isolated.

'Why would they be jealous or suspicious?' I asked inquisitively. Fert chuckled to himself at my reply before dismounting to fall in beside me as we recommenced the gruelling walk along the road by the wall. We led the vanguard for three days and Ruadh moved back into the ranks on the second day allowing Fert to take his position.

'You are an exile. Ceretic marked you a coward and a traitor and you are one of very few survivors of a massacre despite having no fighting experience or training.' He spoke in a very matter-of-fact manner but his words cut deep with a bitter realisation. 'You won't die no matter how many times the king's council try to kill you and you always scrub up gleaming like a silver chalice.'

'You mean Ailean? My uncle tried to kill me not the kings' council?' Fert turned and looked at me perplexed.

'You know they sent you into Luguvalium expecting you to die right? That's why Ailean was the first reinforcements as well. Kill off both the men vying for the highest title in Stratha Cluith except for the king. A supporter of Drest could be appointed as Ealdorman to influence King Ceretic.' He wore a great big smile on his face making me think he was jesting for a fleeting moment. He spoke plainly and I trusted Fert. 'Why do you think they gave you young boys that waited to be hanged or suspected Brit sympathisers?' Each chosen man possessed specific abilities and they were young because they needed to be small. Ailbeart and Muir were certainly not small despite their youth.

'Are you serious?' I asked the question but knew in my gut he was speaking honestly. It was blatantly obvious know.

'I'm just teasing Cal,' Fert smiled at me but I was not reassured. I wanted to keep talking about this matter but our destination came into view. We marched passed countless towns and simple checkpoints along the wall but this fortress was different. The Roman fort built into the wall was a simple design but the steep banks gave it a sense of grandeur. The clay banks led to the sun-baked clay walls giving marvellous character to a dilapidated and abandoned stronghold. One solitary figure stood regally in front of the open portcullis gates. It was Nechtan and we had reached the Red Fort.

THIRTY

'Captain, rally all the commanders for an immediate war council.' Nechtan spoke with urgency and looked concerned. He dashed into the fortress without acknowledging me. In the days of Hadrian, my ancestors obstinately threw themselves at the wall and impenetrable fortification such as this. The walls stood on steep clay banks with short spiked palisades stretching along the top of the wall. The narrow gantry that ran around the entire inside wall could hold many archers or javelinists. The internal building consisted of barracks, training square and a simple clay slabbed hall the other side of the courtyard. This was a Roman military station. I was in awe of the aptitude of Roman efficiency.

They knew how to be flamboyant. They left behind many majestic buildings, picturesque mosaic floors and astonishing statues. They took that ability with them and we will never see such masterpieces again. This fortress was simple and made of little more than the ground that it stood on. Yet it was a formidable obstacle for any foe.

Another settlement roughly a league south of the fortress was clearly visible on that clear fresh summer's day. It would have been a town for the large garrison required to operate a military station as significant as the red fort but was likely to be abandoned and in as much disrepair as this stronghold.

Fert swiftly galloped away to fetch the commanders. A long line of warriors ambled across the summery green countryside. I stood in the square with Ailbeart, Ruadh and Muir admiring the immaculately positioned dilapidated buildings and defences. A steady stream of Lords and commanders galloped into the square and thrust their horse's reins into the nearest warrior's hands as they dismounted before rushing into the simple hall. Talorc cantered into the fort and steered his horse toward me. He leapt from the saddle and stumbled slightly as he hit the ground. I reached out to grab the reins but he handed them to Ruadh. He began walking towards the hall and gestured for me to follow.

'Come Calum, we need a recorder.' Nechtan had someone record every council to study every aspect of every meeting. An unusual practice but it made sense considering how heated war councils often became. Things of great value are easily overlooked when too many authoritative figures jostle for control. Nechtan read anything he could get his hands on except the bible or Mag Mel scriptures. He said he needed to train his mind much the same as he trained his body.

A long and weary-looking banquet table stretched the length of the great hall. At the far end were two tall chairs of equal size and height. Two benches ran the entire length on both sides of the table. Eochaid sat on one of the chairs with Nechtan sat next to him on the bench. Other warlords, men granted the honour of raising their own armies, sat at the far end of the table. My father was the only warlord in Stratha Cluith and Ailean had not remained in control of that formidable force but he was still commanded the Dun Phris Brigade. Ceretic's two living sons now led the remaining two brigades my father controlled replacing my other uncles. All Stratha Cluith units currently marched back home.

Talorc handed me a piece of tattered papyrus sheet, a reed pen, and a pot of lampblack ink before sitting at the far side of the table. Now being the heir apparent to a kingdom, he could have sit nearer his uncles but was happiest amongst his own military rank. Although a quietly ambitious man, his patience was a great virtue to him. He sat amongst his peers biding his time knowing he would he steadily move further up the hierarchy. Drest was always last man to enter the hall. He did not like waiting, so made everyone else wait for him. He had barely sat down before Nechtan stood up and cleared his throat. He addressed the two kings as he spoke.

'I apologise for the hasty council after a hard march. I know you all want to ensure the wellbeing of your men but I have received significant reports from Luguvalium.' He paused for a moment to take a deep breath. 'Notable Brit forces march toward Luguvalium. They approach from the western road missing our army marching along the wall.' I stopped writing and lost concentration.

Concern for both Gazella and Acair overwhelmed my mind. Acair should have returned with Ailean to Stratha Cluith when army marched home but she could have stayed with her father. Gazella lived in Luguvalium. She was young, beautiful and lived in a tavern, which was the worse place to be when brutish warriors thinking of ale, plunder and rape were within the walls. She was a Briton, which should be enough to stop her from coming to any harm, but I doubted it.

Daghda was right. I knew better to ignore a man of the Gods. We marched away chasing the rabbit and the Brits marched into Luguvalium. Nechtan had continued talking but a different voice now spoke. My self-pity drifted my thoughts from the room and I had missed vital information.

'Aniel has an army to defend the fortress. We continue our plan and take more strongholds. If their army march on Luguvalium then another considerable force will not oppose us as we advance,' said Sliabh, ealdorman of Craeg Phadrig. The infamous Dal Riadan warlord spoke confidently staring directly at Eochaid before sitting down indicating he had finished making his point. Noisy bustling and shuffling erupted around the hall as men wishing to speak vied to be the next man standing. Talorc stood first.

'We return to Luguvalium and assist my father. The Britons have decided to face us so we meet them in battle now. If we take more fortresses we dilute our collective strength further.' He spoke assuredly with the confidence of a veteran commander. Before he had sat down Sliabh returned to his feet and spoke again.

'The reports state the Brits number five to seven thousand men. Before spring, they rumoured to number over twelve thousand. If either is accurate then we encounter a force too large to face alone. Our collective strength has already diluted because half of our army has fled home. We should not face the brunt of the Brit forces whilst Ceretic and Eoppa hide away and keep their armies unscathed.' The derision in his tone exposed his feelings about the armies' different strategies.

The ongoing power struggle between the kingdoms had angered many senior lords and commanders who were seasoned leaders but had little influence within a kings' council. The next person to stand was Drest. He usually waited for everyone who wished to speak to have a say before making the judgement. It was rare for him to intervene so early and it was unexpected.

THIRTY-ONE

'We have a dilemma. Valid points have been voiced. We are tired and have the concerns of our armies on our minds. We will pause and consider our points of view carefully. We must not make hasty notions through emotion and fatigue.' He made this last comment whilst glaring at his nephew. He instantly dismissed returning to Luguvalium by from his mind. He walked around the table and disappeared out of the hall.

My stomach ached and I could feel the palpitations of my heart thudding against my chest. I was angry I had not listened to Daghda. He knew what would happen and my ignorance could have cost my beloved Acair and the beautiful Gazella their freedom, their virtue or even their lives.

'What's the matter with you?' I had not noticed Nechtan beside me until he spoke.

I could feel the tears building in my eyes that made me hesitate before speaking. I needed to speak to someone about what I had done and hoped I could hold back the flood of tears as I opened up.

'It's my fault. Daghda warned me Luguvalium would fall. Now...'

'Daghda warned you about what Cal?' Nechtan interrupted me sharply. He rarely interrupted anyone and listened more than spoke.

'The wolves taking Luguvalium and eating the cubs,' I stated as if that made sense. Nechtan looked at me waiting for me to elaborate.

'Try making more sense. Start from the beginning.' Nechtan sat down beside me with his back against the wall. I told

Nechtan the warnings Daghda gave the morning we left Luguvalium.

'The wolves have stirred and taken Luguvalium. Daghda knew it all along.' I took a deep breath and began to relax. My chest was no longer as tight and my heartrate slowed. I was confused when I looked at Nechtan and saw him smiling.

'Daghda does talk to the gods but they don't always talk as simple as you and me. They can talk in riddles Cal. So do you sometimes.' He was calm and reassured. 'As far as I know Luguvalium has not fallen. Daghda said as soon as the fox leaves, yes. The wolves enter as soon as, that was definitely his words, right?' I paused and thought back to that morning. I had not been paying that much attention to him because my mind was reeling from my conversation with Ailean. I was not interested in anything he said and did not realise the importance

'Yes,' I answered hoping I was right. Nechtan's smile lit up his face as if a bonfire had ignited behind his deep emerald eyes. He paused before returning his gaze back onto me.

'Did you see the stronghold to the south when you marched in?' He asked.

' 'Not much of a stronghold, no embankments, the palisades are three paces high. I could reach the top stood on Ailbeart's shoulders. I didn't note any troop activity either.' I hardly drew breath before Nechtan continued. He was rushing the conversation now.

'There is a watchtower on each corner with three men. The two gatehouses have two towers either side with two men on each platform. Another watchtower situates at the centre of both the east and west walls but no gates. I think guards patrol he inside of the wall but cannot be sure though. I reached the walls without being spotted last night but any real numbers would be spotted too easily.' He was talking in a matter of fact manner as if informing a war council of gathered intelligence.

'A troop of the right men might make it. Would the loss of men be worth a small garrison town of an abandoned fort?' I did not have the authority to talk on such matters but Nechtan was

asking for advice for a reason. I spoke as I read the situation.
'That is Coria, the main Roman auxiliary fort in northern Briton. It was created solely to make food, weapons and armour for every Roman stronghold on the wall.' Things began making more sense. The plan was to take the town and use the Brit resources against them. We were on the move for a long time and food was becoming scarce. Weapons and armour would be in a state of disrepair. Horses would have been lost or becoming lame with exhaustion.

'Why did the entire army march into the Red Fort?' I asked, 'That would put them on a state of high alert. They must expect an attack.' Nechtan's grin grew after every time I spoke. A plan formulated in his tactical mind. The three sons of Erb were like the three warrior Gods of Tuatha De. Drest was the brawn, Aniel was renowned for unmatched courage and Nechtan was the strategist. Together they were a formidable force to match anyone, possible the holy triquetra themselves. I saw Drest's plan created as we spoke.

We sat in the empty hall discussing various ideas and possible issues until men started walking back into the hall. Drest walked in and looked straight at Nechtan who immediately stood up to walk over to him.

He turned to me and asked, 'are the pups of war ready to be wolves?' I looked up at him wondering what he was plotting. Alarm bells were ringing in my mind remembering they sent me to Luguvalium to die. I did not want to answer him so I responded with another question.

'What are you going to be?'
'The rabbit.'

THIRTY-TWO

I am going to die. Maybe not this night but I will die young. I sat with my back against a tree in the scorching midday sun binding three lengths of Papyrus rope. The remaining allied armies marched away down the road we had arrived from yesterday. The deafening racket they purposively created during the manoeuvre was in hope of catching the attention of the sentries stood upon the walls of Coria. The town was a league away and clearly visible across the gently sloping meadows in the warm summer daze.

I was glad I was not marching with them despite knowing I had a better chance of seeing tomorrow's sunrise amongst that army. Those men would spend the day marching west in the blistering heat just to loop around and return through the fields and trees after dusk ensuring they avoided any roads. The scorching summer sun sweltered with vicious ferocity as if the fires of Formoria rose from beneath our feet.

I pulled the ends of the rope tight and secured it with a double knot. Ruadh shaped and holed the wood we needed for the ladders and neatly stacked a pile of rungs between Airson and me. I thought about certain failure and impending death whilst I carefully threaded the strengthened papyrus rope through the slot in the wooden rung securing it in place with a double knot either side of the plank. Airson and I worked well together making sure each rung was level before locking it in place. His hands were shaking slightly and I realised I was not alone on this suicidal mission or in having destructive feelings.

My stomach swirled as I remembered the men I led on the Luguvalium assault who did not sit amongst us. I agreed to this mission despite having little choice but my men knew nothing about it until I gave the orders to stay whilst every other soldier marched away. I hastily briefed them as I told them what job they needed to do in preparation. Every soldier should know their role and be confident in their abilities to perform the tasks ahead. Instead of briefing each warrior individually quashing any doubts of their capabilities I slumped against a tree trunk lost in my pessimism.

Nechtan told me to be composed and self-assured amongst my men because confidence breeds confidence. Men who feel they are destined to succeed and believe in their leader fight with passion whilst soldiers expecting imminent and inevitable death rarely see the next dawn. I tried to bury my own despair by taking a deep breath before I spoke. I addressed Airson but spoke loud enough so my entire troop could hear. We all performed individual tasks in preparation for tonight's assault and had dispersed amongst the small cluster of trees upon the little knoll.

'We will be first in the tavern tonight Airson. You won't put your hand in your pocket either. I didn't buy one drink in Luguvalium,' I said casually. I was trying to lighten the natural tension that hung in the air. Mentioning Luguvalium was the wrong option. He smiled slightly but kept his focus on the knot he was tying in the papyrus rope. 'The pups of war will be heroes once again.' I continued my futile attempts of casual conversation. Airson stopped what he was doing and looked straight at me with an unusually grave expression.

'That is an insult. They call us pups because we are expendable children oblivious to the perils we face as if this is a game.' His serious tone took me aback slightly. Airson's eccentric sense of humour, jesting and prank pulling was a regular boost of moral within the troop. He obviously doubted himself, the troop, the plan, and me. As the most experienced man and well into his twenty something summers he knew the threats of battle and raids better than the rest of us. Being from Bryneich, he had fought in Eochaid's army against the Picts and Dal

Riadan's but now sat amongst warriors he faced a few summers ago. His drafting to a Pict brigade was one of many movements intended to create unity between the coalitions. Now he prepared for a desperate raid whilst His kinsmen marched home to Bryneich whilst he prepared for a desperate assault with little chance of success

'I don't care. How many troops have a title? Mention the pups of war and men know whom you are talking about. After tonight it will never insult again.' I spoke with more belief than I felt. The term will not be used again as we would all be slaughtered. Airson did not reply. He continued to loop the papyrus rope through a wooden rung making the ladder's we would need.

'The enemy quivers in fear at the very thought of the pups of war, Airson,' Ruadh intervened. 'Every lord and guard captain is stricken with fear of the pups raiding their town in the midst of the night.'

'Children pretend to be a pup. Breaking into barns as the mythical Muir the magnificent,' Muir had heard the conversation and strolled over.

'And the women will beg for our return dreaming of lying with a legendary pup.' Ruadh's face lit up as he spoke imagining the idea.

The optimistic conversation burst the bubble of tension that had hung above our heads. My men spoke of hopes and dreams for the future. 'Pups of war' was a derogatory term now but I knew it could grow to be a famous and honourable label. Belief gushed through my veins. The commanders may think this mission was destined to fail and have a different strategy for the main army but I knew we would succeed. Luguvalium worked as why not this assault. The knot in my stomach loosened with the conversation having a positive effect on my mind too. We were the pups of war and tonight we would be the wolves that ravished the cubbish Brits.

THIRTY-THREE

The sun disappeared behind drifting clouds at dusk wafting a cool breeze through the stifling summer air. No moon or stars were visible as the fluffy white clouds turned a sinister grey. We travelled in single file mere inches apart to avoid separation as we crept in the black emptiness toward Coria. The firm grassy meadow was damp with freshly formed drops of dew. The clouded sky above quenched every flicker of light or shadow with the potential to give away our movement.

The sky shone bright and vindictive during the Luguvalium assault. We crept inside the river Eden's banks to conceal our shadows but the menacing darkness that night aided our approach. Several flaming arrow soared above us sparking the sky into life. The missiles landed at least two hundred paces to the east near the Roman road. I threw myself onto my belly. Lack of silhouettes around me confirmed my entire troop dropped to the ground to avoid detection.

I remembered a conversation I once had with Ruadh about fire arrows. Flames affect the accuracy of a shot and stop the arrow from reaching its potential distance. These arrows did not lose distance as they sailed into the blackness of the night. The fires of Formoria erupted through the dry and dusty ground as a blaze burst into life on the ground. I had spotted strategically placed poles on the Roman road but dismissed them thinking they were distance markers. A thin line of thatch stretched between the posts. A spark of light raced across the ground indicating thatch and posts were soaked in pitch. Sporadic burst raged into life as the fire reached the next pitch post placing the road into clear view.

I stared in the direction of the hypnotic flames. Something caused those signal volleys. They knew we attacked and had set light to their warning system to hamper our approach. My heart thudded in rhythm with the unmistakable sound of horseshoes on stone. Cavalrymen hunted down advancing warriors but they galloped on the tiled road. The echoes were feint and distant so I glared toward the northern gate expecting a division of horses to appear in the refreshing firelight. A sole rider appeared from the direction of the red fort heading toward Coria.

Creeping doubt emerged in my mind whilst I lay on my stomach waiting for the flames to die. Our awaiting army near the southern gate might mistakenly read the flaming arrows as our signal and begin the assault. I prayed to Oghma the God of warriors that I would not see the returning signal as I stared into the dark cloudy southern sky. No flaming arrow appeared. They were not there. It would take most of the night to make it back. I worried unnecessarily but I knew hidden plots ran deep in every tactic.

Our infiltration into Luguvalium was a ruse to get me killed but my unexpected success masked the plan. I feared this mission had the same objective. The Brits would be on high alert because our army had occupied the Red Fort. Just marching away a day later in the direction was come did not make sense. The Brits know an invading army need to plunder supplies, which made our ruse too obvious.

A metallic screech reverberated across the open plains as the portcullis slowly rose. The sole rider galloped through the black hole now in the wall before the iron grid rapidly slid back into place. An age passed before the flames began to die down although the firelight was too far away to give away our position if we had continued to creep forward. We stayed on our bellies until the flames diminished. We had all night to get inside the walls and make it to the southern gate. Our main objective was to open those gates so anything else we achieved was a bonus.

Dawn of Dark Days

The pitch posts near to the Red fort still blazed but the harsh light dimmed enough for us to continue. I crawled my way to Tamhas and Sti who led the line. These infamous sneak thieves had sparked a manhunt that raged throughout Cathures. The twins infiltrated guarded great halls and noble manors that bustled with servants and slaves stealing lavish ornaments that they saw as ill-gotten gains. Their imprisoned father had failed to pay his levies and remained incarcerated until his debts were paid. His sons paid his dues after their first raid on the administrator's home who had imprisoned him but had discovered they had a hidden talent and continued. The sentence for such audacity was hanging but the mission into Luguvalium offered an opportunity for redemption. They performed their roles with expertise and their advice and assistance assured the success. I depended on their abilities once again.

I waved my hand forward signalling for Tamhas to continue but waited for Airson to pass before falling back into file ensuring Ailbeart followed. We moved with purpose and renewed vigour toward the wooden walls, leaning our backs against the simple wooden palisade as we reached the town. We rested briefly to catch our breath and control the dread that inevitably gripped our souls. All twelve men slammed their backs against the long wooden stakes that formed the strong palisade wall before I gave the order to ascend. The rest gave me time to assess the situation inside because footsteps meant different cause of action. Silence.

I tapped Ailbeart on the knee as I stood before moving towards Sti and Tamhas. Ailbeart and Muir appeared behind me and I placed my hands together on my knee. I thrust Sti upward as he stepped into my grip lifting him his into the air. He was a short slim man but surprisingly heavy but he easily leapt from my hands landing with his knees on Ailbeart's shoulders. Ailbeart huffed as he took the full weight of Sti who sprung to his feet to stand tall on Ailbeart shoulders. I turned to help Tamhas get onto Muir's shoulders as the dark menacing night sky ignited with light once again. We could not lie down and wait

115

here. We were at the palisade and getting into Coria no matter what. It was ever leaving this place again that I began to doubt.

THIRTY-FOUR

The lightening vanished as quickly as it had erupted sending the world back into eerie darkness. Thunder rolled through the blackened night sky. A sporadic burst of light giving a brief glimpse of the day was the last thing we needed. Elada, the demon God of fire sent a message through the storm. He wields a sword moulded from a bolt of lightning in battle but I did not know if he used it to help us see our way or to alert the Brits. Whatever he was doing, I knew it would be malicious and spiteful. I hoped he aimed his toward the Brits this evening.

I took deep long breaths whilst I waited for the long thunderous rumble to pass. Tamhas placed his hands on Muir's head and leapt for the hidden stars as I thrust upwards. He bent his knees as he landed expertly on his feet standing on Muir's shoulders. Ailbeart and Muir both shuffled inelegantly as they turned to face the wall. Ruadh passed the twins the two papyrus rope ladders we spent the day making. They threw the looped ends toward the sharp palisade spikes aiming to hook then over the pointed tips.

'Keep up baby bro,' mocked Tamhas as he slipped his ladder into place on his second attempt. Sti's ladder fell into place after his third throw. Ruadh lifted up two leather jerkins to each twin to layer over the sharp points of wood before they pulled themselves onto the wall. Sti quickly pulled up his ladder and lowered it over the other side. I hoped Nechtan was wrong about the interior patrol because a guard would easily see it gently blowing in the wind as it dangled from the wall. The twins sat perched on the double layer of leather padding assisting each man as we precariously climbed the hastily constructed ladder before shuffling over to the second ladder and climbing into the auxiliary fort.

Jumping was quicker and easier because the palisade was not high enough to cause serious injury as long as you landed right but I did not want to take any risk. The landings could attract attention from a patrolling guard or an eager sentry on the towers. This method took longer but it was safer and stealthier. Tamhas unhooked the first ladder as Ailbeart climbed down into Cario. He climbed down the second ladder whilst Sti threw down the leather jerkins. He unhooked the last ladder before lowering himself down toward the ground. He bent his knees rolling sideways onto his shoulder as his feet struck mud. My men quickly collected the items into neat bundles and strapped them onto the twin's backs. Anything left behind would give away our presence within the wall.

Another flash of lightning ignited the sky making the town burst into view. We hunched low with our backs against the inside of the wall allowing the light to vanish back into the empty blackness of night. The appearing buildings were simple wooden longhouses but a lot larger than expected. The monstrously big storehouses dwarfed most great halls I frequented with my father. The rumble of thunder rolled across the town echoing against the wooden buildings and spiked wall. Elada waited until Sti jumped before creating his flash. He was with us and we were going to achieve another impossible infiltration.

I repeated my instructions to Tamhas and Sti for the umpteenth time. They led the larger section of men to take and hold the southern gate. If my reconnaissance mission failed, the gates would still open and unleash Drest the Brutal upon this sleeping fort. I watched as all eight men slunk along the wooden wall before dashing across the open walkway into the small shadowy alleyway between the buildings. I started casually strolling down the muddy walkway toward the centre of town. I glanced down the dark passage as my men disappeared hoping to see them again. I sent a section to their deaths in Luguvalium. I took a deep breath to swallow my self-pitying before continuing on my path.

Ruadh, Muir and Ailbeart casually strolled beside me acting like four Brit soldiers meandering through the town. Another flash of lightning sparked in the night sky followed by the expected roll of thunder rumbling through the darkened streets. The unexpected downpour lashed down with ferocity. Elada was playing tricks on me. We walked briskly plodding through the quickly sodden mud paths passing two rows of the massive wooden halls before we entered the main square.

I never saw a town square like this before. Squares are stone, cobble or mud but this fenced plot was a lush green meadow. The well-kept short grass had a few yellow patches or muddy puddles showing where an animal grazed too much. It took me while to realise it was a grazing plot but I never heard of a farm inside a fortress before. The field was empty. I bolted towards the nearest large barn as I realised the field was empty. The other rushed to help as I struggled to pull open the giant door. The door slid open enough for us to slip inside. A few loafing pieces of wheat lay on the dusty floor of the empty barn. We checked three more buildings. The floor of one was stained red with dried blood and ropes attached to hooks dangled from low beams that ran width length along the ceiling. All the carcases of the animals were gone. The other two only had mere morsels of grain and cereals left behind like the first barn. Coria was not a fully stocked auxiliary fort the kings thought.

'So what do we do?' asked Ruadh rather loudly in Scottish.

'Stop shouting Scot inside a Briton stronghold,' I replied sharply but barely more than a whisper. A row of small house like buildings stretched along the far side of the meadow with a larger building situated on the corner of the street. The sign dangling above the door rattled as swirling gusts of wind ripped through the town. The dark night sky hide behind the menacing black clouds as the relentless rain soaked through our leather and into our skin. Dawn was a long time off and I could not contact the army waiting outside the gates without risking the mission. I did not know what we should do but I was cold, wet

and thirsty. I headed towards the tavern I spotted.
　　'I think it's time for a drink'.

THIRTY-FIVE

'They will kill us. I do not know how painful the torture for information will be first so let's not be caught. Watch and take note of what you can. Muir, listen well.' I stopped at the corner of the meadow to speak to my three companions. We infiltrated the fortress sooner than necessary to ensure we had enough time. Every plan changes on the first contact. It gave an opportunity to spy for vital information. We scouted the storehouses but the first four were empty so the rest would be too. An opportunity to scout the Brit soldiers was rare and both Muir and I spoke Brit fluently. Taking Ailbeart and Ruadh inside was a concern. Their knowledge of warriors ways might prove useful as they watched whilst Muir and I listened to an overwhelming number of conversations.

The tavern was busier than I had expected. As I pulled open the door a warrior standing square in the doorway shuffled back slightly trying to allow us to enter. We squeezed our way to the bar at the far end of the room. The small tavern heaved with soldiers standing, sitting and crouching in every little nook or cranny. Having so many men inside worked in our favour allowing us to blend in with the mass of warriors. I held four fingers up to the attractive young woman standing behind the bar. Muir handed over coin as she placed four tankers on the sticky damp bar top. After having my wages stopped since Luguvalium, I was penniless. My heart pounded against my chest, my stomach tightened and my mind whirled amongst these foreign soldiers. I knew this was a bad idea but it was too late.

Muir made his way through the crowd to a very small space by a window in the far corner. We stood in a small square whilst Muir and I spoke casually about nothing in particular. I consciously tried to relax and listen to the conversation occurring nearby but I my blaring thoughts drowned out the external din. I awaited the exclamation that we were Scot spies that would inevitable come. We kept the small and discreet weapons we carried over the wall concealed but even armed we would not fight our way out of this horde.   Scabbards strapped to most Brits in this tavern housed their swords anyway. An unusual practice inside a tavern within a fortress but the army seen at red fort had the garrison on edge. The entire brigade was on high alert for any unusual behaviour and I decided to commit this suicidal act.

    I sent eight men to take the towers at the southern gates who were probably already dead. My closest friends were in an overcrowded shack full of drunken enemy soldiers waiting to be killed where they stood. We sipped ale slowly trying to appear as if we guzzled it down. Being intoxicated in this situation was lunacy but we had to keep up appearances. Soldiers drink. We were soldiers in a tavern so we had to be drinking. Ale or wine quells the logical fear and anxiety before a battle but I needed more than beer to quell the engulfing dread flowing through my mind. A large soldier caught my eye and started shuffling his way in our direction.

THIRTY-SIX

'Good evening master,' he said pleasantly. His greeting caught me off guard. Nechtan gave me a second arm ring indicating I was a master but in my head, I was still a troop leader. He said I would be surprised how much more authority the second ring gave. I hesitated before responding and the man frowned slightly. If suspicion had not bought him over then he would be suspicious now.

'That's you, boss,' chuckled Muir in Brit. He slapped me playfully on the back. 'You forgot your promotion already? How much have you drunk?' He spoke with a worryingly convincing Brit accent in a calm and jovial manner.

'Still getting used to it Aurelius,' I responded. I turned to face the big Brit and noticed three arm rings. He was a cohort captain and probably the commanding officer of this garrison. The only man inside the walls that could recognise everyone had just happened to stroll over to us.

'Evening Captain. How are you?' I spoke with the best Brit accent I could muster but naturally dragged my words. Naturally perfect, it appeared I was drunk.

'In good spirits my lad. Congratulations on the promotion,' He said genuinely. He caught the attention of the young barmaid and put up five fingers into the air. He quickly turned back to face me. 'So, whose division are you leading?' He probed suspiciously. If I did not answer, it proved I was lying but answer with inaccurate details and I tripped myself up. I took a deep breath to compose myself and disguised the pause by lifting my tanker to my lips. I thought about Brit Lords I met on the few occasions I travelled with my father.

'I am from Leodus. I fight for Lord Lupus's son.' I remembered the conversation Lupus held with my father last summers end in Luguvalium. His son Canus, a celebrated hero in the Roman army, had written stating he was returning home with some of his men. He proudly told my father about his hero son at least a dozen times.

'Really,' the man exclaimed with too much enthusiasm. 'Canus will be in here soon. He's resting from his journey.' A wave of dread surged through my body. The shock of tripping over the first question ripped my wits away from me. I responded quickly to mask my distress.

'Canus is in Cario?' I asked without thinking but continued. 'He left my troop behind to help garrison Cario when he rode out?' I do not know why I said such a statement. The captain had mentioned a journey but if Canus, I gave this man confirmation of his suspicions.

'He returned not long ago and I just finished my council with him. Please excuse me, I have not introduced myself. I am Feris, garrison captain of Cario. And you are?'

'I know who you are Feris.' I said a little too sharply. 'It's Mendax. We spoke before but you were rather worse for wear.' My too familiar tone took Feris aback slightly. He paused before replying and Muir spoke next.

'I expected you to get onto the bar when the singing begun.' Muir spoke in a calm and jovial manner. Feris paused as he tried to remember an event that had not occurred. Soldiers drink a lot. The likelihood Feris drank himself into a state of absent recall was in our favour because proud men do not like to admit they cannot recollect the events of a previous night.

'Ah yes. I remember now. My apologies, Mendax. The big guy did not speak much then either.' He said as he tapped Ailbeart on the arm. Ailbeart stared into space but I knew he was scanning the tavern for information.

'He hasn't got a clue what is being said Feris. He is Welsh.' I replied quickly. The alliance between the Brit and Welsh kingdoms would undoubtedly cause this common issue. He smiled and turned to Ailbeart. My heart almost burst through my chest as he turned   toward Ailbeart.

'Welsh? I'm from Gwent. How are you, kinsman?' Feris asked Ailbeart in Welsh.

THIRTY-SEVEN

My heart thumped as I felt beads of sweat dripped from my forehead onto the tavern floor. My head twitched in every direction looking for the best way out. Fighting was futile but we needed to get out of this mess. My mind raced. I went to step toward Feris to block the seasoned warrior from my men but stopped suddenly.

'Wet, cold and thirsty,' Ailbeart replied casually as he lifted his tanker to his lips. My mind whirled in the opposite direction. Ailbeart spoke Welsh. He had not told me before. I do not know why but this mattered. I consciously tried to soothe my blaring thoughts whilst I allowed them to talk. I speak five languages fluently including Welsh so understood every word. Feris chuckled at Ailbeart's response

'Where is home?' His probing moved onto Ailbeart. Ailbeart remained as cool, calm and collected as usual. He rarely became uptight even in the heat of battle or in a potentially fatal situation such as this one.

'I'm stationed in Leodus,' he responded politely enough 'but raised in Gwynedd.' He looked through Feris speaking at him rather than to him. My beating heart slowed when Ailbeart spoke of the town I previously mentioned. Ailbeart held well under scrutiny. I considered joining in with the conversation to help take the pressure off Ailbeart. Muir stepped in at the right time to help me gain my wit and knee how much of a relief it was. For some reason I wanted to watch the conversation unfold without my involvement.

'I am of Caerwent in Gwent. I've never been to Gwynedd.' Feris' tone softened slightly.

'Closest I've been is Plas Coch in Powys.' Both men spoke icily.

'Plas Coch?' Ailbeart's face naturally lit up as he recognised the town, 'Do you know Bwlch?' he asked with a warming tone.

'Every Welshman knows that weird man. The little drunk is hilarious,' replied Feris as a smile appeared on his face.

'He's not so funny when you upset him. I've got the bump on my head to prove it,' Ailbeart joked merrily.

'He knows how to fight,' Feris relaxed as the conversation continued. The barmaid appeared gripping her fingers around the handles of five pitchers. Not a drop spilt as she shimmered through the small gaps between the bustling crowds. Feris thanked her as he passed the tankers around. Ailbeart began a story about the first time he met Bwlch and ended up in a bar brawl. They spoke about other people who they both knew with surprising detail. I listened intensely to the peculiar conversation unfolding before me. Ailbeart had not told me he even spoke Welsh, let alone knew half the kingdom.

His relaxed manner and tone gave his lies a genuine feel whilst he spoke freely with the Brit captain. He fabricated his way through the conversation with extraordinary storytelling skills. Terror raged in my mind forcing me to doubt everything I knew about this exceptional liar. I suppressed my doubts trying to concentrate on the task in hand. Once we took Cario, I would find out the truth from Ailbeart. He gained an instant rapport, discussing kinsmen whilst laughing and jesting naturally. I tensed instinctively when Feris' spoke with a serious tone.

'Fight with me this morn?' he asked Ailbeart. 'By my side when we assault the Red Fort.' My heart smashed against my rib cage as his words sunk in. A Brit attack on the Red Fort was not part of Nechtan's plan. Only a division of cavalrymen remained in the dilapidated stronghold to keep up the ruse. Is the army had marched away then a garrison would have remained. The outnumbering Brits would slaughter them in their sleep. Ailbeart was lost in his own web of lies as he responded.

'Of course captain. If my master permits?' Ailbeart looked at me. I wondered why he would alert Feris that I understood Welsh.

'Take Aurelius with you,' I replied indicating Muir. I sent two of my men and closest friends amongst a brigade of adversaries. Not the best of ploys but for some reason I did not want to leave Ailbeart alone with this man. Opening the southern gate had to be my priority until the task was complete. I knew Sti and Tamhas successfully took and held the watchtowers either side of the gate. News of any failed attempt would have reached the tavern by now. I listened intently whilst Feris briefed Ailbeart on the Brits plan to sneak up to the Red Fort on foot just before dawn. Nechtan must be expecting this obvious plot but I feared it was an unusual oversight. I made my excuses saying I needed to muster my division and left with Ruadh. I looked over my shoulder at Muir and Ailbeart as I slipped out of the tavern door hoping I would see them again, alive.

Brit soldiers followed us out of the door emptying the tavern. Deserted streets soon bustled with optimistic armed soldiers trudging toward the northern gates eager for the impeding raid. Ruadh and I ran as soon as we turned the corner at the end of the street. I needed to forget the Brit raid on the Red Fort and concentrate on my duty. The Brits may retake the fortress and kill Nechtan's cavalry division in their sleep but we would hold Cario when they returned. The provisions we needed were not here which meant this assault was a waste of time but we would control another Brit stronghold. If we successfully opened the southern gate.

I could see some shadowy figures on the eastern tower as we dashed down the cobbled main road. Sti waved in greeting whilst Tamhas just put a thumb up. Ruadh darted up the rickety wooden staircase that led to the platform of the western tower. Three flaming arrows soared high into the lightning blue night sky. Three fiery streaks replied indicating Drest's army waited outside. I signalled to Tamhas to start lifting the portcullis gate and allow the pandemonium of battle to begin.

THIRTY-EIGHT

The Cavalry stallions thundered into Cario shaking the ground splashing through the sodden mud paths. The spine-chilling warhorses bounded past before the portcullis was halfway open. The leading riders' ignored my desperate pleas as I demanded attention. The rain slowed to a misty drizzle hampering visibility and although the black sky faded to a gloomy blue, the sun was yet to appear. Blocking their path was the only way to stop them so I could redirect them toward the red fort.

These magnificent but brutal animals trained to charge perilous shield walls of metal, wood and flesh whilst ignoring the sights, smells, tastes, and noise urging their natural instincts to flee. One senseless soldier barring their way was an easy obstacle to ride through and any attempt was pure stupidity. Horses galloped in pairs until expertly wheeling in opposite directions at the crossroads. They followed the muddy patrol path ran inside the palisade, cutting down the Brit soldiers standing on every guard post and tower. Warriors determinedly stared into the black abyss beyond the walls whilst being attacked from within.

My arms were waving frantically as I screamed for someone to listen. Highborn elite cavalrymen were resolute in their task ignoring the lunatic frantically waving his arms around screaming commands. Thick mud flung up from the horses hooves as they bolted past covering me from head to foot. An unsaddled soldier dressed in simple leather with no clear emblems or sign or high authority was an unimposing figure and dismissed as insignificant.

The horses galloping through the gate no longer headed

down the patrol paths instead slowing to a steady trot forming into elegant columns of six. The main road running from Cario's' northern gate to the southern gate would be the direction the expected garrison approached from to be confronted with an elite unit of cavalry.

Nechtan was renowned as the innovative tactician of the Scots but his brothers' possessed astute military minds as well. Drest's men confronted the guards on the wall quickly and efficiently blocking their route to sound the alarm whilst the remaining cavalry marching in ranks of six could deal with a blockade, a cavalry charge, a blood-curdling shield wall, or frenzied ambushes. All of these scenarios would have been likely and considered but no confrontation would come because the garrison had already left Cario. The Brits abandoned Cario in pursuit of retaking the red fort.

My mission of opening the southern gate was complete but now I had a new task. The Brits marched toward Nechtan's singular division, with Muir and Ailbeart in tow. I thought about rushing toward the northern gate to help but I could not make it in time on foot and was little use on my own. The advancing Scot infantry rushed toward the gates as the final straggling horses cantered through the muddy swamp the entrance had become. I could not see them in the harsh half-light of the fresh dawn because the misty rain hampered my visibility but I could hear the commotion and cries of an advancing army. Three horses slowly cantered through the gates. The Brits were on foot so could still be caught but I needed to get to the northern gate.

The insufferable elitist cavalry would not listen so I must warn Nechtan. I yelled for a man riding a majestic black horse to stop as he cantered within striking distance. The soldier gave me no consideration as the horse continued past. I stepped forward grabbing the riders leg determined to unhorse him. The torrential rain had soaked my leather jerkin and my hands were slick with thick mud giving me little grip. The rider swung his right gauntleted fist striking my cheek. The horse continued without faltering as the glancing blow hurled me back. I landed hard and ungracefully in the muddy swamp.

Ruadh stood and watched my foolish bravado from the roadside but trudged his way into the boggy road to help me up. He gripped my shoulders pulling backwards but slipped and slid in the sludge. He continued to yank at my limp body as I lay in turmoil not helping at all. I was distraught no one listened to me and was back in a dark despair lost in my own mind. Men needed to ride straight through Cario and back out of the northern gate to warn an unsuspecting Nechtan that he was under attack. Nechtan said he was the rabbit but now the foxes were rabbit hunting whilst they rested in an oblivious slumber. A permanent slumber if no one helped.

THIRTY-NINE

'The Red Fort! The Brits attack Nechtan. Ride to the fort! Ride now!' I screamed hysterically. Ruadh regained his feet and dragging me out of the boggy sludge. The three horses wheeled around and sped back toward us. My legs kicked frantically pushing myself out of their path but I kept shouting the same words over again. The horses rode straight at us but the rider of the jet-black stallion leapt down before the horse thundered by. He landed with a splash in a deep puddle but managed to stay on his feet staring through the thick mud mask that covered my face.

'Say that again, Calum.' It was Drest and he recognised my voice.

'The garrison marches on the Red Fort. You must help Nechtan.' I was in a frantic state and unaware I was giving commands to a king. It did not seem to bother him as he clasped my wrist and pulled me to my feet.

'Get on the back of Tal,' he barked at Ruadh. He quickly leapt into his saddle as his horse cantered back toward us and gestured for me to get on. Ruadh sprinted to the rider next to him who helped him onto the rear of the horse. The rider was Talorc.

Drest's magnificent war beast stood tall at sixteen hands. I put my hands on the horse's hindquarters trying to thrust myself upwards but pain ripped through my exhausted shoulders. Drest grabbed the back of my jerkin and pulled me up before clicking his heels against the horses flank. I barely sat down as the horse galloped away. I awkwardly grabbed Drest by wrapping my left arm around his stomach and grabbed the

Dawn of Dark Days

back of the saddle with the other, somehow managing to stay on. The horses wheeled expertly left at the crossroad and then an immediate right without any obvious signal from the riders. A good cavalryman has a special relationship with his horse allowing them to move as one.

'Hold on Nechtan,' I found myself shouting as we galloped through the empty streets. We effortlessly took another Brit stronghold and my role in its capture was once again significant but I could only think of Nechtan, Ailbeart and Muir. The horses approached the open northern gates but no Brit was in sight. I leapt from the horse stumbling to my knees as I landed awkwardly because the horse was a lot bigger than the mares I learnt to ride on. I starred through the gates into the gloomy blue abyss that masked a ferocious battle. A soldier raced down the steps leading to the towers that housed the portcullis winches. I turned and drew my sword as he reached the bottom but his sword angled by his side. He yelled toward Drest.

'The guard posts are taken my king but these gates were open on arrival.' The man spoke with an authoritative tone and wore three arm rings. He walked straight up to Drest as he continued his report. 'There isn't ...' Drest nodded as the man spoke but barged straight past him and bounded up the rickety wooden steps three at a time. Me, Ruadh and Talorc quickly followed. Eochaid, the third rider, stayed saddled on his horse. Drest stood on the small tower platform with two other warriors so I stayed on the top step not wanting to overcrowd the king.

'It's too quiet. Calum, were they on horses?' Drest continued to look into the bleak nothingness as he spoke.

'No, on foot,' I replied.

'I wish I could see better, where is the damn dawn?' The dark looming clouds cast a foreboding shadow across the plain. No sun, moon or stars were visible in the deep blue sky. The drizzling rain hung in the dawn half-light causing poor visibility.

'Ruadh! Pitch posts on west side,' I ordered quickly as soon as the idea sprung into my mind. Ruadh pushed by me,

Drest and the two other warriors as he made his way to the small fire pit built into a stone slab at the far end of the platform. He pulled four arrows out of his quiver placing them into the smoking embers. Drest frowned but stepped aside to allow Ruadh through. He did not say anything just watched. Ruadh fired two arrows that arced into the darkness and quickly died on contact with the sodden ground. Setting fire to an arrow affects its distance and accuracy and Ruadh aimed at an insignificant target he could not see. I have never met a more skilled or luckier archer than Ruadh and luck was in his third arrow.

    A ferocious flame burst to life bringing a little light to the gloom. Two small flickers of flame raced across the ground in opposite directions. The pitch posts were designed to show the road during the night. Feris would not use the path so we were unlikely to see his whereabouts because the harsh firelight only shone onto a little ground either side of the road. Tiny blazes ignited along the path. Drest glared at me as if he was waiting for my next move or waiting for the purpose of this order.

    Cario was roughly a league away from the red fort. On a clear summer day, you can see one fortress from the walls of other. This murky morning there was no way of knowing how far ahead the Brits were. Drest waited for me to continue my plan for a few moments before realising I had no other ideas. He pushed past me and bounded down the staircase. Ruadh, Talorc and the man giving the original report stood on the steps behind me but Drest struggling by them to reach the bottom step just as the cavalry formation came into view. They trotted slowly through the main road of Coria formed into ranks of six awaiting opposition. Drest used the side roads to reach the northern gate quicker. The man nearest to us in the front rank looked perplexed when he saw Drest on the staircase. Drest turned and pointed through the open gates as he bellowed a command to his men.

    'Charge!'

FORTY

'Charge the Red Fort!' Drest bellowed urgently. 'Charge, Charge!' The cavalry kicked their heels and galloped through the northern gates in search for the battle they had expected inside Coria. The thin flame raced into the darkness still lighting the pitch posts ablaze. The fires sprung from outside Coria but would continue to light the way for an entire league. The Romans designed the warning signal for the two garrisons to communicate. There ingenious method now aided us. I stared at the small flicker of flame in the distance and hoped it was enough to alert Nechtan. Nechtan would have guards on the walls that would see the flickering flame as a warning, if it reached the red fort in time. I doubted they would be ready for the impending assault.

I saw Drest, Talorc and Eochaid dash through the gates toward the ensuing battle. I regained control of my heavy breathing and calmed myself down. I smiled. Both forts would be under Scot control before the sun fully awakened. Ruadh appeared beside me with a smug grin beaming on his face. I tapped him on the shoulder.

'Good shot,' I said not taking my eyes from the distance. The murky sky quickly cleared as the sun erupted from beyond the horizon. The darkened clouds faded away taking the drizzling misty rain with them. Shadowy figures appeared in the distance. Horsed riders chased down men on foot. The fighting raged a few hundred paces from the red fort and the shadowy figures were as small as tiny ants foraging in the dirt.

Horses galloped south from the Red Fort revealing Nechtan was aware of the assault. I was unsure whether our warnings had alerted him or if this was part of his plot all along. His mind worked in mysterious ways and the enemy did exactly what he wanted. The Scot shield men reached the north gate after finding Cario deserted. My stomach whirled as the first men raced through the open portcullis to join in the melee.

'Halt! Stand fast, halt!' I commanded with as much authority I could muster. Every man on foot in the open plain was a Brit. The scots swordsmen would cause chaos and confusion when they reached the fray with Scot cavalry mistakenly cutting down their own kin. They ignored my orders and sprinted into the distance. The captain who made the report to Drest now stood by the gate. He repeated my orders with a natural air of authority forcing the men to turn and face him. The soldiers awaited further orders but the captain remained quiet.

'Form line! Form line!' I had no idea what I was commanding or why but could not risk the Scot infantry causing confusion in the simple scuffle taking place.

A thin single ranked wall without the heavy wooden shields quickly formed as the captain repeated my command and took charge. It was a matter of moments before the superior cavalry slaughtered the Brit soldiers on foot. Riders wheeled their horses around and head back toward Cario whilst others headed toward the red fort. Brit soldiers scattered in disarray soon abandoning any attempt to assault the Red Fort. The cavalry advancing from behind dispersed them effectively as they tried to outrun the horses in vain.

A pang of disloyalty emerged as I realised Muir and Ailbeart were on foot. My men were out on foot. I watched as cavalry chased down and killed foot soldiers with relative ease and wondered which where my friends. One man sprinting toward Cario made good ground and his antics caught my attention. As a horse approached, he knelt on one knee and lifted a small object high above his head showing it to the advancing soldier. The riders thundered past allowing the fugitive to continue his sprint. I smiled as I realised it was Muir.

Another horse galloped toward Muir without slowing.

Muir had knelt like before displaying his object above his head but suddenly stood up tall as if accepting his fate. My heart sank when the rider shifted his weight in his saddle leaning with his right foot dangled underneath the animal for balance. The horse cantered past without slowing his stride. Muir leapt in the air kicking is right leg high and straight. The rider grasped Muir by the waist and pulled him onto the rear of the horse. The horse faltered slightly but regained his stride and galloped toward Cario. The rider was Talorc.

The manoeuvre was complete with expertise and I was in awe of both men. Talorc was a natural leader and would be a king I could see myself pledging my service to. Muir was a boy in age but already a skilled swordsman with a fantastic mind for war. The cavalry returned to the fortresses but I remained on the wall starring into the fresh summer day. The plain was empty except for the dead, dying and a fiery streak splitting the lush green meadow in half. Then I spotted a most peculiar sight within the middle of bodies.

FORTY-ONE

A scuffle between two sword men raged a few hundred paces from Cario. It was hard to make out the men's identities but I knew it was Ailbeart and Feris. They dodged and parried each other with ease lunging with too much aggression. Ailbeart lunged forward belligerently. Feris feinted to the right instead of bringing his sword back towards Ailbeart and slicing towards his torso, which was unguarded. Feris threw his elbow forward and smashed it into Ailbeart's face. He stumbled backwards tripping over a fallen Brit and tumbling to the ground.

My heart sank for Ailbeart knowing Feris would pounce on this advantage and finish the contest but he hesitated for a fleeting moment. He lunged with his sword overstretching his stride as he stepped. He should step short and drive the blade down into his opponent's exposed flesh. Ailbeart sprang back to his feet. Feris advanced bringing his sword down in a slicing motion. Ailbeart bought his swords up blade edge broadside on. He held the hilt with both hands easily parrying Feris' strikes. Ailbeart pushed hard on Feris' blade struck forcing Feris back.

Neither man fought with menace. I felt like a spectator of a sparring match between two champions or a tournament duel. Something was out of place. They rushed toward each other clashing their swords together echoing metallic clangs across the open meadow. A lone rider galloped toward the melee from the direction of the Red Fort. Feris feinted to the right and Ailbeart foolishly lunged leading with the point.

I often made the same ploy during sparring sessions and he fell for the ruse every time. My usual move was the exact same Feris used now. Ailbeart's hefty bodyweight carried him through the lunge as Feris continued to step beside him. Feris placed his arm onto Ailbeart's back shoving him forward as he bought his knee up. Feris' knee struck Ailbeart in his stomach as he fell forward. Ailbeart landed on his back. Feris twisted his body around moving his feet expertly to correct his stance lifting his sword up with both hands. The thrust downwards would glide through the fault line in Ailbeart's armour and easily slice through his throat.

I screamed hysterically. I chose the cowards path again and watched from the ramparts whilst I sent my friend to die. A deep guttural wail reverberated across the plain. The blood-curdling scream made my goose pimples shiver despite my distance from the source. Feris looked up to see a horseman quickly bearing down on him. Feris had time to thrust his blade through Ailbeart before turning to face the cavalryman but he did not.

He turned to face the oncoming horse with his left foot slightly in front of his right. Feris was a defensive fighter. He wore leather although his rank indicated he could afford better armour. Some soldiers preferred not to wear the metal suits of the Romans or the chainmail suits of Scot nobility. They greatly affect movability and fighting style. Feris' agility was his armour. That becomes a little more difficult when facing cavalry.

The rider sat proud and purposeful on his horse with his sword angled by his side. Most cavalry lean across to cut down a foot soldier in a similar way Talorc had rescued Muir but the advantage gained from being on horseback was lost with the rider being in an unbalanced position. Feris expertly rolled away from the horse as it thundered past. The horse wheeled left and cantered toward Ailbeart. Ailbeart got to his feet and pulled himself onto the back of the horse before the cavalryman galloped toward the Red Fort. My heart sank.

Feris was a highly skilled swordsman and an asset to the Brits. An opportunity to kill him vanished as the horse galloped away. I knew at that moment that we would pay for that mistake. A few Brits managed to return to Cario. I watched in awe as

Ruadh and a few other archers fired their barbs of death into the men. Feris walked back toward Cario but stopped when he saw the bloody spectacle of arrows ripping through flesh and bone. He stood lost and alone in a meadow of slaughter.

    A lone rider approached from the edge of Cario. Only the Scots were on horses but this man was a Brit. His gold plated armour belonged to Roman Brit legions. The rider's metal suit glistened in the fresh sunlight of the new day as he gently cantered toward Feris. He dismounted a few paces in front of him and the two men embraced. He must have been the rider we saw early that night on the cobbled road. If it was Lord Canus then we had let the two most influential men in Cario escape. An error that would haunt us come summers end.

    We controlled three Brit strongholds before the sun had fully set. The pups of war were instrumental once again. Our reputation grew. A few horses without riders frolicked in the blood-soaked meadow grazing on the enriched grass. We lost few men in the melee but an obvious sight of fallen comrades still upset me. My mind slipped back into despair. Every other Scot in Cario was overwhelmed in triumph. Something concerned me stopping me from enjoying this victorious glee. I felt its significance. Only one detail was missing. What was it that had me so worried?

FORTY-TWO

I tried to make my way toward the steps leading down but the small platform was overcrowded. The courtyard and adjacent streets were crammed with warriors and horses wanting to be near the action as it concluded. Soldiers are inquisitively nosey. News spreads like a wildfire because of it. I weaved my way through the masses and down the rickety staircase that was in a state of disrepair. I hurried down desperate to reach the bottom before the staircase collapsed but was careful not barge expecting the weak railings to give way. I saw Drest return and needed to talk to authority.

A thread of thought in my head unbalanced me. I began to push my way through the crowds as my feet found solid earth. I headed in the direction I last saw the king. Someone grabbed my arm with an unforgiving grip. Another attacker seized my legs and steadily lifted into the air. The men around me were screeching and wailing with hysteria. Someone pushed my backside and I found myself on the shoulders of another man. I stopped struggling when I realised I was perched upon Fert.

'The hero, Calum the Cur,' bellowed Fert. Muir was on Talorc's horse when I last saw him galloping back toward the walled town. Now he floated toward me in the distance. An unusual frenzy engrossed the crowd of warriors. These were not lovers, families, friends and common townsfolk welcoming returning heroes. Seasoned and battle-hardened warriors excitedly squealed my name. Cheers for the pups of war erupted behind me.

Airson rested on the shoulders of two large men being too heavy for one man to bear. I held my hand up in greeting and he smiled back. We passed the time yesterday afternoon joking about sending the army into rapture and being celebrated as heroes but had not expected it to occur. Airson had needed a little confidence. This scene was beyond our imagination. I heard shouts again.

'Quiet, Quiet everyone. The Cur wishes to speak.' Someone called for silence. I looked around and realised everyone was staring toward me. The crowd misinterpreted my hand movement but I was no leader and certainly not a speech giver. I cleared my throat as my father did before beginning a toast at a feast. I thought it was to ensure he spoke clearly but suddenly realised it was an opportunity to think of something to say. It did not work. This situation had caught me off guard. I have never been one for praise, and do not think I ever will be. It gives me the warming sensation, as it would anyone, but public displays make me feel vulnerable. Therefore, I passed the vulnerability on to the strongest man inside the walls.

'Drest the Brutal! Drest! Drest! Drest!' I began another chant. The rapturous warriors erupted again echoing my cries. The crowd began to divide snaking a pathway in my direction and a horse trotted through the emerging space. Fert lifted me over his head and assisted me back onto my feet. The crowd went silent. The warriors in front of me tried to shuffle back into space that did not exist. A small ripple of shuffling surged through the horde of soldiers as they moved backward creating a space for the rider. Drest was in a sombre mood. He only as he advanced toward his next victim during a battle with his hand gripping a bloodied sword. He was a ferocious man with a true thirst for a massacre.

'Fall out,' he barked the command viciously dispersing the crowd quickly. 'Prepare to march.' He turned his gaze to me as he leapt from the saddle of his huge horse.

Intensity builds deep within a soldier on the eve of battle. Anxious excitement with dark desires for blood curdled with an apprehension of impending violent death. No genuine battle robbed our army of any real release of tension. Another successful skirmish and two more strongholds without severe casualties or loss of life made this day a triumph but hyped warriors needed to discharge. The frenzied celebration was the resulting release but my reputation began that day. Drest's epithet was brutal, which suited his stubborn, merciless ambition. I liked the idea of being Cur though I had no idea what it meant. The crowd dispersed to allow Talorc's horse through. He dismounted beside Drest before they walked toward me.

FORTY-THREE

'You did well,' Talorc proclaimed. 'But bravery has its place. Attacking the king is beyond lunacy even if your intentions were good' He was a very different man to his uncle. An emotional man quick to temper but was commonly found smiling. He smiled now but without warmth. His inexperience showed through his tired, bloodshot eyes.

'Thank you,' I responded unsure if he congratulated me or reprimanded me. I knew how Drest felt.

'The next time you attack me will be your last moment in this world.' Drest spoke without anger or aggression. He stated fact. He looked over my head and addressed Fert as he spoke again. 'Captain, disperse these men.'

'Do we march soon?' Fert asked after hearing the command Drest gave to disperse the crowd.

'Soldiers disappear surprisingly quickly when they think we march soon captain,' Talorc answered for his uncle. 'A war council meets in the Red Fort so expect your orders soon.' Fert nodded in acknowledgement. Talorc expected to march immediately. We all knew Drest's desire for Pons Aelli. The formidable stronghold had been a symbol of Roman strength and ingenuity and Drest knew the reputation he would hold if he captured it. The march was inevitable. Drest pulled himself back into the saddle and wheeled his horse toward the northern gate. Talorc followed his lead.

'Lord Talorc, return this to Lord Nechtan please,' I called after him. I held out the second arm ring I borrowed for the infiltration of Cario. The authority a second arm ring possessed was immeasurable. Feris would not have addressed the situation in the same manner if a troop leader were the highest rank present in the group. Talorc looked at Fert.

'Does he need that, Captain?' he asked in a manner of a rhetorical question.

'Yes, Lord,' Replied Fert. '...and he needs these.' Fert held three thin crudely made arm rings. Confusion spread across my face as I looked back at Talorc. He trotted down the cobbled road following his uncle to the red fort. 'Choose your leaders wisely, Master,' he bellowed with a beaming grin on his face. Talorc formed Fert's Cohort when he gained his brigade but gave him three divisions. Most cohorts have four divisions. I smiled as Fert affectionately cuffed me around the side of the head. He turned around and barked an order at a soldier sat on the bottom step of the tower. Fert gave him a list of names before the man leapt to his feet and sped into the alleyways of Coria.

'...immediately means immediately Neadh,' Fert shouted after the soldier. He turned his attention back to me. 'Muster your troop Calum, the rest of your division is being found.' He briskly walked away but paused to give one last piece of advice. 'Choose wisely.'

'I will,' I answered. All my men remained in the small courtyard inside the northern gate. I walked toward them when I heard a familiar mocking voice.

'Did he really think so? He didn't, did he?' The questioning tone was infuriating enough usually but knew he was talking about me by the derision in his voice. 'Do you think he makes a good cur?' He spoke with his usual group of sat with their backs against the   palisade wall, relaxing in the sun before the heat of the day got too hot. I spun round to confront Roinn. We were both divisional masters now but I still should not allow him to rile me. I took a deep breath to calm down as he looked toward me. I just shook my head casually from side to side.

'Everyone knows what you are now, boy. You don't like that, do you?' he snarled.

'A hero,' I answered back. My men who stood the other side of the gate began walking across as his entourage lethargically began getting to their feet. I knew better than to rise to provocation but there was no reason why this man should have a problem with me. His aversion toward me was infuriating.

'You're a devious mercenary. Do you have any loyalty?' He continued to goad me.

'I am a sworn and loyal master serving the same lord and king as you.' I snapped angrily. Roinn knew cur was derogatory.

'I have served the same lord and king my entire life. How many have you had? Is it three or four, already?' Roinn was speaking calmly now. He saw my shoulders tense as tiredness and emotion took its toll leading me to bite at his taunts. 'You are no noble and not a soldier. Have you killed anyone yet?' I had no response. My wit evaded me. A crowd of my new soldiers arrived behind me and this was not the example I wanted to set. I turned away allowed him this small victory but vowed to seek justice for this ridicule. I bellowed for my men to fall in and my troop formed the front rank.

FORTY-FOUR

I looked through the ranks of my new division. Their natural discipline was pleasing as they quickly fell into formation behind the pups of war. My troop infiltrated the fortress last night but still stood tall with their chests pronounced. They looked battered, bedraggled and unpolished but proud of it. Despite their youth, they looked like battle-hardened and seasoned soldiers. My new infantry warriors were not involved in the skirmishes but looked filthy and fatigued, old and battle worn but not in the same aspiring manner. Most of these older veterans slouched their shoulders and stood forlorn hardly making an effort to stand at attention as I spoke.

'Congratulation pups of war for another successful raid. You deserve the reputation and prestige that awaits you.' I spoke slow and deliberate. The number of men that stared back at me with adjudicating eyes overwhelmed me. 'Welcome new companions and kinsmen. Honour and glory await us all.' I found myself scratching around the emptiness of my mind trying to find something inspirational to say. Nothing emerged. Talorc was awe-inspiring the first time I had met him. His speech surged an ambitious desire throughout the new brigade. These seasoned soldiers doubted my capability to lead them. I needed the gain their respect and prove my authority but my desperation showed I was not ready.

'Ruadh! Muir!' I barked my closest friend's names more abruptly than intended. 'Quick... March!' I had not briefed either of them but they competently approached as I stood several paces in front. I gave no order as they halted together with discipline. I smiled uncontrollably as I handed them an arm ring each seeing the glee in their eyes. Their beaming smiles were infectious. I thought of no awe inspiring or inspirational words so dismissed the division. Both Ruadh and Muir huddled around their new followers as I did when I first took command of the pups. It was pleasing to see their devotion to their new men. We were a close unit whose bond created a unique troop. We claimed the slur of pups of war and made it our own badge of honour. My reputation was growing as Calum the Cur.

FORTY-FIVE

Five days passed. Five thousand men busily prepared to march on leaving little time for rest and recuperation. Eochaid appointed a Dal Riadan commander as Lord of Cario with his senior captain given command of the red fort garrison. Skeleton garrisons remained behind but the majority of men marched as the conquest gained pace. My men set up a rough camp to the west of the northern gate and worked on digging a ditch in front of the palisade. We knew the flaws in the stronghold and immediately worked to correct them but knew the march to Pons Aelli would continue soon.

Enthusiastic anticipation hung in the exhilarating air masking the evolving tension. The majority of these soldiers met Ceretic and Eoppa's desertion with derision. Their cowardly decision to follow alternative tasks proved they lost their nerve. They hid in fear whilst the remaining army ripped through Briton. We captured two strongholds and now marched on the impenetrable Pons Aelli.

Ailbeart found the encampment as dusk set on the first night. He made no fuss about our growth in numbers. He did not seek after me instead finding Airson and setting his pit next to him. I kept myself apart from the division to watch new bonds and tensions form within my men. I did not drill them and gave few tasks except digging the ditch, allowing a brief time for a quiet respite before the conquest recommenced.

On the eve of the fifth day, Fert sent ale, wine and meat as reward for the small victories. I suggested a small celebratory feast to reward their admirable behaviour in Cario. They worked hard during the days and remained sober at night. They sparred with each other, tended to their kit, and completed various other soldiering tasks rather than drinking feasting and fighting within the walls.

Four troops make up a division but I only led enough men to create three. The fourth troop usually consisted of cavalrymen and scouts but I possessed no horses. I held the last arm ring for my final troop leader in my hand. My fingers nervously spun it around gently as I approached the campfire. Sti and Tamhas lay sprawled out the far side of the crackling fire. Ailbeart sat on the damp ground next to Airson. His calming assurance was a real comfort to me demonstrating this was the right decision. A nagging doubt about his loyalties plagued me for a few days but there was no foundation in my suspicions.

I crept behind him before sitting down calmly. He smiled in greeting but said nothing. I smiled back. An unexpected tension fizzled between us in the refreshingly cool night air. The third arm ring rested in the palm of my hand. Ailbeart glanced down at the authoritative bauble watching the rough bronze edges glisten in the firelight. Tamhas and Sti recited their version of assaulting the southern gates. They argued about every little fact and kept interrupting each other's sentences. This was the fifth time I heard the story and it became more elaborate every time. They were a funny pair but good men. Ailbeart sat staring into the fire watching the flames flicker in the cool night sky.

'I didn't lie to you Cal,' he spoke calmly but with discomfort in his tone. He stared into the flame as he spoke twiddling his fingers nervously. 'Not telling you something and lying are different.' He paused for a moment leaving behind an eerie silence. The twins chattering seemed distant. 'My mother was Welsh. I was banished, like you, but I deserved mine.' He took a deep breath struggling to continue. I allowed him to compose himself whenever the tenderness became too difficult. He never paused for long fighting through his emotional agony.

'I went to my uncle in Gwynedd but my heart stayed in Stratha Cluith. I learnt of the Scot truce and Drest's desire for Briton. I went to Nechtan for a pardon. He offered me the

Luguvalium raid. I did not expect to survive.' An eerie silence followed only broken by his short heavy breathing. We sat side by side like so many nights before but an invisible gulf appeared between us. My shoulders loosened and chest relaxed as Ailbeart spoke as if his omissions placed a weight onto me. I felt empowered as my friend crumbled beside me.

'Why were you banished?' I asked after a pause. Ailbeart took a deep breath followed by a quick intake of breath. He was crying. The streak of tears running down his face glistened slightly in the harsh light of the fire. I waited a few moments for him to gain enough composure. His icy distant tone was unexpected when he answered.

'It will be a great honour to lead the pups or I can pledge my sword to another. The decision is yours, but if I stay, you never ask me that again.' We sat in silence.

Memories flooded my mind filling in huge gaps of the picture in my mind, like the stunning mosaics on the floor of the grand white stone building in Luguvalium. Every member of my original troop was dispensable. He appeared self-assured and poised on that first assault but he had accepted his fate. He rode to Luguvalium for redemption and expected to die.

The rustic arm ring slid across my fingers tips as I sat perplexed about the decision I faced. Our bodies practically touched but we had never been further apart. No one else deserved to lead the pups. It dawned on me I knew very little about any of my men despite believing we were a close unit of brothers. Not knowing or understanding frustrates me and fills me with a sense of inadequacy. I must know the source of the anguish that tormented my friend. Rumours would be rife amongst the seasoned soldiers who would tell me but to enquire would be a betrayal on my part.

I walked twenty paces before looking behind. The arm ring lay on the grass where I left it. Ailbeart stared as it glistened in the firelight but did not pick it up. The decision is yours, I thought to myself as I walked away.

FORTY-SIX

I got drunk. My young body was not used to ale so it never took much but I drank a lot that night. The conversation with Ailbeart left me more perplexed than before. I meandered through the encampment aimlessly finding myself in the company of Fert. I stormed over to the trunk he sat on whilst talking to one of his soldier, Maoidh.

Fert was the second son of Bane of Eta and a nobleman but preferred the company of lowborn soldiers rather than his cavalrymen peers. He was fond of those with weird or fanatical traits with Maoidh being a perfect example. As Banes bard he accompanied him into battle to witness his fantastic feats and audacious deeds to put them into song. He now leads one of Fert's divisions and sings about his own actions. Either a sword or a lute remains nearby, usually both. Born a farmhand he ran away to be a druid. The gods did not take to Maoidh and his whimsical ways. They command us and we cannot connect with them unless chosen. He turned his back on them after they rejected him to become the strangest of all beings, Christian.

I stormed over to Fert in a fearsome rage. I knew the vile meaning of cur but I was no scoundrel or mongrel. I heard a different villainous term every time I passed Roinn or a group of his cronies, a wretched worm, a cowardly snake, a blackguard bum.

'So I'm a good for nothing rat am I?' I snarled aggressively looking down as he remained seated.

'Excuse me?' Fert replied with a hint of annoyance at my abrupt approach.

'Roinn and his men la...,'

'Cal,' Fert interrupted calmly, 'how many of those imbeciles have a nickname?' His composed tone under my erratic salvo made me pause. 'It takes reputation and prestige to gain a tag Calum,' he continued with his peaceful explanation 'and you have neither' Fert was a strange but well-collected man. Every action had purpose but I could not understand why he ignited the frenzy after the red fort skirmish.

'Why am I a cur?' I asked politely.

'A cur is a mix-breed, someone without origin or allegiances.' He continued in the same calm manner remaining on the trunk. I looked at him puzzled trying to understand his point.

'So I am a disloyal scoundrel? Is that what you think?' He obviously thought little of me, yet he promoted me the same day he labelled me with this despicable term. He shook his head reprovingly.

'Rifts are rife throughout the four separate armies. Most of these soldiers have vowed vengeance against another Scot over these past few years.' Fert spoke to me but watched Maoidh quietly strumming a lute. 'You are not a man of Dun Phris, or Pict, or Rheged. The Scot coalition needs a common hero. Being the cur will help as your reputation grows.' He turned back to face me and smiled before passing a pitcher of ale.

'I am no hero Fert,' I replied defensively.

'You are not even a warrior yet, Cal. No man yet to face a shield wall knows the desolation of a soldier.' He had returned his gaze to Maoidh with a smirk across his face. He was already drunk and babbling. 'Only you are blind to your potential capabilities. The name will grow on you, trust me.'

Maoidh carefully placed his lute on the soggy grass and stood up swaying his arms aimlessly. He pranced barefoot around the campfire. I was unsure if he danced or performed a ritual but he was funny to watch. Fert and I giggled loudly as we conversed in a jovial manner. This was fun. I needed more fun.

FORTY-SEVEN

Maoidh stumbled over to sit cross-legged in front of the stump I shared with Fert. His luscious brown hair flowed to the small of his back and he wore a long black gown. His gentile facial features and feminine manner would commonly mistake him as a woman if it were not for his long shabby beard and troubled eyes. He pulled out a small roman vase from somewhere in his cloak and pulled the cork stopper with his teeth.

`Do you know the best thing about being a druid, Calum?' He lifted his vase to his lips and took a sip of whatever substance was inside shaking his head like a wet dog climbing out of a river. 'The gods choose their followers Calum. Some are touched within their soul and can speak to them. I was not so lucky.' He spoke matter-of-factly. He did not seem emotional or upset about what he spoke of he was just stating how it was.

'And some are touched in the head,' Fert bellowed with a chuckle. He tapped his own head but gestured toward Maoidh. Fert started singing a song about a druid that annoyed the gods jesting with Maoidh. Maoidh just stared at me ignoring our other companion.

'It's the elixirs. Some heal the body, some rectify the mind, and others cleanse your soul. This one...' he paused to indicate the delicate vase before he lifted it to his lips once again 'harms the body, mutilates the mind and blemishes the soul. Nevertheless, it is bliss. Some say it sends you to Mag Mel.' Meeting the gracious gods would enlighten any man but if you reached Formoria, you would certainly return a malicious creature with dark desire. He leant forward slowly as he spoke staring into my eyes. I felt a little uncomfortable but could not turn away.

'Being Christian I know gods entering bodies and trips of the soul is a heap of fish swill. I get drunk and have wondrous dreams.' He sat back with a reassuring smile across his honest face. I sat and listened in silence occasionally swigging from the pitcher of ale I held. 'A Christian also knows a soul in torment. We listen well and advise better Calum. Please tell what ails you.' He stopped talking but held his hypnotic gaze. His eyes were almost completely black. The little remaining white glistened in the firelight.

My worries are mine to bear and should remain locked inside not to burden others. That night I spoke of anything and everything, even concerns I had not realised bothered me. I began with the ambush that took my father and brother. I spoke about my exile, the gauntlet that nearly took my life, the incapacitating dread infiltrating Luguvalium, Ailean's plots to kill me, my concern for Acair and Gazella's safety. The Coria assault poured out exposing how afraid I had been that night, not scared of death but failure.

Fert swayed back and forth in a drunken stupor singing one of Maoidh's tunes not listening. He occasionally refilled my pitcher as I revealed my world to a virtual stranger. My head pounded and my heart ached before I began on the most recent cause of my turmoil. Ailbeart had not told me of his troubled past and it inexplicably infuriated me. His life was nothing to do with me but I cared about my men. Maoidh slowly leant forward and knelt before me. His feminine face had a warming glow initiating truth and honesty in a conversation. He closed his eyes and whispering quietly to his sacrificed god repeating the words healing and compassion a lot. He made the sign of a cross on his own head and chest and then did the same to me before opening his eyes and lifting his vase to my lips.

'Drink my child, drink.' He spoke assertively as he poured the thick tonic into my mouth. I naturally gulped the surprisingly sweet elderberry fluid. Maoidh occasionally sipped from the vase but poured it down my throat as if I was drinking water.

My head swirled, stomach ached and heart raced. The substance splashed into the copious amounts of ale already in my stomach.

The world got gloomier as the ground beneath me revolved. I slipped from the trunk I sat on and curled into a ball shivering. The cool night air became bitterly cold but I hands became clammy with sweat. Tears ran down my face as I closed my eyes. I could not concentrate on any thought for longer than a fleeting moment as my mind raced of control. The ground span faster preventing me from grasping a single thought. My mind fell into darkness as the movement stopped. I took a deep breath and opened my eyes.

FORTY-EIGHT

Unexpected harsh daylight stung my eyes. My arms clasped around a beam with my ankles wrapped around each other locking my legs tight around the wood. I gripped tighter realising I was high in the air. My head rested against the beam of the barn. I lifted my head gently from the beam it rested upon to discover I was in a small barn. No horses stood in the three stalls, only a young boy raking out the one nearest the large open barn door.

He whistled a gentle tune as he worked hard. Sweat speckled over his muscular bare torso. He was ten or eleven years of age but looked strong and agile. He finished sweeping the filthy straw into a neat pile and straightened his back resting the pitchfork against the back wall before walking toward the stall entrance.

I took a sharp breath when I saw he was Ailbeart. No, this boy was too young and small to be my friend but they looked so similar. Not just in look but his mannerisms too, his head held high assuredly. Ailbeart never told me about a son but he hid a lot of his murky past. Ten years separated the lads making it unlikely Ailbeart was his father but maybe brothers.

He bent down next to a small bale of water sitting by the open door taken sips from cupped hands before splashing his reddened face. He stood up straight turning his head at a noise outside before hurrying back toward the back of the stall. He picked up his pitchfork and scuttled to the second stall ensuring the gate locked shut behind him. He no longer worked or moved at all. His knees were tight against his chest with both hands clutching his legs as he shook, petrified. He sat huddled right in the far corner behind a pile of soiled hay.

He hid but easily visible from my vantage point. The noises outside got louder. Light clatters of metal on wood, horses cantering into the farmstead, the odd person talking blended into a calamitous racket. Wood split and metal scraped against the ground as a deep guttural growl exploded into a fearsome rage. The rampant voice grew louder and the metal chinking became rhythmic.

A tall man dressed in a tatty and battered leather jerkin clanked into view. Rusted and worn cuisses protected his upper leg but with no greaves attached instead donning long fraying leather boots to protect his lower leg. I could clearly see his face because he wore no helmet. He too looked a lot like Ailbeart despite already being roughly thirty summers old. My uncle's companion, Leyn, appeared in my mind for a fleeting moment. The man's lush brown hair flowed down his back but Leyn was bald. I chuckled lightly at the odd sight of this angry man who looked like several different dismembered warriors sewn back together. None of his armour fitted properly suggesting none of it was originally his. The man stormed toward the first stall gate kicking it open.

I looked around my surroundings realising things mismatched here too. The stable was small but to possess such an annex suggested wealth despite the state of disrepair. The young boy wore simple cloth slacks and went barefoot. The angry man's attire was aged and mismatched but he owned armour. The two young women who chased after him were dressed in simple apparel but both possessed an air of grace that becomes of a noble lady. Their heads held high and backs straight as they scurried after the raging warrior but kept their distance. They pleaded with him desperately but he ignored their hysterics as he stomped toward the third stall kicking that gate too. He struck it so hard that it slammed against the stall wall before slinging back toward him. He steadied it with his hand as he walked through.

'Sach come inside,' the elder of the two women said assuredly 'Sleep it off, he can wait'

'Leave him alone!' The younger one wailed. She hid behind the bigger woman whilst she screeched aggressively. 'You've just got back and started already.'

The man stomped out of the third stall stumbling back towards the second stall. He hissed at the women in defiance before grabbing the gate to steady him. He was drunk. He casually pushed the gate open and walked in. The small boy's attempts to hide were futile.

FORTY-NINE

'Ail, you little maggot. Stand up and be a man.' He spat with venom. Easy for you to say to a small boy I thought. Try being so confident confronting me. Something stopped me from intervening despite the urge to help. I did not know where I was, how I got here or why this was happening. All I knew was I did not care much for the brutish bully. The foolishly courageous boy steadily unfolded himself from the ball he screwed himself into and steadily got to his feet, holding the pitchfork firmly in both hands. He held it across his body with the menacing three prongs pointing away from his aggressor.

The man clenched his fists as stepped toward the boy who instinctively stepped his left foot backs turning inwards. His stance was flawless exposing he knew how to fight. He spun the pitchfork round to aim the sharp spiked toward the man who paused taken back. The watching women gasped when the bully regained his confidence and rushed the brave child.

The inexperienced boy pointlessly jabbed the pitchfork at his advancing assailant but the seasoned soldier easily sidestepped the waning shot and punched the boy squarely on the chin. The blow took the youngster straight off his feet. He landed with a heavy thud three paces away. The boy was stunned but I saw a gritted determination in his eyes. The muscular man was drunk but surprisingly quick. He dashed toward the boy kicking him in the chest preventing the boy's attempts to sit up. The leather boot snapped the wooden handle of the pitchfork the boy tried to block the kick with but the weak wood gave little defence. The foot remained on the boy's chest as he slammed back onto the ground. The man knelt down on top of the child leaning with his body weight as if trying to cave in the lad's chest.

The man has his back to me hampering my view. A bone-tingling wail erupted from below. The mere scream of a boy's desperation possessed potential for a world-shattering war cry. The youngster's hands arced upwards toward the man's head but his assailant saw the glistening prongs of the pitchfork curving toward his face. The man grabbed the thin wrist twisting it vindictively. The boy dropped the pitchfork, which clattered to the floor. A high pitch squeal of pain and anguish reverberated through the small, dilapidated annex. The other hand moved with control and precision making the warrior ignore the threat.

The broken piece of handle sank deep into the man's beefy neck spurting a stream of bright red blood arcing across the stall with fatal ferocity. A weak guttural sound developed into a breathless choking cough as the brute slumped over the boy's shoulder. The women were wailing hysterically. The older of the two stood in the stalls entrance whilst the younger, maybe fourteen summers, rushed toward the bloody scene. The stall floor quickly flooded with glimmering red goo. The man died the instant the stake struck him. The boy scrambled back pushing with his feet to shove his way free from under the large man. I gasped as I looked into the boy's eyes. I looked into the same eyes last night. They were red raw, glistening with tears, giving the deep brown colour an endless appearance. The boy was   Ailbeart.

FIFTY

The young girl splashed into the gory scene thrusting her body into the man to help Ailbeart wriggle free. He stood up in a daze staring at the younger woman. The older woman stood in the gate with her hand over her mouth sobbing like a toddler who had scrapped their knee. She took a deep breath and began snivelling.

'Oh, Ailbeart! What have you done?' she said with very little emotion. 'Oh, Ailbeart. You stupid boy, come here.' The woman cautiously stepped forward trying to avoid the sludgy blood puddle gently ebbing across the stall floor like a coastal tide. The younger woman caped in blood stood up to challenge the older woman.

'Run Ail! Run,' she screamed. She kept her eyes on the older woman. Ailbeart leapt to his feet rushing toward the stall gate. The woman tried to grab him by the shoulder but her hand slipped from his blood slick skin as the boy dashed by. He headed for the door but stopped whilst his quick eyes darted around the stable before turning swiftly.

He headed toward the solid rear wall in a desperate panic. He kicked over a poorly stacked pile of buckets revealing a small hole before scurrying through and disappearing just as two other people ran through the stable doors.

The tall muscular man was probably twenty summers. He sprinted into the stall ignoring the congealing slick red blood on the floor. He knelt down beside the man but was faced the woman who tried to stop Ailbeart. I gasped again. I stared directly into Leyn's brutal eyes.

'Where is he? I will kill the little runt.' He said standing up.

'No Leyn. It wasn't his fault,' pleaded the youngest woman. She gently grabbed Leyn's hand but he quickly pulled his arm away.

'Not his fault,' he aggressively snapped at the girl. 'First, he splits our mother in two, drives our father to an early grave and now decapitates our brother?'

'I warned Sach to lay off the boy. I told him he would fight back one day. Not like this though. Not like this.' The woman who arrived with Leyn stood in the stall entrance next to the other woman.

'I'll murder the little bastard. Seorsachadh should have drowned the piss sodden maggot at birth.' He headed toward the door as he spoke. The woman he had entered with stepped in front of him but he scowled at her and gritted his teeth. 'Damn it woman! Don't try to stop me. Meadhan fetch for the returned men. Tell them to saddle up again. We have a murderer to kill.' The older of the two women that witnessed the atrocity sped away. She could not escape the terrible scene quickly enough.

'He's our brother Leyn and not at fault.' The woman blocking Leyn's path spoke assertively with an assuredness I have witnessed in few men, let alone a woman. Leyn barged past her and headed for the large door. The youngest woman ran to the other, embracing as they both started crying.

'I have no brothers. They are both dead,' Leyn spat as he walked out of the stable. I sat up sharply. Ailbeart and Leyn were several summers younger and Leyn had hair verifying I watched events of the past. This is impossible, what had Maoidh given me? I must stop Leyn from catching Ailbeart. I leapt to my feet but misjudged the width of the beam I perched. My left foot landed firmly but my right foot carried on past the beam into thin air hurling me toward the hard stone floor below. I closed my eyes. Is this how I die? I asked myself as I hurtled to the ground.

FIFTY-ONE

I flung open my eyes when I felt the ground beneath me. The world spun with nauseating ferocity. My head was throbbed and eyes stung as the harsh sunlight forced me to close them again. I blinked slowly allowing my eyes to adjust. Tears rolled down my cheeks. My stomach felt like it was trying to leap through my chest during sporadic spasms. I rolled over on all fours unable to gather my surroundings. The ground was soft and wet and I could make out a hazy green vision through my water-filled eyes. I was not in Ailbeart's Stable and found myself somewhere else again. I heaved.

The repulsive stench that emanated from the thick yellow bile caused me to heave further. The smell filled my nostrils stinging my inside as I took deep breaths. I stayed in that position until my vision focused. I crouched next to the stump I sat on last night and was back outside Coria. The atrocity I witnessed was too vivid in my suffering mind to be a dream or my imagination. The smells, the noises, the gory scene that unfolded before me was too real.

I sat back onto my knees straightening up but lurched forward as my stomach reeled and I began vomiting the sticky steaming bile again. With my stomach emptied and my throat burning, I collapsed back in an exhausted heap closing my eyes allowing my mind to drift back into the darkness.

The chilled water was refreshing after the shock of being drenched subsided. I gradually opened my eyes to the harsh sunlight to see the distorted figure of Ailbeart slowly come into focus. Not the boy Ailbeart, my friend. He stood before me with an empty pail in his hand. He wore a stern look on his strong face. I struggled to kneel as I tried to speak but my burning throat made it too painful to talk coherently. I coughed and spluttered a few unrecognisable words.

'How's the gut this morning?' The voice that spoke was calm and friendly. I felt rage bubble inside my fragile stomach. My head spun again forcing me to take a few deep breaths to calm down. Ailbeart stepped forward and grasped me under my left shoulder whilst Maoidh grasped the other. I saw Maoidh nod toward Ailbeart before they simultaneously thrust me forward. The force propelled me to my feet but I stumbled unable to control my legs. My left leg faltered and I dropped back to one knee.

'How is he going to march?' I heard Ailbeart ask Maoidh, 'he can't even bloody stand.' The world still spun but not at such a ferocious pace. I struggled to my feet taking deep breaths. The fresh morning air stung as it entered my chest. Maoidh wore a wide grin forcing me to suppress the urge to punch him in the face to wipe the mocking smirk away. In truth, I would have struggled to throw a punch. I stumbled forward clumsily, placing my hand on Ailbeart's arm to steady myself. My hand struck metal making me smile at the sight of his arm ring.

'So we march today?' I managed to ask with slight croakiness.

'Most brigades have gone Calum. Fert waits on you before he reports to Talorc. He told me where you were. A good night was it?' He chuckled to himself with a mocking tone.

'Report to Fert. Tell him I am on my way. I need to talk to Maoidh.' I tapped him affectionately on the arm and loosened my grip. I surprisingly stayed balanced. Ailbeart looked at me perplexed. He was one of my closest confidants and rarely excluded him but suddenly excluded him from everything. He smiled and nodded casually walking away toward the encampment. I was smiling as he walked away but stopped turning back toward Maoidh.

'What did you do last night? And how?' I spat the words with more spite and venom intended. Maoidh's shoulders tightened stunned with my ferocity. His face became stern but remained calm as he started walking toward the brigade. He spoke with a surprisingly soothing tone.

'I did nothing but calm a man in distress.'

'How did I see what I saw?' I snapped back not interested in his justification.

'That elixir clears the mind generating a deep and healing slumber. After I listened to your distraught rambling, I thought you needed a good rest. I certainly did.' He continued his explanation. 'The side effects will wane quickly leaving your body and mind stronger than before.' We ambled side my side. Anger and frustration built up inside my weakened body as he repeatedly misunderstood my questions. I felt anger and frustration build up inside my weakened body.

'How did you send me to a different place and time? What sort of magic is that potion?' I spoke as assertive as before but without the spite. Maoidh paused for a moment.

'You stayed there all night Calum? I am not a magician and wasn't even a good druid. Wherever your dream took your mind, your body remained here all night.' My head still throbbed and stomach churned but the ground had stopped moving from under my feet.

'What I saw was not true?' I asked in desperation. Maoidh carried on walking beside me considering the situation.

'The elixir clears the mind allowing you to envision things you struggle to understand or hide from. I didn't say what you saw was false just that you did not move.' He talked in a matter of fact manner and faced forward as we walked.

'I watched a young Ailbeart kill his brother. Leyn is his brother too.' I continued probing not satisfied with his answer.

'You can't see what you don't already know Calum. Your pieced together what you refused to see.' He turned and gave a coy smile as he spoke. Two cavalrymen dashed toward us with two ponies in tow. More questions burnt in my mind but Fert and Talorc interrupted.

'Hurry up, boy. You've made us late. If you can't handle your beer then don't drink.' Fert was understandably angry. The orders to march came at dawn, to my surprise it was already approaching midday. The army left us behind. Maoidh leapt into the saddle of a beautiful chestnut brown pony. She looked like a young foal stood next to Talorc's mighty war stallion. I struggled to pull myself into the saddle of the spotted grey and clicked my heels to follow the three men who already sped away.

    I still did not know if my intoxicated dream were true events. I must ask Ailbeart, I thought. If I did then I broke the agreement I accepted when he donned my troop leader arm ring but I had to know. It may cost me my friend and the loyalty of a great warrior but I had to know.

FIFTY-TWO

My entire body ached as if I had faced another gauntlet. I trundled beside my division on the pony as we marched at a gruelling pace for the first day without many pauses for respite. We needed to catch the rest of the army who charged determinedly toward Drest's desired stronghold. My men struggled along in the scorching summer sun whilst I rode on horseback. Guilt engulfed me but I would certainly slow the pace on foot. Fert took the pony back mid-afternoon as we approached the rear-guard of the army.

I joined my men leading from the front as we marched at a swift pace. My body felt fresh and revitalised and my wits returned. I could not asked Ailbeart about those events whilst we marched surrounded by other soldiers. It was not the time or place to discuss such matters and I would talk to him privately when the time was right. He did not seek after me during respite, which was unusual. I did not see much of Fert or Talorc either.

I irritated them by making the brigade last to march. They were livid with me as they sped away after bringing me the pony. Rumours spread around the troop that we were heading for this place or that. Airson heard we marched on Eta to punish King Eoppa for desertion. Rumours always buzz through an army, even the ridiculous ones. Everyone knew we marched on Pons Aelli because of Drest's obsession of its supremacy. I did not know our exact destination because Nechtan excluded me from the war councils. He probably replaced me as the recorder due to my promotion but I no longer felt as influential as before.

A chestnut pony swiftly appeared from behind as dusk began to set. The scorching sun already disappeared behind the rolling green hills on the horizon that shone with a deep orange glow. The horse slowed to a trot to walk alongside me. It was Talorc. The wealthier lords owned more than one horse each with an individual purpose. They swapped between them long campaigns keeping them fresh. His scouting horse was very quick and agile but struggled when she carried Talorc in his armour or his kit packs. She was his usual choice for marches and I was not surprised to see him riding her. He stayed beside me for half a league without saying a word before dismounting and leading the magnificent pony by her reins walking beside me.

'You are either a senseless incompetent traitor or a witless and naïve fool.' He spoke with a surprisingly calm tone considering the words he spoke. He walked beside me but faced forward. 'Think carefully before you respond because my patience with you is running thin.' Such harsh behaviour for being drunk was unexpected. I am rarely considered witless or naïve although I was young and naive in truth. 'You were warned to choose wisely Calum. You have promoted three men whose loyalties are as shadowy as yours.' I suddenly realised they were angry about my promotions. My mind raced into the darkness searching for reasons why. Talorc told me.

'Ailbeart?' Talorc stopped talking allowing me the opportunity for a defence.
I took a deep breath considering my reasons carefully.

'He is a talented, self-assured swordsman with a strategic mind. He proved himself brave, strong and capable in two assaults of Brit strongholds.' I spoke assertively confident with my selections.

'These traits are also good in a spy. You allowed him to make contact with a kinsman and left them alone with someone who could not speak their tongue. Are you part of his unit? Are your loyalties with the Brits?' He snapped the accusations with cruel aversion. I did not reply. He said to think carefully before I replied. I did.

'He is as loyal to our cause as I am and we will keep proving it despite your suspicion.' The constant doubting of my men and me was exasperating.

'He's a murderer, a scoundrel, and a foreigner. Test his loyalty Calum and prove your claim before you become suspect again. Do it soon.' As he spoke, he elegantly flung himself into the saddle and clicked his heels disappearing into the harsh orange sunset.

Fert appeared beside me moments later ordering my division to halt and set up an encampment.

'Rest well tonight,' he bellowed as my men bustled busily, 'Tomorrow we reach Pons Aelli.' He continued down the line halting each of his divisions but soon returned.

'You are a fool boy,' he stated as he sat next to me. I was lighting a fire whilst my troops created a triangular encampment. Most divisional encampments were square but I had only three troops. 'You are showing that you can lie, sneak, fight, and think. Great attributes if your loyalties are true. But you keep falling foul of their tricks too.' I listened but focused on my task not looking at him. He leant over and blew on my flint and steel. 'I know it's not you. I'm not convinced it is Ailbeart either. That farce of a fight with the Brit captain looked staged.' I continued to concentrate on the fire as it finally began to smoke. 'There is a traitor amongst us and Ailbeart is the prime suspect.'

'Why is there a traitor?' I snapped. I glared into his eyes with an anger that Talorc had ignited earlier. 'We are trying to find enemies within and not fighting the Brits.' Fert smiled at me with false warmth.

'There are always spies and men with false loyalty Calum. Do you have one man in your division that does not have a greater loyalty? They are all Talorc's men, or Nechtan's or Drest's. Not to mention loyalties within the other three kingdoms.' He was stating opinion as if it was fact. I felt like a child being taught a nonsensical lesson that the tutor thought invaluable. 'The pups were created from suspects to flush out spies. Most think it is Ailbeart.'

'They mistakenly decided I was the traitor at springs end and I've got the scars to prove it.' I snapped. Despite our phenomenal infiltrations into two walled towns, the hierarchy still distrusted our allegiances. My loyalty for my men developed into a bond I could not explain especially for the few that assaulted Luguvalium with me. Flames sparked into life. I sat back away from the blaze carefully placing my flint and steel back into my kit bag. Muir approached from behind and sat down.

'My troops sorted Cal. I've sent three men into that nook of trees, rabbiting.' He pointed to a small cluster of trees with bushes running along one side like a small hedge. It was infested with rabbits and I was famished. Fert looked down at the grass flicking a daisy head like a child at play. We did not speak further on the spy issue but I knew the problem would not go away. As Talorc had said, it was up to me to prove there were no false loyalties. I must and sooner rather than later.

FIFTY-THREE

I opened my eyes quickly as I heard a twig snap close by in the black summer night. I sleep shallow and stir easily whilst encamped but someone crept through my men. The dull moon shone determinedly through the overcasting clouds directly above. I lay still but gripped my right hand around the dagger hilt which always slept by my side. I listened in the eerie silence but whatever woke me had stopped. The moonlight casts deceitful shadows as the animals of the night scurry around in the dark.

I closed my eyes again and loosened the grip on the dagger. I always slept with my dagger held loosely in my hand. A firm strike against my boot made me sit up grasping my dagger and bringing it in front of me. I was staring directly into the reddened and distressed eyes of Talorc. My daggers tip a mere inch from his nose.

'Walk with me.' He was not requesting. We would likely see fighting tomorrow, I did not want to be tired but my commander wanted me to accompany him, and I could not refuse. I put the knife by my side and reached for my leather boot. Talorc passed me my second boot before I had pulled the first on completely. I stood up slipping the dagger in the scabbard that ran alongside my boot and picked up my leather jerkin. The nights cooled as summer began to change into autumn. I did not want to be cold the eve of a battle.

Talorc carefully walked ahead of me creeping around my sleeping men. Some men stirred but turned over and drifted back to sleep quickly. I felt anxious about returning to Pons Aelli. My life changed immeasurably just a few months before reaching the formidable fortress. Talorc and I walked side by side toward the knoll where some of my men caught several hares as dusk set. Talorc did not say a word until we passed the first tree.

'My father is dead, your friend Murdoch too.' He spoke in a matter-of-fact tone with little emotion. His tender eyes gave away he had been crying. My chest felt heavy as if my heart turned into iron pulling it toward my stomach. Fert left for a war council shortly after warning me about Ailbeart but that was long before dusk set. We expected to reach Pons Aelli or an enemy force tomorrow and councils last longer before battle. I suspected it finished a while ago and Talorc struggled alone with his grief before finding me. I said nothing but kept walking beside him in silence.

'We should have gone back. We knew Luguvalium was besieged and should have gone back.' I could not focus. The Brits had bitten back. This changed tomorrow's plans. Luguvalium was in the hands of the Brits. These should have been my biggest concerns. Acair and Gazella clashed together as they both occupied my mind. My heart split the day I met Gazella. I had only ever had feelings for Acair before, but now I cared for two women. If one died, I could stop feeling guilty about the other. I realised what I was thinking and my guilt intensified.

Acair would have left with Ailean but Gazella stayed. Luguvalium is her home. She was a Brit but I doubted that would keep her from harm. The townsfolk welcomed the occupying army into the town demonstrating how poorly the Brit Romans treat their people. My concerns were of angelic smiles and the warming glow they gave. Talorc was deep in his own grief.

'If they were reinforced they would not have been defeated.' Talorc was in the dark despair of self-pity.

'How did Luguvalium fall?' I asked insensitively. I was more interested in the women inside rather than the town or soldiers.

'My father faced the Brits shield wall to shield wall. He broke through the Brit wall of five thousand men with less than two. They broke but a Brit lord rallied the retreating soldiers and regained control. The Scots broke and retreated into Luguvalium.' He gave a report as if addressing a war council repeating the exact words he had heard.

'I am returning to Luguvalium.' He stopped walking turning to face me. 'Join me.'
It was not a request. He was my Commander and if he gave the order, I would march with him. Yet he would have to get the permission from Nechtan, his Lord and I knew that would not happen. Talorc had little information and consoled himself privately, which puzzled me to the reason he bothered waking me in the midst of night. We were hours from attacking Pons Aelli.

'The pups go through the grate and let the rest of the brigade through the gate again.' He was thinking aloud rather than talking to me.

'It won't work.' I responded 'Murdoch would have repaired that grate by now.'

'I am king of Rheged and will avenge my father,' he continued. He was speaking aggressively with grief clouding his judgement. He breathed heavily and his shoulders were tight. 'I need to take Luguvalium back Calum. I don't know how.' He spoke with an innocent calmness now. 'All I know is I need your help.' I placed my hand on his shoulder reassuringly and looked into his distressed reddened eyes.

'I am without king or title. I pledge you my sword and allegiance. We will you take all of Rheged together, on two conditions.' I paused letting what I was saying sink in. 'I am released from my pledge when you control Rheged to return to Stratha Cluith and reclaim Dun Phris.'

'When we have taken Rheged I will support your claim to Dun Phris.' He was smiling as he spoke.

'Secondly, you let me go back to bed. I need sleep before we take Pons Aelli tomorrow. We do not discuss further plans until Nechtan has released you from the Pict army.' I was newly promoted to divisional master and had no right to speak to a prince, commander and king apparent in such a manner. I always spoke plainly, which is why authority would seek my advice so often. He nodded in agreement. We turned back toward the encampment.

I kept my arm on his nearest shoulder and he placed his arm along my back. He did not say a word as we walked back in an awkward embrace. I felt uncomfortable but he needed support. The weight of a foreign kingdom fell onto his shoulder and in turn, he had slammed it onto mine. I crawled back into my pit, closed my eyes pushing all thoughts of future battles and hastily made pledges out of my mind. Tomorrow would be another world changing day.

FIFTY-FOUR

A thin red line appeared on the horizon when I opened my eyes that seemed moments later. The days beginning approached. I rolled out of my pit still dressed from my midnight stroll with Talorc. I woke my three troop leaders before returning to pack my kit. Airson lit a fire from the remains of the wood from last night and water boiled. He knelt by the cauldron preparing salted fish whilst the stale bread soaked in water to make it easier to eat.

I noticed how frayed the edges of the small leather bag was as I stuffed my kit inside careful not to aggravate the numerous tears. My entire division need paying and my equipment needed replacing. I hoped I would plunder before days end, if I saw days end. I sat in front of the fire and ate the scraps of the meal Airson prepared. As master, my share would be the largest portion but it barely appeased my hunger.

I formed my division into the front of the cohort eager for the march to recommence. Talorc strolled along the line wearing his usual smile and looked awe-inspiring in his splendid suit of metal that glistened in the juvenile sun. The distressed Talorc from the night before had disappeared and replaced by his commander and future king guise. He nodded in greeting but spoke no words. He walked the length of his brigade every morning before riding to the front but we marched almost two leagues before he galloped past. It took longer than usual probably spending the time seeking out the captains, masters and leaders he wanted in his vengeful quest.

Suddenly feeling tricked, I pushed the thought out of my mind needing to focus on the events of today. I pledged my sword to an uncrowned king, bound to free a kingdom that had never been under Scot rule. My heart was as heavy as when I first heard the news about Murdoch's death. Flashes of Acair crept back into my mind. Her slick dark hair flowed eloquently to the small of her back. Her deep blue eyes that could keep you transfixed in a gaze for hours. Her innocent giggle after she had made an innuendo. The memory of Gazella's touch barged its way into my head. Her face reddening as bright as her hair as she lay under me, biting her bottom lip to hold back screams.

My thoughts had not been my own since springs end on that fateful day scouting toward Pons Aelli that sent my world into a frightful spin. Everything changed quickly. The dusty haze could not settle before something else sent my mind reeling again. We marched east across a meadow as my mind drifted back to the day my old life ended. A world of treachery, violence and bravado shattered my privileged infancy as I plunged into adulthood.

The lush green grass was not as long as neighbouring fields but shone with a richer green. My gaze kept returning to the small embankment that rolled the length of the northern edge. I stumbled to a halt as I recognised the meadow we stood in. The cloudy overcast day had pelted us with a relentless heavy rain. We marched at a quickened pace without the suns blistering heat bearing down. The sun suddenly blistered through the fading cloud. The moist grass shimmered, enriched with the blood-soaked mud that filled this land last time I was here.

My new life began in this field. With shoulders raised and chest pronounced, I took a deep breath continued on my new path. My division continued to march forcing me to quicken my pace and catch up. The quaint Romans wore the same tunics and armour marched in time. We moved as one unit but some men naturally stride further than others do. My breathing was heavy as I slid back into position next to Airson. He looked at me worryingly.

'Cramp,' I lied pointing to my lower leg. He smiled and faced ahead. My nostrils flared with the smell of death that still clung to the air. I could taste the dirty metallic residue that landed on my tongue. I heard the dying screams of men whispering in the wind. I saw my brother charging toward King Constantine II.

The majestic king was ageing and his grey hair was thinning on his head. His face wrinkled with the wear of regulating an empire. His reactions slowed but he turned and thrust his hunting spear upwards whilst dropping to one knee. The steel point ripped through my brother's eye and scraped the back of his skull. He stepped forward with the force of a warrior half his age. He had let go of the spear, propelling my brother two paces. He landed in his final resting place with a spear marking his grave.

My father was the second man over the embankment that day. He tried with desperation to reach my brother before it was too late. I saw him skilfully cut down two Brit warriors with natural ease. They fell without slowing his advance toward the high king. I witnessed my brother fall before turning to find a less prolific figure. I saw the back of the immense blonde giant. My stupidity of attacking such a man ended my battle that day.

I watched the shadows of men fighting that simple scuffle as I continued marching. It had not been a great battle of many armies, a chance encounter between a large hunting party and an inexperienced scouting party. To me, it was the battle to end all battles and the most horrific day I had ever had the displeasure to survive.

We were no more than two leagues away from Pons Aelli. I scouted the horizon expecting the towering walls to come into view as the sun passed directly above us. We reached the southeastern corner of the field that was my father's eternal resting place. The brigade ahead had already halted for lunch. I left this field the first time as a tired, battered and lonely child with fear and hatred in my heart. I walked from this place the second time as a leader of men, a proven warrior, and future hero. I once again vowed I would be a scourge upon these Brits.

FIFTY-FIVE

My heart skipped a beat. A splash of water spilt from my canteen as I jumped nervously. The rolling drumbeat erupted unexpectedly with fearsome savagery. Drest's vanguard brigade marched to the rhythm of the war drum. The offensive on Pons Aelli began.

Before the physical conflict came the battle of hearts and minds. I heard drums at feasts and tourneys throughout my childhood but never heard a malicious racket like this. These drummers were not here to entertain at a banquet or create tension as two combatants competed in a duel of skill or strength. They struck fear and doubt deep within the souls of the most seasoned and stern warriors. The noise was like the thunderous collapse of Formoria as the corrupt and sinful gods of spite and greed exploded back into the world.

We wanted our enemies to know we were coming and were not afraid, daring them to face us in the field of battle. It spread confidence through our ranks making our blood pump round our bodies in eager anticipation. Some kings and lords employed banner-men to let their adversaries know who came to kill them. Warriors seeing the banner of Drest the Brutal or Maol the Mauler quivered at the thought of facing champions of great reputation.

My father never employed banner-men saying he would rather put a sword, axe or pike in the hands of a man on a battlefield than a big stick with cloth blowing in the wind. My proud father told me soldiers knew if they were fighting him without needing to see a sign.

Our adversaries would turn to ale to strip them of fear

and gain the unparalleled courage needed to face a shield wall. It also rids the man of the keen sense of danger and drains him of his training and skill. We marched as the drumbeat thundered on numbering five thousand. The majority were foot soldiers and the first men on a field of battle. They saw the fear in the enemy's eyes, smell the alcohol on their breaths, and taste the sweat pouring from their brows as they charged toward them. The noble cavalry usually waited until the victory before venturing forward.

Every military leader adopts unique tactics and strategies. Some use missile launchers as the enemy infantry charge toward them. Others wait until the shield wall breaks and uses the archers pick out the retreating fugitives. Some place them amongst the ranks of their shield men to pick out any man displaying baubles of authority. Every army needs strong leaders, take them out and armies crumble. I know some warlords who have no missile launchers within their ranks.

The latest reports placed the majority of the Brit forces at Luguvalium. The numbers greatly differed in every report but the likelihood of meeting a force of equal our numbers was minimal. The Romans took all men of fighting age back to Rome leaving worn out veterans, untrained boys and militia to defend Briton. A traditional battle of horde versus horde would be too much. We had superior numbers, skill and experience to force our way over the walls. We would receive heavy losses but we remained the more likely victors.

I found myself wondering why Ceretic and Eoppa left the invading forces. We invaded unprotected land with guaranteed victory. If the coalition had broken and the truce annulled then Drest and Eochaid had a very different problem before winter arrived. Bryneich and Stratha Cluith bordered Briton cutting the kings adrift from their kingdoms. I realised if I was Ceretic or Eoppa I would be marching into Pictland and Dal Riada whilst their kings and armies were preoccupied south of the wall. A wave of uncertainty surged through my body.

FIFTY-SIX

We marched at a blistering pace aided by the clouds casting cooling shadows above us. The walls appeared on the horizon accelerating our speed further. The cavalry cantered steadily causing the foot soldiers into a brisk jog. Our thunderous clatter, the flags of legendary warriors, our display of speed and agility, it was all a display of bravado aimed at striking fear deep within the ranks of the men stood watching our approach. This was my first manoeuvre of this magnitude and was yet to taste the sourness of true battle. The audacity of our approach intended to spark confidence and believe in our own ranks too and it worked for me.

I was the son of Bruce Dun Phris. I was born a warrior and destined for greatness. Drest's army wheeled left forming a tight line shoulder to shoulder with shields overlapping. They did not form as tightly as a battle line but was still an intimidating sight. I called for my division to halt.

I stared at the walls of the notorious Pons Aelli stretching to the menacing grey clouds above. This was not a derelict fortress guarded by simple wooden palisades. I could make out small shadowy figures on the crowded wall. They must have increased the number of guards on the ramparts as a show of force when they heard our advance.

I stood beside Airson and Ailbeart and could not think of two better men to be fighting alongside in my first shield wall. I assumed it was Ailbeart's first shield wall as well, but in truth, I had never asked him. Airson faced many shield walls but now stood next to the men he had fought. I hoped it would not be the last time we fought alongside each other.

Eochaid's army wheeled right and began the tedious task of forming a line. The portcullis gate stood prominently in the middle of the wall across the lush green meadows. We stood on the crest of the hill that led to the town and was maybe half a league away. We watched as the grated gate lifted fully open revealing a darkened passageway into the walled town that was sinisterly inviting. Our drums beat our song of strength and we banged our swords or pikes against our shields. Some were screaming vicious taunts despite the watching guards not being able to hear them from the top of the walls.

A disciplined rank of soldiers appeared from the shadowy entrance. They wheeled right to form a line just in front of the walls. The awe-inspiring men marched out stepping at the same time, all wearing blood-red tunics with gold plated chest plates and gold cuirass with greaves. They were unified. I hoped they did not fight as gloriously as they looked. Four hundred Roman uniformed Brits stood in the shield locked, blood red and glistening gold wall. They stood undeterred from our superior numbers smashing their hilts against their steel shields thundering their sound across the plain. The smaller numbers of the Brits had performed the battle of hearts and mind efficiently. We matched every single Brit soldier in that wall with twelve Scots. I still feared the command to charge.

FIFTY-SEVEN

Drest, Eochaid and Talorc sped across the lush meadow to greet three Brits on horseback. Drest led our entourage with the two younger kings tucked in on his flanks in a tight arrow formation. It was customary to match an entourage with the same number of men and three Brits approached our lines revealing they knew not all four kings were present.

The leading Brit lord was a short stocky man with cropped grey hair and was clean-shaven, customary for Roman soldiers. He nodded in greeting to Drest but faced toward Talorc. My eyes transfixed on the Brit on my near side who sat on a gigantic black stallion at least seventeen hands tall. The towering burly frame of the blond brit monster that knocked me down at springs end made the horse look like a pony.

My men talked between themselves as the scene unfolded and I listened intently as the experienced veterans named our opposing lords. The oldest man was Lord Viopprimes of Lindum. The blonde man mountain was Magnus, Ealdorman of Pons Aelli. The third man was the one conversing with Talorc but the other horses blocked our view. Viopprimes' horse snorted and tossed her head as she stepped back. The horses were skittish with the inevitable electric tension in the air. I gasped.

Talorc was talking, or arguing, with Feris of Cario. Feris rode here after the infiltration of Cario and the red fort, which is why they expected us. Talorc spoke Brit allowing all three adversaries to understand his demands. It was customary to have an interpreter so Feris' replied in Scot. Feris spoke at least three languages. A pang of uneasiness ripped through my heart.

My father spoke several languages and travelled extensively but rarely faced battle despite being the most influential man at Ceretic's disposal. My father was a spymaster. The comparisons between my father and Feris were obvious as I watched the calm and assured captain negotiating with kings and lords being relaxed amongst the most powerful of men.

He fought aggressively with Ailbeart outside Cario with senseless rage and Ailbeart's combative style was different too. The contest appeared farcical and staged. I no longer felt as comfortable or safe as I had moments before with the men on my flanks. Airson I trusted.

Drest spat at the feet of Viopprimes stead before wheeling his horse around and galloping toward our lines. I was furious with Talorc after he branded one of my men as a murderer, a scoundrel and a foreigner. His words raced through my mind. I regretted not asking Ailbeart about my elixir triggered vision now. It explained the reason he fled Stratha Cluith as a boy but gave cause to be Welsh in allegiance. No one from Stratha Cluith or Pictland ever did anything for him.

His brother abused him and then they hunted him as a malicious murderer after he defended himself. Leyn surely followed him to Gwynedd with demands and threats but his Welsh family obviously gave him protection and shelter. He was alive. His skill with a sword and shield showed he had a better life in Gwynedd than in Stratha Cluith. It was odd he fled a life in Gwynedd to fight for a kingdom that exiled him. Nechtan could have executed him immediately but he still took the risk. My loyalty and friendship clouded my judgement.

I shuffled closer to ensure our shields were locked substantially enough to sustain a clash of iron and steel. Drest, Eochaid and Talorc returned. The kings wore grave expressions usual for Drest and Eochaid but Talorc rarely appeared concerned. Talorc offered safe passage for the garrison to abandon Pons Aelli. Feris' terms were for us to return to Pictland free from pursuit. They mentioned Pictland and not Scots as a collective telling us they knew the coalition failed. Both unacceptable terms instantly rejected. To offer a good deal suggested the opposing force feared defeat.

Viopprimes rode back to the wall disappearing through the open portcullis gate. Magnus and Feris walked closer to our superior army. Magnus wore a purple tunic underneath slick white metal plate armour. He shouted in defiance issuing a challenge to anyone to face him in single man combat. No one moved from our disciplined lines. Some men would be tempted because defeating a respectable and known fighter gave the victor instant reputation and prestige. Lowborn shields man could rise to lords with enough victories. I knew my father promoted Murdoch from troop leader directly to captain after defeating an Irish lord in single combat.

' … Piss sodden maggots and cowards.' Magnus finished his rant of insults. He grabbed his genitals and gestured himself toward us before he continued his barrage. 'Are you all gutless women and babes fresh from suckling your mother's teat?' The usual displays of bravado continued. Another part of the mind games before the true fighting began. Despite the desires for status, it would have been ludicrous for any Scot to accept his challenge. Our superiority was too great. Feris walked directly toward our line not shouting insults or threats but issued a single challenge.

'Ysbiwr, face me in single combat. Answer for your crimes.' He repeatedly bellowed the challenge as he walked closer.

'He is calling me Ysbiwr,' Ailbeart said with fear in his tone. 'I don't want to fight him Calum,' he said pleadingly as if the decision was mine. I spoke Welsh and knew Ysbiwr meant spy. Feris confirmed my suspicions. I was his superior so the decision was mine. I regret saying these final words before he stepped forward.

'Go Ysbiwr. Face him and answer for your crimes.' He gave no reply. Ailbeart stepped forward nervously and sauntered toward the confident looking captain.

FIFTY-EIGHT

Ailbeart's shoulders relaxed and head lifted higher with every step he took toward Feris. He knew his abilities as a skilled swordsman. Ailbeart feared no foe. Fighting a friend and his spymaster was a different situation. Feris glared at Ailbeart but walked backwards towards Magnus who fetched the horses and rode to meet him. They spoke briefly with Feris still facing Ailbeart. Magnus galloped back to Pons Aelli leading Feris' horse by the reins.

Feris strapped a small circular iron-rimmed shield to his left arm and gripped a short sword firmly in his right hand, angling the blade defensively. At fifteen paces away from Feris, the long wooden shield clattered to the ground after Ailbeart cut the strap. The shield covered a soldier from head to shin and was a formidable barricade. The edges curved inward allowing the shields to interlock in the wall. In single man combat, it was a burden so Ailbeart charged without it.

He wailed a defiant battle cry as he rushed toward Feris holding his longsword in both hands but he angled it too high. He usually fought well one on one but now acted erratically. I favoured him as a sparring partner because his fighting style changed trying to force a mistake. Fighting a single opponent is completely different to a shield wall or a frenzied melee. A cavalryman galloping past would not slay your assailant. An unseen arrow would not sail through the sky and lodge into the opponent's eye. Most men fall in battle by a strike they do not see.

When facing a lone soldier discipline and strategy was everything. One of Maol's lessons sprung into my mind as I watched my friend's irrational advance. Let the opponent defeat themselves. Fighting too aggressively overexerts the body leaving you fatigued and vulnerable. Ailbeart forgot this lesson but Feris remembered.

Ailbeart's sword slashed upwards as he rushed within striking distance. Feris slid his right foot across to steady himself before pushing the blade away with the full face of his shield. He followed through the turn bringing his left foot round pushing hard with his shield striking Ailbeart in the chest. Ailbeart stumbled back in the sodden mud. Ailbeart bought his long blade across his body as he managed to stay on his feet. Feris lunged forward in a desperate attack sensing his opponent was unbalance but Ailbeart reshuffled his feet to recover quickly. Ailbeart parried the lunge confidently as he stepped back into his natural fighting stance. Feris' front foot slid forward on the drenched grass.

Both men paused to check their stance. A metallic clash resonated across the luscious green plain as the blades collided during long arcing motions. They both tried to force the other combatant off balance matching each attack with an equal stroke. Ailbeart's hefty long sword being wielded with a two handed grip forced Feris to slide back after each impact. He continued his frenzied beat attack wielding his blade swiftly with aggression. Feris' short blade lacked the force to resist the rapid blows.

Feris remained on the balls of his feet keeping his stance despite sliding back. He turned his blade in shorter arcs to deflect Ailbeart's brutish swipes with ease. Ailbeart bought his blade back again but this time Feris pulled his sword back dropping to one knee to catch the force of Ailbeart's strike with his small iron shield. Ailbeart stepped forward after every strike forced Feris back to keep momentum and control. This time Feris caught the strike with his shield freeing his blade but Ailbeart stepped within striking distance.

Feris flung himself forward pushing off from his bent leg thrusting his shield against Ailbeart's sword. He plunged his sword forward aimed at Ailbeart's stomach. Ailbeart slid his left leg behind his right to face Feris side on. Ailbeart leant back slightly as the sword edge skimmed his leather jerkin.

Feris' thrust carried him too far forward. His front foot slid in the saturated ground underneath him sending him back to one knee. He instinctively bought his shield arm over his head as Ailbeart quickly shifted his weight slamming the sword down with frightful ferocity. Feris swivelled on the spot aiming his sword edge back toward Ailbeart's front leg.

Ailbeart bought his front leg back to avoid the strike but his arms remained extended. Feris stood up thrusting his body weight through his shield pushing Ailbeart's hefty longsword up whilst his feet were unbalanced. Ailbeart stumbled back with his sword held too high. Feris moved with speed and precision ensuring his feet held firm in the slippery sodden mud before striking toward Ailbeart. He swiftly manoeuvred his short blade from side to side ensuring Ailbeart was not given the opportunity to use the full length if his blade. Ailbeart could not wield his lengthy blade with Feris' at such close quarters. Ailbeart shuffled his feet backwards as he deflected the strikes of Feris' beat attack but could not regain his stance in the sopping sludge the ground had become.

His back foot slipped hurling him hard onto his back. As Ailbeart's shoulders hit the ground, he kicked his legs upwards allowing the momentum of the fall to carry his body backwards. I was in awe as Ailbeart's large body agilely rolled back as his legs flew over his head. The unintentional move paused Feris' frenzied assault. Ailbeart was on his knees with his heavy long sword was in his left hand angled away from his body. Feris lifted his sword as he stepped forward. Ailbeart's open chest invited Feris' final strike.

FIFTY-NINE

Ailbeart threw himself sideways onto the long summer green grass. His sword still gripped in his outstretched hand. He rolled down the slight incline they fought on heading back toward our lines. I later learnt of Feris' legendary reputation for swordplay amongst the Roman Empire. I knew Ailbeart's capabilities with a blade. Neither man fought well that day.

Feris advanced on Ailbeart's rolling body slicing his sword downward ripping up the lush grassy plain. Ailbeart's tactics gave him no awareness of his opponent's whereabouts or intentions. Feris' should thrust blade into the space just behind Ailbeart allowing him to roll into the fatal strike. Instead, he chased him across the meadow frantically slashing his sword with every stride. A childhood image flashed into my head.

The milkmaid erratically chased down rats from the cowshed using a broom, her feet, a pitchfork, whatever was closest at hand, by whacking the ground in front of them as they scurried away. We rushed down to the cowshed every morning to watch this hilarious spectacle. We offered to kill the rats for her but she flatly refused.

'If I wanted them killed I would do it myself. I just want them out of my shed,' was her daily reply. I missed aimless childhood days.

I watched a battle to the death that my friend was gracelessly losing. Ailbeart rolled at an animated pace with renewed purpose in his plight. Feris took three quick short steps forward and raised his blade vertical gripping the hilt with both hands. His blade glistened in the autumn sun as it plunged hard and fast toward Ailbeart's mid-drift. Feris checked himself as Ailbeart's roll faltered. He rolled over onto his back cumbersomely and straightened his arms above him as the blade tip plummeted toward his body.

Feris' destructive blade strike split through the wooden long shield burying the short sword up to the hilt. Ailbeart rolled once again yanking his shield as he went. The short sword ripped from Feris' hand. Feris' stumbled over Ailbeart's rolling body as his momentum carried him forward. Ailbeart rolled again but tumbled over his right shoulder releasing the long shield. Feris landed on his knees with no weapon. His round shield was still strapped to his left arm.

Ailbeart rolled just once more but angled his roll onto his right shoulder. He sliced his long sword inches above the grass as his left knee struck the ground. The sharp blade edge sliced through the little bit of flesh above Feris' ankle. Ailbeart let go of his sword but sprung to his feet with rejuvenated belief. Feris lurched forward with the unexpected pain that ripped through his ankle. Ailbeart's swift, powerful uppercut struck Feris under the chin lifting Feris off the ground as all of Ailbeart's brute strength surged through his jaw.

A ferocious roar erupted from our watching ranks as the glamorously armoured captain soared through the air. The clatter resonated across the plain as his metallic armour crashed into the damp soil. Feris lay still. Ailbeart took a stride forward leaning over to pick up his sword. Ailbeart's blade would slice across Feris' throat before he ever woke. Ailbeart stumbled to the right as he bent down clasping both hands to his stomach. He took a few short awkward strides before collapsing back into the muddy ground.

The victorious cheering turned into an eerie silence except for a few groans of concern. Ailbeart rolled his shoulders a few times in a feeble attempt to get back up before laying still. Dead still. Feris' blade pieced Ailbeart's stomach when it splintered through the long shield. A gut wound is likely to kill a man but never quickly. A fatal blow to the head or a chest wound usually cause instant death. A punctured stomach meant a long and painful wait for the darkness to ascend as blood gently seeps away slowly draining a man of life.

Neither warrior moved for an age. I looked around for a senior soldier to give an order but none came. An unwritten code of honour about single man contest and pre-battle etiquette specified no man intervened during these challenges but surely, this fight was over. I was eager to charge. We fiercely outnumbered the glistening Brit soldiers and the passageway portcullis remained wide open.

Feris rose to one knee and paused. I realised he was struggling to put weight on his shattered ankle. He stubbornly found his feet and stumbled toward Ailbeart's longsword. Ailbeart dropped it as he rose like a phoenix from the flame to punch Feris off his feet. Feris uncomfortably limped toward Ailbeart's lifeless body pausing as he placed weight on his left leg. He fought the urge to give into the pain and slump back to the ground. He raised the mighty longsword above his head as he stepped into striking distance of Ailbeart's lifeless body.

SIXTY

A war cry capable of curdling the blood of Gods' resonated across the rolling hills. A few fleeting moments passed before I realised that bone-chilling shriek filed with anguish was mine. It was the first time I used a war cry and its magnitude was fear provoking. I sprinted forward cutting the straps of my long shield as I raced toward my friend. I did not need to look around to know I was not the only man that broke our disciplined ranks but Muir was the only man ahead of me. I was quick and slight so soon thundered past him.

Feris looked up as the deafening noise erupted. A lone cavalryman galloped hastily toward him as he awkwardly inched back trying to stay up on his crushed ankle. Magnus' gigantic black stallion wheeled around Feris shielding him from my view. Feris struggled onto the back of the gigantic stead before it wheeled around and galloped back toward Pons Aelli. I carried on running. A pursuit of such a magnificent horse was futile but I was looking at the red and gold glistening line standing before me. I would take one hundred lives in recompense for my friends. The stallion thundered across the green meadow and disappeared through the gaping black hole.

The portcullis gate inexplicably remained wide open. Alarms started ringing in my head but I continued to race forward regardless. The Brit line held steady. Some soldiers hesitantly sidestepped or gave glancing stares toward the open entrance into the fortress. The formation broke when the leading soldiers were roughly one hundred paces away. They should have broken earlier or stand and face us but they left it far too late. Men desperately filtered through the dark tunnel as the first Scots ripped through their rear ranks cutting them down from behind. I had unwittingly slowed my run and moved barely quicker than a brisk walk.

I gained my wits as Scots poured into the fortress as if the Brits ushered them along. The men on the walls fired arrows and javelin but for every man firing outwards, there was two facing in. The Portcullis had not moved. The winch should have released slamming the iron grid shut.

'Stop!' I screamed with sudden realisation. 'Halt. Get back. It's a trap.' I urged the warriors thundering past to stand fast. The iron grid grated an eerie screech as it slid down its housing. The spiked iron slats sliced into some warriors who were directly underneath the gate as it clattered shut. I looked behind at army line with sudden guilt and regret.

The charging soldiers came from Nechtan's army and the gaping hole in the Scots line was where Talorc's brigade had stood. Few men from the other armies ventured forward but the men around me had taken my lead. Screams and clattering reverberated from within the walled town as the Brits butchered soldiers like cows in a slaughterhouse. It was my fault.

I saw a magnificent chestnut horse galloping towards me. It charged toward me. I saw Drest's scowling stare but not his foot until it smashed me square in the face thrusting me back onto the ground. He leapt from his horse with ease. My body felt like it smashed through the ground into my undug grave as his metal-clad body landed on top of me. His metal fist flew toward my nose. Wet thick claret sprayed the air before me. This is the least you deserve, you fool, I thought.

SIXTY-ONE

We stood with locked shields, shoulder to shoulder, from dawn to dusk, for five days. Summer faded fast. The blistering heat subsided to reasonable warmth with a pleasant breeze. Occasionally the clouds opened to drench us with a refreshing shower. Men fatigued and resources became scarce. Cohorts took turns to eat, drink and sleep whilst the remaining army stood firm facing Pons Aelli. We besieged a town with plentiful resources, resting well whilst hidden by the wall.

Drest the Brutal was the last leader I expected of delaying an inevitable attack. His bizarre desire to capture Pons Aelli drove the Scots here. Now we weakened our strength and resolve whilst the Brits were well fed and rested. A sombre mood engulfed the encampment after we fell afoul of the well-executed trap. They baited us and we bit hard causing needless death.

Muir was the only man to move before me. The loyalty we had for each other was unbreakable. I was angry I doubted Ailbeart's oath. My swollen nose and split lip caused by Drest's boot and gloved fist subsided to a dull ache. Neadh stood beside me in Ailbeart's place. At roughly thirty summers, he was an experienced shield man and a former troop leader in Drest's army, but lost favour. Nechtan offered him a refigured opportunity amongst Talorc's newly formed brigade. His invaluable experience was ideal to lead Ailbeart's troop. I handed him the arm ring commanding to lead the troop. He calmly pushed it away back toward my chest.

'I will lead Ailbeart's troop whilst he recovers. I will not take a man's rightful place.' He spoke with a calming authority demonstrating I possess another natural leader within my ranks that I would need to call upon in the coming years. We lost fewer soldiers than I first feared. Any was too many trapped behind the iron grid as the gate slammed shut. It was the bravest and quickest I led to the slaughter. The gaps in the shield wall filled effectively enough. The Brits standing on the ramparts staring across the newly mudded plain would see we were still a formidable unified foe. The sun disappeared behind the forts casting a foreboding gloom across the meadow. Drest's Royal Guard Captain rode along the line issuing new orders.

'Fall your men out, Master. Rest well. We begin the wall breach at dawn,' he muttered abruptly. He slowed as he rode past but did not stop. I tried so hard for these men to accept me. My own king cast me aside and taken everything I knew away from me. A dark desire to prove my worth ignited inside me. My substantial role in vital victories this summer was indisputable. My instinctive reactions and naive stupidity threw doubt back into everyone's mind. I had marched to Pons Aelli as a hero because of Cario. The rejection and snubbing had resumed over the last few days.

The breach tomorrow morning gave me another opportunity to show my worth. Our food depleted yesterday. The little water we had I decided to leave until the morning to quench our thirst before the fighting began. We had no ale, mead or wine since Cario. Every Scot would face the wall sober without a drop of ale, mead or wine left throughout the army. Alcohol slows reactions and numbs the mind, which may give us the advantage. It also provides unparalleled courage in the face of an impending gruesome death.

Darkness spread across the meadow shielding the wall from sight. We laid our shields down gently and moved with caution. The noise of an army would be heard on the ramparts just a few hundred paces away. The thunderous racket reverberated across the empty plain as five thousand men noisily manoeuvred around the encampment. The noise was atrociously loud. Too much noise could give our intentions of an assault at dawn away to the unseen guards.

I lay my head upon my tattered and frayed leather kit bag and closed my weary eyes. Cheers of elation erupted around me. I sat up to discover the cause. One thousand soldiers marched into our rear-guard. The absurdity of armed soldiers advancing upon another army in the dark was apparent to me, but all I heard was joyous voices of men greeting returning kinsmen. I heard the distinctive sound of horse hooves thudding in the moist ground. I sat up as the captain rode into view. He grinned uncontrollably in a jubilant mood.

'King Eoppa has returned, boy so orders have changed. Move your division to the left flank and report to King Eoppa immediately.' He spoke giving plain instruction but with an exuberant glee in his tone. 'Congratulations. You lead the breach over the wall.'

SIXTY-TWO

The kings' council planned to kill me. I was unproven in battle but consistently chosen to lead infiltrations into fortresses. Each time I survived the fires of a raid they threw me straight back into another flame. It was no coincidence. I was capable yet expendable. I rolled out of my pit and pulled on my leather breeches before donning every item of clothing I possessed. It was the easiest way to carry it. I strapped my scabbard around my waist and threw my tattered kit sack over my shoulder. I felt the presence of someone stood behind me.

'Be the first on the wall, Cal, for both our sakes.' Talorc spoke jovially in a light-hearted manner but I knew he meant what he said. The unexpected glimmer of his full golden metal suit momentarily blinded me as I turned around. It was a dark sinister night as the rain thundered with hateful intensity. No moonshine or starlight broke through the thick grey cloud. The little light there was shimmered from Talorc. He seemingly glowed in the dark. His new helmet had a thick gold band running along the crown with a regal plume of green dyed feathers lining the top of his head. He dressed for battle although dawn was a night away. He regularly donned his armour stating he was learning to take its weight but he was not an egotistical man. Tonight held an air of arrogance unusual for Talorc.

'I don't seem to have much choice,' I replied unenthusiastically.

'I asked for your division to take a ladder Calum so you could be the first.' He answered with a smile.

'So now you're trying to kill me as well,' I said a little too bitterly.

'No Cal, I'm making you a hero. We have big plans remember.' He smiled but I sensed something irked him from his unusual mannerisms.

'What's happened?' I asked suddenly realising I was focusing on my self-pitying again.

'The three kings are besieging a wall each. I am not crowned so don't count, apparently.' His jovial tone vanished. He spoke with unusual bitterness. I knew Talorc was eager to avenge his father's death and claim the Kingdom of Rheged. 'My brigade is disbanded across the three armies.' He stood looking as regal as an uncrowned king could. His glistening golden gloves rested against his hips. It surprised me to discover Talorc had thrown me into the flames of the breach but suddenly realised why. Eoppa's unexpected arrival knocked him down the chain of command with a bitter bump. If his men successfully lead the charge then it reflects well on him. If we fail then he was not in command.

'Let's grab the rest of your stuff. I will walk with you.' He looked around for the rest of my kit as he spoke.

'I've got it all.' I responded, shuffling past him. I saw a smile appear back on his handsome face through his open face piece.

'Do you know why low ranked warriors fall in battle and commanders survive more often? Soldiers make fortunes through ransom.' He changed the subject. It had never occurred to me that poorer soldiers died more often than the richer. I did not know if this was true. I remembered how I knew Nechtan, as my father's prisoner. It suddenly made sense. Talorc would stand out shining like a rare jewel in a sea of ragged warriors tomorrow. Men would fight to wound and capture but not kill him.

'So?' I was missing the point of this conversation.

'A lord does not wear a leather jerkin. You don't even own a helmet. You've gotta get better armour and trinkets. Your position commands better attire.' We walked side by side toward Eoppa's men. They busily settled after a long march trying to rest before a hard breach and an unforgiving battle tomorrow. He was speaking informally. I nearly responded with a sly remark about his glow in the dark metal suit but was not in the mood for jesting.

'I'm a forsaken Lord. A penniless divisional master pledged to an uncrowned King of a foreign kingdom. I think owning a leather Jerkin is respectable.' I chuckled trying to lighten the sombre mood that engulfed me.

'You...,' Talorc snapped and then took a deep breath, '...are a usurped Lord with royal backing to reclaim your birth right. If you don't look and act like a lord then men will soon forget Calum. Remember who you are.' He nodded his head before rushing toward another soldier. He wore a simple tunic and tried to carry all his armour as well as the rest of his kit. Talorc dashed over to help when he noticed him struggling. He was a kind-hearted man who had a desire to be a king but lacked the ruthlessness needed to lead.

My men trudged behind me. I paused to allow some to catch up so the majority of my division reported to Eoppa's flank together. Two warriors walked in the opposite direction carrying a stretcher. The wounded man propped himself up on his elbows to look around.

'Halt!' I snapped the command. The two warriors stared at each other and then at me. They stopped and gently lowered the stretcher to the ground.

' How are you Ailbeart?' I asked gingerly. Guilt panged my heart for commanding him to fight Feris.

'Unfortunately I will live,' he jested with a smile. 'No battle for me tomorrow. Maoidh put some grass or something on the wound. Says it will help. Stings like a bitch though.'

'I'm sor....' I had to apologise for my actions. Ailbeart interrupted.

'No need Master,' he said assertively. 'Nechtan has discharged me so I return to Gwynedd, Know anything about this?'

'No!' I blurted a bit too aggressively. 'I will speak to him,' I promised. I could not lose a friend or warrior like Ailbeart. I had my quivering doubts but was now adamant he was not the mole in my division. If there was one I would find him, but it was not Ailbeart.

'No need Cal,' he spoke assertively but with a defeatist tone. 'I am not welcome, haven't been since the day I was born.' He looked down at the ground as he spoke.

'My sword is pledged to you but I ask you not to call upon it. Goodbye dearest friend.' With this, he gingerly waved his hand. Ailbeart winced as the warriors carrying the stretcher lifted him into the air surging pain through his healing stomach.

'Goodbye friend,' I said, little more than a whisper. I would lead my men onto the western wall to prove my worth and demand Ailbeart's return as the reward. Talorc's words surged back into the front of my mind. Remember who I am. Calum map Bruce Dun Phris, the Cur, raider of fortresses, and tomorrow I add Pons Aelli to that list.

SIXTY-THREE

The sinister night sky was as black as pitch. Drizzling showers continued throughout the night. Dark clouds casted gloomy shadows intensifying the nervous tension. The lightening blue sky signified daybreak was upon us although the sun was yet to appear on the horizon. Three flaming arrows streaked across the cobalt blue sky toward the north. My thumping heart pounded against my chest as if attempting to escape this miserable situation. Three responding arrows soared high directly above. Moments later another three flaming streaks were visible far to the east.

The signals appeared so far in the distance. All faction stood as close to the wall as we did. I looked to my flanks as the formation stumbled awkwardly forward. Ailbeart and Airson usually stood by my side and it felt strange looking downward. Tamhas and Sti wore the same belligerent grimace on their parallel faces. Slight for warriors but both possessed unimagined strength. They were quick, agile and daring, the perfect pair to follow me on the ladder.

Our unusual formation hampered our approach but we kept moving cumbersomely. The first missiles clattered against our thin wooden long shields that the rear rank held clumsily above our heads. The larger warriors, like Airson, normally stood in the front rank to use their raw power when the shield wall clashed and shoved against each other. Their brute strength kept the hefty shields resolutely above all three ranks protecting us from the sharpshooting archers and javelin throwers. The small circular shield held in front of my face impeded my view making me shift my head slightly to get a better look.

I naturally flinched as a well-aimed arrow ricocheted from the inner ridge of my shield. A gentle but menacing gust wafted onto my face as the missile flew by an inch from burying itself into my eye. Normally leading from the centre of my front rank, I placed myself as the second man from the right flank in this formation. The ladder would be raised from this position and I would be first to attempt that vital task.

We held the smaller circular shields as close to the tips of the long shields above our heads as possible. Our unprotected lower legs left inviting targets for the missile launchers high up on the wall. Better an arrow in the fleshy leg than in the eye. The long shields hindered our ascent whilst the circular shields would deflect the rapid onslaught of arrows and javelin inevitably launched toward us as we cautiously climbed the uncertain rungs.

The two outer posts of the poorly constructed ten pace long ladder were straight tree trunks. Five-ply papyrus rope held thick branch rungs securely in place. The rope was thick and awkward with several knots looking unable to hold weight. The greenest men carried the ladder in the middle rank. Those that faltered in battle before or yet to prove their worth and gain experience had the significant task during the wall assault. Cowardice spreads like wildfire and any man can be spooked when nothing but bloody, death and destruction is before them. I knew every man within that line could find the inner iron when needed. They met the unprotected onslaught of missiles whilst raising the ladder before thrusting their bodies against the bottom as the front rank perilously climbed.

The torrential onslaught of arrows and javelin persisted. We attacked the fortress on three sides stretching the garrison. They held the paramount advantage high and secure upon the wall during the initial assault. Many men would lose their lives today. Breached the wall to open the gates and the tables turn in our favour instantly.

Fert's last words of advice surged through my min. 'Reach

the base of the wall before breaking formation. My pounding heart ached within my chest as I pushed the nauseating dread deep into my stomach. This was the last place I wanted to be throwing up. A ladder sprung up to my far left not far in front of our position but I knew we were still too far away. Incapacitating doubt crept through my body darkening my mind. It is now or never. I took one more step, one more deep breath, one more fleeting thought that today would be my last.

'Now!'

SIXTY-FOUR

My shield lowered to my side as I sprang forward. I thrust my arms back and forth propelling ahead of my men. Sti and Tamhas dashed a pace ahead shoulder to shoulder. Ruadh tucked into me on my left flank whilst Airson sprinted directly behind holding the long shield with his large shoulders above all our heads. We broke into a smaller unit. My men wrapped themselves around me working as one. A secure glowing sensation surged inside forcing me to smile despite giving the order too early.

We reached the foot of the wall and knelt down on one knee. I turned to look behind. I planned to begin the manoeuvre roughly fifteen paces from the wall despite Fert's instruction. The erection of the ladder required space despite leaving men vulnerable. I lost my nerve and gave the order at about twenty-five paces, too soon.

The middle rank tried to sprint away at individual paces despite carrying the ladder impeding them. The barricade the ladder made trapped the rear rank behind. Those seasoned warriors angled their long shields offer the ailing middle rank and shoved into their backs urging them forward. It was an abysmal manoeuvre. I realised we required extensive practice on different tactics and manoeuvres but now was not the time to plan further than the next split moment.

The left flank reached the wall first and tried to place the curved edges on the sodden ground ripping it from the grips of the men at right end. I bellowed for them to stop. The right flank regained a firm hold and heaved the ladder in an arc motion whilst the central soldiers gawkily side stepped pushing the ladder upwards. The ladder swung in the air before clattering against the wall a pace short. The ladder straightened swiftly locking the curved edges into place. Soldiers stamped on the iron-reinforced bottom rung to sink it into the sodden soil.

I leapt to my feet pushing them aside throwing myself on the second rung before continually springing two rungs at a time. I felt Tamhas grab my leg instead of the trunk and felt reassured I was not alone. My left arm rested on my head with my elbow tucked into the shield as best I could. I leapt two-footed then leant into the ladder to help my balance as I let go with my free hand to regain a higher hold. I moved swiftly. I raced toward the grey clouds in the deep blue sky high above.

My archers fired their arrows toward the ramparts forcing the Brits to keep their heads down stopping them from pushing the ladder away from the wall. The flying missiles abruptly stopped indicating I was approaching the top of the wall. Ruadh's knew to stop his men firing when I reached the point of dismount. It was too risky to have arrows flying so close but also gave a clear signal to me. I meticulously planned every fragment of that assault but could not fathom a way of getting onto the wall from the ladder. My head dunked tightly into the shield blocking my view. Now the moment had come and I still had no notions.

I firmly gripped the ladder as it moved away from the wall slightly. My warriors below pushed hard. The sheer weight of soldiers clambering up the rungs thrust it back hard against the wall. I flinched expecting the ladder to splinter and crumble beneath me but the stricture possessed a concealed strength. The ladder came away from the wall a second and third time. I watched two scots to my left flail there limbs erratically as they fell toward the ground. Their ladder arced past my field of vision. I heard screams of pain and desperation before the thud as the ladder crashed to the ground. A triumphant cheer erupted upon the wall as more Brits rushed in my direction determined to thrust another ladder successfully from the wall. Move Calum move! I heard myself screaming in my head.

Sti's voice screamed in a desperate wail but I was unable to hear clearly. The missiles stopped clattering against my shield allowing an opportunity to peer round my shield to scan the situation. I stood on the second rung from the top but three men stood behind both trunks of the ladder. I heard counting. They worked out a coordinated shove would push the ladder past the point it needed to fall to the ground. I would not make it to the ground in time, leaving me a single option.

I leapt up when I heard a deep Brit voice yell two. My left leg bent as it landed on the top rung enabling me to pull my dagger from my boot scabbard with my right hand. There was no room to draw my short sword. The word three resonated between my ears. I straightened my left leg swiftly thrusting all my body weight forward. I focused on the repulsive grimace of a large man leaning over the wall anticipating my move. I swung my left arm toward his chin with my shield angled to strike the top of his neck.

The shield had not made contact before I turned my attention to the next foe stood in my path. My right foot landed on the top of the stone rampart as my shield collided with the first Brits neck. I pulled my right arm back across my body sending the second foe stumbling back as the sharp edge of my dagger glided across his throat. Blood trickled down his neck reminding me of how I came to possess this weapon. It pierced Leyn's neck in a similar way.

My shield strike thrust the man to my left backwards pushing two soldiers behind him onto the cold floor. A fourth Brit fell from the wall into the crowded courtyard below crushing his kin as he fell. I was thinking instinctively allowing my limbs to move freely but with purpose. The sound of wood striking the ground resonated behind me indicating the ladder had fallen. I was on a wall overcrowded by Brits baying for my blood alone. Calum map Bruce Dun Phris against three thousand Brit warriors. I smiled.

SIXTY-FIVE

Our next objective was to open the northern gates and lay any doubt of our certain victory to rest. The towers either side of the gate housed the winch mechanism. The swiftest of glances toward my distant left could be my last with adversaries stood on both flanks right. The plan changed. Survive.

The sharp tip of my dagger pierced a Brit warrior's jaw stood directly in front. I repositioned my shield angle to take the force of a kick from my left but the blow ripped the dagger from my grip leaving it lodged in the jawbone of the man in front of me. He fell back pushing another man from the wall. I deflected a second lacklustre kick easily forcing the assailant to slip back hindering the horde of Brits charging forward.

The dead Brit with my dagger jammed in his jaw laid entangled with the man whose throat I slit as I leapt onto the ramparts. Soldiers desperately tried pushing past the muddled men but they hindered each other's approach allowing me time to deal with the threat on my right. I pulled my shield back tight against my hip angled slightly downwards and left as I stepped forward with my right foot.

I pulled my sword out of its scabbard as a glistening object lunged toward my head. Quickly twisting my elbow to bring the sword across my body, the attacking sword's edge glanced down my blade striking the hilt guard. I thrust my elbow forward pushing the blade away but the edge nicked my chin as the soldier stepped through with his attack. I bought my leather-clad knee up striking him in the groin lurching him forward. My left arm flew upwards smashing my shield into his head and left shoulder forcing him to fall sideways hitting his head on the stone ramparts as he crashed to the floor in a heap. The cracking sound indicated he died on impact.

Fallen bodies littered the pace wide stone passageway hindering the Brits advance. Only two Brits could attack me at once but that was more than enough if they coordinated their assault. I could not defend against simultaneous attacks from opposing directions. The steady stream of assailants continued with each man seemingly waited his turn to charge the solitary opponent.

A sword from the left arced upwards trying to bend around me shield. My right arm deflected the strike arcing upwards with my blade as I struck up with my left knee but the Brit saw the manoeuvre and shifted in front of me. I tucked my shield in tight against my body as another warrior advanced from my right with an axe held above his head leaving his torso open. I swivelled my rest as I naturally drew my right arm back before plunging my sword tip into the axeman's chest. The Brit to my left manoeuvred around my shield slicing his blade toward my exposed torso. He slipped on the sludge oozing from the crack in a fallen comrades skull landing hard the clammy blood drenched stone floor.

The iron rim clanged against the stone rampart as I slammed my shield rim down hard and fast severing his ankle. I pulled my sword out of the axeman's chest. Wet claret misted the air as the fuller sprayed blood to aid the blades withdrawal as I pulled my sword from the axeman's chest.

A young lad stepped forward frantically swishing his short sword in an arced beat attack. I easily parried the repeated strikes swiping my blade efficiently to deflect the feeble attack. I pulled my shield tight against my hip as I lifted it from the fallen Brits leg but my focus was on the erratic attack to my right. A dark shadow suddenly cast over me from the left as I realised another soldier advanced. I flicked my sword up just before the blades clashed. The inexperienced soldier's eyes glazed with shock as the blade sliced through his throat ricocheting off his strong chin.

A large Brit with the stale stench of ale on his breath stepped within striking distance on my left. His raised mace plunged hard and fast toward my head. Freed from the attack on my right I turned my attention, instinctively throwing my shield arm up to catch the blow. The sheer power of the impact forced my left leg to buckle and my left arm numbed from fingertip to shoulder. He raised both hands above his head once again. He drove the spiked mace down aiming to force me through the dank stone floor. The metallic spikes of his mace glistened in the dawn sunlight inviting me to the after-world.

SIXTY-SIX

An iron clash resonating above my head dazed me but the spiked ball did not bury deep into my skull. The assailant slid backwards as my saviour leapt onto the ramparts. Muir angled his war axe above my head. He easily swivelled the axe with his strong arms driving the heavy head up toward the Brit slicing the sharp edge through my assailant's chin and splitting the man's face. The thick red ooze and pink slush steamed as his heads insides spilt onto the clammy stone ramparts after his lifeless body slumped to the floor.

Muir rested the blood-dripping axe head above his shoulder as he stepped forward to my right challenging another on rushing Brit. I regained my wits swivelling left on my knees before thrusting back onto my feet. Airson stepped onto the ramparts miraculously still gripping the long shield he held during the charge to the wall. My men replaced the fallen ladder with speed and efficiency to come to my aid.

Airson dropped to one knee concealed behind the long shield. Splinters flew into my face as I heard a woody thud. Airson stood up effortlessly swinging the large rectangular wooden shield to the left flinging two Brits over the wall. A horde of Brits stood on that wall but stopped advancing as my warriors rushed up the ladder baying for blood filling the space Airson's sweeping shield movement created.

I concentrated on my breathing as Maol taught but struggled to catch my breath. Every drop of air filling my lungs stung my chest and throat as I quickly exhaled. I knelt down and removed Nechtan's dagger from the Brit warriors jaw, closing his eyelids to cover the icy vacant stare. I became cool, calm and collected during that momentary pause. The Brits were less calm, and drunk

'Form line,' I bellowed as Ruadh appeared on the wall. Men leaping from the ladder onto the ramparts already formed a shield wall on my right flank under the guidance of Muir. I looked at Airson who nodded in response without giving the order. The length of the large shield covered the entire breadth of the passageway as he swung it round. Ruadh, Airson and I firmly leant our shoulders against the wooden blockade.

'Now!' I commanded hoping my men knew my plan. They did. We charged forward swiftly keeping our head and limbs tucked behind the shield. I planned to smash the wooden blockade into the disorganised Brits pushing them back until our makeshift wall came to a shuddering halt. We shoved the disarrayed warriors back hurtling many over the wall. A few shrewder soldiers leapt onto the parapet to attack us from the side but the men behind us unbalanced them effectively forcing them to fall.

The wall kept moving as we stepped over, onto and through the fallen Brits. The brits fell back onto the passageway knocking their own men off their feet allowing us to keep thrusting forward. The men behind us crouched stabbing their blades into the fallen men we stepped over ensuring every man we knocked down was dead. Our progress slowed as we pressed the Brits into a tighter and stronger obstruction. We stumbled on the fallen bodies. I gasped as I felt a blade edge slice the front of my lower leg and ricochet off my shinbone.

A raucous clamour surrounded us. Brawls raged on the wall both in front and behind. Other Scots had breached the wall. A wave of relief flowed through my body realising we did not fight alone on the wall. I was exhausted. Sweat poured from my brow stinging my eyes. The flesh wounds on my chin and leg were superficial but pain ripped through my fatigued body. I took a deep breath clearing my misting mind. The objective changed again, not just to survive but thrive upon this wall of death, decay and destruction.

SIXTY-SEVEN

We drove those Brits back as if we were the gracious Tuatha De gods expelling the vindictive Formorian's back into exile. They were the scourge of humanity making us the just and virtuous cure. Many druids have recounted to me the tale of how our world came to be.

The Gods once lived amongst us in our world in peaceful harmony. They were righteous and divine but some wanted to control us. A vicious war of Gods ensued, battle after battle. Bres the usurper overthrew Nuadh the King of the Gods and chopped off his hand. Lugh, Daghda and Oghma, resolute for vengeance, trapped the Formorian Gods by the sea. A colossal battle of darkness and holy righteousness raged but the Holy Triad triumphed.

Nuadh sent the malicious Formorian's through the earth, stone and fire banishing them to the underworld known as Formoria. The Tuatha De expected restored peace but Balor the Blighter, King of Formorian's, had turned humankind's hearts dark and sinful. His mortal followers were loyal to his cause.

Realising the war had just begun Nuadh created Mag Mell, a land for the virtuous gods amongst the clouds. He and the Triad of Heroes keep a watchful eye on the Formorian's whilst Dana, mother of us all, could guard woman and children against the wicked workings of Balor and his supporters.

The immortals left our world allowing humanity to destroy each other. I did not know if we fought for the grace of Nuadh or for Balor the blighter to be unleashed back into our realm. That day, I did not care. I was just and virtuous and sent those villainous Brits to their deaths.

SIXTY-EIGHT

The blockade stopped. The mass of Brits now shoving back matched our collective attempts. Airson looked across at me concerned. I nodded in response before taking a final deep breath.

'Ready…' I commanded the men around me with an order they had never heard is if they could read my mind. 'Now!'

Ruadh and I stepped back with our trailing led dragging our front foot along the floor. Airson launched the wooden the shield into the distant sky before it dropped into the heaving courtyard below. The men behind had not understood my idea but we managed to create enough space to allow Airson to remove the obstacle. The Brits fell forward still against the removed shield. I bought my shield arm up stepping forward to strike an unbalanced Brit. The man fell forward gasping for air as his the iron rim struck his throat crushing his windpipe under the force of the blow.

Ruadh stepped beside me driving his sword toward another Brit. The blade ripped through his eye socket lodging in his skull. The man fell back ripping Ruadh's sword from his grip. Another assailant saw Ruadh unarmed and leapt toward him with eager anticipation. My right arm already moved in an arcing burying the blade deep into the fleshy part of his chin. He fell over the man I killed with my shield blocking the path of other Brits behind him.

I yanked hard at the dagger embedded in the Brits jaw needing a greater effort than expected to pull it free. I stood up quickly as another Brit advanced upon me swinging my right arm up to bury the daggers blade in the man groin. The man with Ruadh's sword jammed into his face struck his head against the stone as he flew back. He placed his boot on his tranquil face and pulled back thrusting forward with his foot. The Brit warriors head pushed into the stone whilst Ruadh yanked his blade free. Ruadh put his foot down in a thick vile puddle of red and pink ooze. The repulsive odour clung in the air as the steam rose and dissipated into the clear blue sky.

I stepped forward to meet the charge of a big Brit with blood splattered over his face and matted in his neatly trimmed brown beard. He checked his stride but I read his feint and moved my circular iron shield across my body as he thrust his blade toward my stomach. My shield movement parried the blow efficiently as I buried my sharp-tipped dagger into his chest. I switched my feet as his powerful sword strike deflected from my shield forcing me back slightly.

Another man stepped forward aiming an overstretched kick toward my groin with the sole of his foot. I sidestepped with ease moving beside his straightened leg. Twisting my wrist, I buried the pointed tip into the fleshy bottom part of his chin. I felt the tip clink against the man's skull before I pulled my dagger free. I stepped back as my adversary fell gracelessly to the stone floor.

Neadh and Grannd stepped in front of me to defend the next wave of advancing Brit warriors. The towers rising high above the ramparts in the far distance appeared no closer than when we had begun. We needed to support the Scots I could heard breaching nearer the towers. I gave myself another new objective. Get to the next breach point. All we had to do is get to the next breach point.

SIXTY-NINE

We advanced quickly moving with a natural discipline the Brits could not match. A constant trickle of Brit soldiers attacked as individuals. Neadh and Grannd instigated the perfect manoeuvre. Airson and I stepped in front of them to challenge the next wave of assailants. Grannd dispatched of his foe quickly and stepped forward with Ruadh. We isolated the Brits. We fought each man individually but moved as one fluent and dynamic unit. We taught the Brits a valuable lesson that day. A lesson they carried into the after-world.

A big burly man with a matted black beard swore at me in Welsh as he stood before me. I realised we did not fight the Brits on the walls. These men were clad in chainmail, mismatched armour or leather not the Brit adopted the Roman uniform. He stepped with purpose.

I rushed him slicing my short sword toward his right shoulder hard and fast. He sidestepped easily running his blade down the edge of mine throwing his elbow upwards. He struck me in the face hurtling me off my feet. He stepped forward again thrusting his blade toward my chest. Grannd's kick caught him off guard. The Welshman fooled me easily without any real effort to feint displaying he was a natural swordsman. I felt relieved I would never face him again. Grannd bought him down by kicking his right knee from behind forcing him to the ground. Airson stepped beside me drawing his sword across the man's throat with a backhanded stroke. He gurgled and spat a warm mist of red spittle before collapsing to the ground.

I leant forward onto my knees lifting my arms in the air roaring in triumph. I held both arms high into the air intoxicated by bloodlust. I possessed a feeling of invincibility. I voiced my immortal strength as I bellowed with triumphant glee. A Brit soldier stepped forward angling his blade with proficiency. He advanced swiftly with a resolution to punish my egotism. I lowered my arms but realised it was too late.

My assailant became motionless like one of the perfect white statues the Romans had built. His eyes glazed over as he opened and closed his mouth like a caught salmon desperately trying to find air. He made a guttural sound as spittle's of blood spewed onto my face. A blade tip stuck out of his stomach glistening in the fresh day's sun. The glimmering tip disappeared allowing the man to drop to his knees. Maoidh stood in his place with a wide grin on his face and a bloodied blade in his hand. He nodded in greeting before turning back toward the way he came.

There were no Brits or Welsh, only Scots leaping onto the ramparts ready to join the brawl to find no assailants. We had taken the wall. My gaze turned to the town far below us. Every street, road and alleyway congested with warriors reminding me of the disciplinary display I had the misfortune to be a part of in Luguvalium. These were not drunk or hungover men dragged out of the taverns.

The matching gold and red uniforms sparkled in the sun beaming above. Dawn was a distant memory but the battle had hardly begun. Airson and Ruadh appeared beside me. I bent down to place my dagger in my boot scabbard. We stepped forward to join the long line of Scots awaiting their turn to help our advance toward the tower. Maoidh calmly stood in front of us. My mind raced. I was shattered, sore and suffering but there was much more suffering to endure that day.

SEVENTY

Bodies carpeted the stone ground high up on the wall. Dead, dying and wounded dishevelled leather clad Welshman. I recognised a face realising Scots rested upon this cold rock surface too. We threw the bodies over the wall as we went launching them over the inner parapet toward the awaiting warriors below. Ruadh and Grannd knelt down to shove a large unkempt man over the wall. A gory gash spliced open his stomach revealing his innards. I darted over and pushed Ruadh away but harder than intended. He stepped forward to retaliate but checked himself.

'He is Stratha Cluith. He rests here!' I demanded. Ruadh's face was stern with a dark glint in his eye. He unclenched his fists and rushed toward the next fallen body dragging it toward the side. In hindsight, the man was no longer Stratha Cluith. He was a creature of the after-world. The men following behind would push him off the ramparts anyway. The fallen comrade lived in Dun Phris. The sight of fallen men that I had known surged a spine tingling chill down my spine. Grannd looked at me perplexed before rushing to help Ruadh haul a fallen Brit soldier over the wall.

The tedious advance slowed. Enough Scots breached the wall ahead to give a welcome respite. We took the chance to recuperate some stamina for the fighting to come. Time is a rare entity in the midst of battle but I wanted to get back into the fray. The charge developed into a shoving contest as the static shield walls clashed.

I leapt onto the outer parapet and edged my way forward carefully. Stupidity but I needed to be closer to the action. I barged my way back onto the rampart three ranks back from the opposing shield wall. To balance on the wall edge that close to the enemy line was more than stupid. The tower now loomed high above me casting a dark sinister shadow from the refreshing autumn sun.

The Brits formed a shield wall on the edge of the platform that joined the tower, the staircase and the ramparts. I found myself locked into the third rank of Eoppa's shield wall heaving against the Brits. A despicable roar of defiance erupted in front of me making me look directly ahead. A large man with a shabby beard thrust his sword through the belly of the Scot ahead of me. His gaze fell onto mine but I held my glaring into his eyes. I lifted my knee high as I stepped forward allowing me to easily slip my dagger from my boot scabbard. The shield wall was moving forward now as the formed lines began to break.

I took another stride as I bought my arm across my body flicking my wrist upwards. The large Brit stepped back to withdraw his blade from the Scots stomach before stepping toward me spinning his blade round to lunge at me. Another Brit advancing on the breaking Scot line knocked into his arm forcing his strike to sail above my head. I ducked seeing the upward motion his sword arm made and stepped within touching distance. A thick spurt of deep red blood sprayed down my arm as I buried the blade into the man's flabby chin. He tried to bring his long blade round in an arcing motion but the other Brit had unbalanced him. He fell hard to the cold stone ground as I pulled my dagger out of his face.

I continued forward not breaking stride during my assault. The platform widened and I found myself in open space. Three shields locked together on my right but no Scot faced them. They stood a little lower and I realised they stood on a step. The Brit line retreated to the stairwell allowing the Scots to break through. Some of their warriors locked in the shoving battle of wall against wall could not break free and retreat. We surged forward overpowering the braver warriors who had stood and fought who now fell valiantly in a disorganised melee of death. More Scots rushed forward to fight on the carpet of the dead.

The archway entrance to the tower was in clear view and unguarded. Two young Scots desperately tugged at the wooden pegs of the winch. A young man dressed majestically in red and gold dashed toward the unsuspecting lads who focused in the geared mechanism that opened the portcullis gate. He moved quickly thrusting his blade toward the spine of one of the men.

'Behind!' My yell was too late. The blade buried deep into the spine of one of the Scots. The Roman uniformed Brit withdrew his blade from the Scots limp body already turning. I alerted him of my presence by shouting my warning but I still dashed forward with a ferocious pace. I swung my dagger toward the man's armpit aiming for a fault line in his superior armour. A chest plates defended well against most sword strokes but even the best armour has fault lines.

The seasoned Brit in his glistening Roman finery saw my obvious attack and shuffled his feet to face me side on stepping away from my sword strike. He instinctively smashed his elbow into my face instinctively brining his right arm back across his body in a swiping motion. I thrust my left shoulder forward struggling to keep my balance after the elbow strike. His sword glanced from the rim of my shield. Both arms unnaturally drooped to his side as they went limp. His dark vacant eyes stared through me before he dropped to his knees.

The second Scot from the winch wrenched his sword free from the small of the Brits back. The other young lad hunched in the corner of the archway. His eyes remained open but the deep glare showed his soul already departed. My saviour grabbed his friend by the elbow lifting his limp body up. He screamed and wailed for him to get up. I calmly moved over and gently shut his eyelids. Pulling the other man gently by the arm I asked for his help turning the winch.

We rushed across to the winch and pulled the pegs but it too stiff. This mechanism had two winched and without the other spinning as well, the gears were too difficult to force open.

Shaun Green

Another two men darted across to help as the brawl on the platform outside subsided. With one man on each peg, the winch finally began to give way. Slowly the mechanism began to shift.

SEVENTY-ONE

The gates screeched eerily as they rose. I left the other men to keep control of the winch before heading toward the steep stone steps leading to the town below. A flimsy wooden guardrail spanned the length of the platform and down the staircase.

The Brits shield wall curved around the small tunnel that led to the portcullis gate. A small curved shield wall locked in front of the dark passageway between the portcullis gate and the heaving courtyard. The entire Brits army locked tightly behind ready to fill any gaps the Scots created. I paused for a fleeting moment expecting to witness the onslaught of on rushing Scots. Drest's shield wall stood firm on the crest of the hill outside issuing a challenge to the naive Brits inside the impenetrable fortress. The void left behind from the charging army gave room for Eoppa and Eochaid to surge into trapping the Brits.

They patiently waited until the frenzied Scots rushed through the narrow arched passageway to clash into their tightly packed shields. The fallen bodies would create a wall of flesh, metal and wood hindering next wave of assailants. The Roman strategies of war stayed in Briton as had their discipline.

The Brits on the stairwell held their discipline too. Individual scots charged the three soldiers standing firm on the second step with shields tightly locked together rather than working as a unit. Two of Eoppa's men rushed the barricade. The faster man jumped aiming a kick at the fault line between the middle and right hand shields. The central soldier shifted his weight allowing the Scots foot to break through the shield wall colliding against the wooden edge of the long shield. A gloved hand gripped the man's thigh before he was hauled forwards disappearing into the crowded steps.

The second man rushed toward the man on my left holding his shield low and his sword angled too high. He clashed into the long wooden shield attempting to force the warrior back. The Brit waited until he shoved with his full body weight before thrusting his shield forward and left. The unbalanced Scot collided with the rickety wooden guardrail before toppling into the waiting army below.

That flimsy wooden rail on the inside staircase was an obvious weakness. Most Scots had cut the straps of their shields during the melee after breaching the wall. Some still gripped the small circular iron rimmed shields but created little defence for our legs in a clash of shield walls. The inner parapet formed a wall flanking the far side of the stairwell creating a formidable obstacle. The obvious flaw in the Brit barricade was the unprotected stairwell. I placed my dagger in my boot scabbard and scraped my short sword free.

'Wedge! Form Wedge!' I commanded sprinting to the centre of the platform. Ailean used the spearhead to break a shield wall in Luguvalium. A wedge was the best formation here too.

I felt the body weight of two larger men press hard against my shoulder blades. We moved with purpose toward the Brit closest to the stone parapet wall. The weight of men following tight behind reassured me. I drove toward the wall aiming to force the shield toward the dilapidated wooden bar that supported the left flank. I shoved the long shield with my short circular sword thrusting my shoulder through the drive.

I dropped my right-hand low sliding my short sword through the insignificant opening created too eager to force the gap between man and stone. The Brit soldier tucked tight behind his shield prepared for the attack on his vulnerable side. My intent was to force the opposing soldier to shuffle left and not to stab him.

The Brits soldier slammed his shield rim and body against the broadside of my probing blade. I tugged trying to free the blade but the Brit held it firm against the solid wall.
Men behind me thrust hard trying to force me through the shields with sheer brute strength. I pushed with my left shoulder trying to force the man I tussled to lose his footing but he stood strong. The usual pushing contest of most shield walls began once again.

I cursed realising Scots were spreading out to create a shield wall the length of the steps. The soldier beside me slumped to the ground whilst deep scarlet blood pulsed out of a gaping wound in the side of his belly. Something glistened in the fresh sunlight as a searing pain ripped through my ankle. An assailant's blade sliced through my leather boot and glanced off bone.

The man on my left must have moved his shield slightly to allow a soldier behind him to slide his blade along the stony ground. I swivelled on the balls of my feet sliding my shield left whilst still clashing against the long shield. The Brit tried to slam his shield back into position but my blocking shield prevented the gap from locking shut. I jerked forward with the sheer force of the collision. My preoccupied arms spread wide apart locked into position. My chest was wide open for a fatal strike and I had created my own demise. The Brit soldier's eyes glinted with glee realising my predicament.

SEVENTY-TWO

The Brit moved instinctively shunting his shield forward recreating the gap I had stopped from closing intent on burying his sword into my chest whilst I stood vulnerable.

I reacted quicker countering his strike the only way possible. I let go of my sword. The shield and wall trapped the blade rendering it useless Forcing me to free my hand. I threw a punch aimlessly, fist clenching as I swung my arm across my body. The sword glistened with menace as the Brit lunged forward but his slow motion allowed me to strike first. My fist struck his wrist forcing the blade to twist upward as I felt the small joint snap. The sword swung vertical. I threw my head back avoiding the unexpected change in trajectory.

I slid my shield hard and fast slamming the rim into the man's ribs before lifting the iron edge up into his exposed armpit. The Scot behind stepped beside me as I quickly shuffled left plunging his body weight against the long shield allowing me to make the necessary manoeuvre. The force of my shield blow forced the Brit back slightly giving me enough room to step into the opening.

I was amongst the Brits shield walls first rank but unarmed. I tucked my shoulder into my shield as I leant fiercely into the unbalanced soldier forcing him back against the second rank shields. Each step dropped several inches. The Brits placed their long shields on the ground pushing hard against the stone step creating a strong rigid barricade. I grappled the Brit pushing with my body weight as if trying to crush him to death.

The shield we rested against slid up above the step holding it in place. The weight of the Brit and me forced the shield to arc up as we unbalanced the shield man flicking us over his head. I flew high above the Brit horde that stood on the steep steps. My exhausted body collided against heads, helmets and shield rims as I ricocheted through several ranks of Brits standing on the stairwell.

An erroneous sense of security surged through me as my body struck the cold stone ground with a painful thud. The soldiers on the crowded steps shoved and kicked me further down the steps pushing me out of their way. The lack of solidarity baffled me. They took me for an ally, or their blades would have driven through my tumbling body, yet they hurled me down the cold stairs discarding a fallen comrade.

A throbbing sensation ripped through my shoulder as I came to a halt with a jerk. My shield caught on a wooden post holding up the flimsy guardrail running alongside the staircase. Pain ripped up my arm and surged through my chest when I slid off the stone step to find myself dangling from the post.

My shield straps wrapped around my forearm and wrist held firm. I reached up above my head with my free hand to try to grab the thin leather strap that ripped through my skin. The sweat lathered leather slipped through my fingertips twice as I failed to get a stable grip. I slipped back to dangling from the wooden bannister. I took a deep breath before thrusting up one final time, desperately needing to free myself as the leather broke my skin. My nails dug into my skin as I clutched my fingers around the thin leather straps before I yanked. Snap!

My shield flung into the distance as I fell to the stone courtyard below. My feet struck an upturned wooden shield but I continued to fall landing on my back on the curved wood. I fell no more than two paces before colliding with the shield, which swiftly lowered to the ground. Six blades rested above vulnerable parts of my body. Any of those strikes would be fatal. My head spun after tumbling down the unforgiving stone steps.

'Friend or foe?' a large warrior dressed in the majestic gold and red uniform calmly asked in Brit. I paused. The dark dread drifted into my mind causing that incapacitating doubt.

'Friend or foe?' this time he barked a command. I was out of breath and tired so closed my eyes to drift into the darkness. Another voice spoke in Welsh.

'Answer him. Say anything,' the Welshman shrieked with desperation.

'I don't understand. I am Welsh,' I pleaded. The men stood staring at me. They were all dressed in the adopted Roman uniform except one. Their swords remained menacingly hovered toward me.

'Who are you fighting for?' the sixth man at the bottom of the shield asked in Welsh. He was clad from head to foot in leather with long matted hair and a shabby beard. I did not know whom I dealt with and needed to be astute. Think, Calum, think!

'I am a man of Powys. I fight for Prince Vortigern.' I used my limited knowledge of the Welsh hierarchy desperately hoping I was not stating an obvious lie. Any man that knew these men would sense my false story.

The Welshman smiled. He lowered his sword and used his small circular shield to lower the Brits soldier's sword standing to his left. He nodded at the Brits gesturing them to lower their blades. The Brits turned to face the direction the gate as the weapons lowered. The Welshman lowered his sword arm and I grabbed his wrist. He helped me up and then patted me on the back.

'Ready to go again?' He asked nodding toward the passageway at the front of the congested courtyard. Brits began charging through the archway leading to the lush green meadow. Soon that meadow would turn into a swamp of mud, blood and sweat. I stood amongst the enemy as they headed toward my army. We would win because the Brits fell for Drest's trap.

SEVENTY-THREE

The congested square instantly emptied of soldiers. For every man rushing through the archway another waited in the side streets and passageways to fill the void. The adrenaline of the crowd swept forward taking me with them. I moved shoulder to shoulder with the Welshman. Eager soldiers jostled and shoved their way toward the dark sinister archway, focusing on the route toward battle and anticipating glory. Impending death lay in their path.

I shuffled backwards as another leather-clad soldier pushed between the Welshman and me taking the chance to rid myself of my unwanted companion. An onrush of Welsh soldiers blocked us from each other's view as I shuffled back.

Eochaid's men fought high up on the eastern wall making slow progress still a considerable distance from the widening platform by the tower and staircase. Eoppa's men enjoyed greater success continuing to push the Brits down the staircase with ferocity. The vacuum of space suddenly around me felt erroneous as I glanced in every direction. I took in all the information that was flooding into my clearing mind.

The soldiers on the western staircase abandoned it quickly with military precision. The infiltrators charged along the parapet flooding the platform before racing down the staircase. Eochaid's men forcing their way down the stone steps gained vast ground in hardly any time at all moving with rapid velocity. The Brits retreated clinically and effectively with a planned and practiced manoeuvre losing significant ground but moving with purpose.

Well over one thousand soldiers erupted through the

darkened archway into Drest's killing ground to clash shield wall with shield wall. The enormous courtyard stood empty. I stared ahead with dread darkening my soul as the retreating Brits formed a shield wall along the southern edge of the square. Those clever scoundrels allowed us to gain a false belief and our arrogance led us into a well-orchestrated trap.

Scots breached the walls and rush down the stone steps. The archway rammed with men formed up inside the tunnel a pace into the darkness trapping us inside the fortress. Iron and wood, sword and shield, gold and scarlet barricaded the streets of Pons Aelli. An urge to lead my men out of the death-pit made me step forward.

Two ranks of men stretched the entire length of this enlarged courtyard with their backs pressed against buildings. The streets and passageways bustled with hundreds of reinforcements patiently waiting to serve justice to the unwelcome invaders. A breach in front of a building blocked our own path but breaching into the streets released a vengeful army.

We fought and struggled our way into Pons Aelli with many good men losing their lives but it was easier than anticipated. We faced the expendable Welsh hordes becoming battle fatigued whilst the disciplined Roman Brits waited for their trap to close. Scots rushed into the awaiting death pit driven by bloodlust. Bloodlust takes over your mind and senses allowing you to conquer your fears and fight invincibly. Fear is a soldier's friend. Fear stops you from charging against a rested superior foe in an advantageous position.

Warriors rushed down the suddenly empty staircase charging toward the disciplined soldiers of gold and red. We attacked rapidly and fell quickly. The fallen bodies impeded the next wave of on-rushers creating an embankment of flesh and bone for the next Scots to conquer. We fought against strategic masterminds.

I took in a deep breath that stung my throat and lungs, quickly exhaling the metallic air filled with blood, salt and sweat that left a pungent aftertaste in my mouth. I stepped forward struggling against the urge to heave.

I leant down scraping my small dagger from the boot scabbard as I marched forward with purpose, heading toward the impenetrable barricade standing before me. My senses overloaded with information. Trust my body to act naturally and I survive. The trained Roman Brits executed their strategic trap with perfection as Scots flooded into the orchestrated killing ground throwing themselves onto swords and pikes.

The central Brit warriors did not watch the flanks were the battle raged. They were preoccupied with the suicidal approach of a young man in simple leather attire holding his head high and his shoulders rolled back demonstrating pure arrogance. The Scots flooded into the courtyard navigating the barricade of dead companions and quickly fell increasing the obstacle for the next Scots down the stairs. The Brits and Scots alike must have thought me mad with bloodlust as I prepared for my charge to a premature death.

SEVENTY-FOUR

'Form line.' The order resonated across the empty courtyard and through the congested streets. The deep echo bounced from the buildings filling Pons Aelli with hope and dread. The Brits were steadfast. Not one warrior stepped out of position or even faltered upon my approach. The trapped us inside these walls taking our blades out of the fight that raged in the outside plains.

I stopped twenty paces away from the formidable shield wall bellowed the command again. Scots stopped advancing on the wall at the bottom of the staircase and raced to the centre of the square. Soldiers jumped from halfway up the staircase to join me. My eyes transfixed before me made me unaware of how many warriors stood beside me but I did not care.

These elite well-trained troops stood before us for a reason. This Roman unit stood before us committed to crushing the inferior Scots and maintaining control of the streets of Pons Aelli. The elitist Brit soldiers were about to face the wrath of Calum the Cur.

I stepped forward with half strides but with purpose drawing a breath of relief as the men on my flanks stepped with me. My first shield wall in battle was against an obviously superior foe and I was leading the way with no shield and an eight-inch blade. Some Scots held the smaller circular shields and a few longer shields purposefully designed for wall charges dotted amongst the front rank, but not enough. A straight line was not the best formation but I felt the men beside me pull in tight with their shoulders touching mine and realised it was too late.

Now was not the time to worry about strategy and positions. A battle is dynamic. Things change quickly with every plan becoming obsolete upon the first contact. I spoke to the two men beside me. I did not bellow the command from the pit of my stomach but spoke so they would clearly hear.

'On my command, shoulder barge the man in front of you. Aim for the far top corners of the shield and strike together.' It was a simple order to understand but neither replied. I was young. My two arm rings dictated a little authority but not enough to lead a clash of armies.

'Barge!' I bought my short blade vertical, tip facing up, as I bellowed. My strange sword position gave limited defensive or offensive options in the heat of the conflict but I knew I intended a certain manoeuvre.

The two flanking soldiers struck the large bronze-rimmed red wooden shields. The Brits behind took the full force of the shove and reacted instinctively. The sun reflected from a golden breastplate that appeared in my view to my right. The Brit thrust his shield forward to clash into the Scot as he charged creating the small gap I needed.

My wrist twisted brining my small blade horizontal to the ground. I stepped forward sweeping my rear foot as I lunged. The glistening silver blade buried deep into Brits vulnerable armpit. The Scot to my right fell to the floor, cut down by the Brit to the left of his assailant. I twisted the blade from the Brits armpit and it pulled free.

An unexpected metal clash resonated inches from my nose. A Scot warrior stepped forward into the gap on my left flank and caught an arcing blade aimed toward my head with his sword. A sense of vulnerability surged through my mind. A soldier from the Brit second rank stepped forward lunging a pike. Another searing pain ripped through my thigh as the circular tip sliced through my leather trousers. It was a glancing blow with the pike continuing forward. I slide my blade edge across the man's throat as the force of his strike carried him across my path.

My body ached through exhaustion and fatigue as too many open wounds seeped out my lifeblood with every movement I took. The knowing feeling I was about to die surged from the pit of my stomach. Deep dread took over my mind but the feeling of certain doom suddenly different. I led this melee proving I was no coward. I was Calum map Bruce dun Phris, the Cur, raider of fortress, scavenger of the Scottish army and I would die a hero.

SEVENTY-FIVE

Death and destruction filled every sense. The bloodcurdling squeals of a man's final moment in this world broke the colossal din of metal clashes, wood splintering and flesh slicing apart. The expected eye-watering stench of blood, sweat and urine had an evil pungency that clung onto your nasal hairs. My nose, mouth and throat burnt with every desperate and raspy breath taken as my fatigued body grasped for the air it needed to continue. I was praying to any and every deity to help me endure this malevolent chaos and end this everlasting pandemonium.

My desperate strategy broke through the ranks of the Brit shield wall but a barricade of wattle and daub blocked our progress. Entire Brit cohorts crammed into the streets and passageways making it impossible to breach through. A chaotic brawl ensued in front of the blocking building. Scots turned the Brits on both flanks forcing our way through the thin line sideways on. Brits broke rank to peel round trying to trap the penetrating Scots. Scots still rushed from the ramparts to join the fracas that raged at the heart of the courtyard.

The autumn sun scorched directly above like a beacon showing the entire world where we were. I fought that day. I did not fight well, using the correct sword strike and holding stance. My mind remained three steps behind my body as I moved instinctively. The scots spread through the thin wall with rapid ferocity, like the destructive flow of a river bursting through its banks amidst a storm.

Both men flanking me during the charge fell and did not return to their feet. Their sacrifice would not be in vain. Every split moment etched another gory scene into my eternal memory. My left shoulder pressed tight against the wattle and daub wall with my back pressed firmly against another scot's back. I trained regular in this technique during sparring sessions. The soldier behind obviously knew of the unplanned manoeuvre.

I stepped forward toward an adversary and a split moment later, I felt the reassuring force of his body back against mine. He stepped forward and I made a conscious effort to shuffle back. We slowly moved west in the back rank of the shield wall. We drove into the gaps that appeared as Brit warriors broke rank.

A horrific screech erupted into the air. A large Brit warrior with his head down charged toward me. The sun reflected from his gold-plated helmet into my eyes dazing me. I felt a hand shove me in my back as fell forward, out of the way of the Brit charging like a trapped bear. The Brit warrior's legs sprawled out in front of me but his torso disappeared into the building behind. The Scot fighting back to back with me screamed in agony as the unmistakeable splatter of a blade being stabbed repeatedly into flesh resonated through the ringing in my ears.

I grabbed the Brits foot with my left hand as I pulled myself to my knees. I buried my blade through the fleshy part of his lower leg until the tip clanged against the stone courtyard below. I stabbed again just above the knee as the man turned awkwardly swinging a feeble punch toward my head. He missed his strike but turned his body so his torso was wide open. I bought my blade across my body by twisting my wrist and drove the tip toward the bottom of his metal breastplate. I plunged my dagger into the crease between his breastplate and his metal cuirass.

The man fell forward dragging my arm down with him forcing me to release my dagger as I struggled to my feet. The Scot who saved my life lay face down with a gooey puddle of blood congealing around him. His hacked leather jerkin mangled with blood, flesh and sinew. I stood inside the building that the Brit had drove my dead saviour through and gazed around the interior. The single room home obviously belonged to a servant.

The small wooden table had one chair beside it. A small hearth stood in the centre of the room with a small cauldron dangling from a coarsely made tripod. Tightly packed straw strewn against the eastern wall showed where an entire family slept. For a brief instant amongst all this carnage, I felt ashamed.

My highborn status gave me a carefree childhood. This family would work their fingers to the bone from dawn until dusk, children included, doing what they could to survive. We attacked their hometown desiring more power and prestige. The thought vanished from my mind as quickly as it erupted. The door flung open and a Brit soldier charged toward me.

I instinctively picked up the fire poke resting against the wooden table gripping it like a sword. The man chuckled as he charged toward me. I swung my left foot kicking the cauldron. I hit the small pot up and not toward him causing the Brit to catch the vessel as I stepped into striking range plunging the sharp poke into his left eye. The Brit soldiers hands clasped around the cauldron as he fell back against the hard mud floor. Two more Brits stood in the doorway. An entire horde waited in the passageway and they knew where I was.

SEVENTY-SIX

'Here! Boy!' The authoritative shout arose from behind me. I shuffled back a few steps knowing it was guileless to take my gaze from the soldiers. The Scot standing in the hole was not large but spoke with power and held his head high. Two rank rings on each arm showed he was a commander. He threw a pike toward me. I felt the smooth wood of the javelins shaft touch the palm of my hand before I closed my fingers around it firmly. I allowed the pike to follow its direction and stepped through taking a firm grip. The metallic spike clinked as it glanced off an advancing Brits cheekbone.

Several Scot warriors followed the commander into the small dwelling. I pulled the javelin back a few inches before sliding it into the Brits gaping mouth. His eyes glazed instantly as the sharp tip buried deep into his brain. He dropped to the floor in a lifeless heap. More Brits rushed through the door challenging the onrush of Scot warriors.

I kept my head up and eyes flicking around me as I stooped down to pick up the fallen Brits sword. I lost too many weapons that day. Weapon retention was something I needed to improve on. Battle moves quickly and a good warrior will hone in on any weakness or advantage they detect and not having a weapon was a major disadvantage.

An influx of Scot warriors charged into the hole in the building eager to press our advantage. War is not pretty. Bards sing of valiant warriors and their noble deeds securing victories. Vile, unforgiving rats took advantage of every opportunity instinctively without contemplating the risk of their own lives. They moved from victim to victim leaving them lying soulless on the ground. Scoundrels with an inert luckiness of survival secure victories in battle.

I, Calum the Cur, was a scoundrel. I closed my mind once again before stepping forward to face a large Brit. He spotted a young soldier stood observing this mayhem as a sign of my inferiority taking me to be cowardice and easy prey. He was wrong and fell to the edge of my blade, as did several others that rushed towards me in that chaotic melee. The brigade commander forced his way through the doorway and into the packed streets.

A young man with cropped black hair and a platted short beard leapt from the table kicking a large Brit soldier in the side of the head knocking him unceremoniously to the ground. He landed on his back next to him but my eyes locked onto the gaze of another Brit who had lifted his sword vertically. He thrust his sword down aiming at the stupid lad who flamboyantly leapt around like a child at play. I corrected my stance quickly and sliced my blade up in an arcing motion running the sharp blade edge across his face. His head split into two before he fell to his knees crashing face down into the sludgy mud floor.

I held out my hand and the young man grabbed my wrist. He thanked me before turning to face another onrushing assailant. He lunged awkwardly leaving his body wide open. The Brit stepped forward to end this man's colourful antics but I was quicker. I stepped beside the Brit as I threw an elbow up towards his chin. The Brit fell backwards under the force of the strike onto my blade that I arced toward his back.

I yanked my arm backwards as I felt his body weight crash into the sharp weapon to pull the blade free leaving a gaping wound in his lower back. The young black haired warrior disappeared through the doorway and into the havoc ensuing in the crowded street. I did not see him again that day but will never forget my first encounter with Drest the younger. I quickly followed him through the door into the cobbled street.

The space in the empty passageway was unexpected. An entire Brit brigade stood shoulder to shoulder in this street a moment before but no Brits remained. I stared into the distance in the direction of the southern gates. Scots ran down the street chasing the mass of Brits who retreated through the open gate and into the distance. I did not know what happened to turn the tides in our favour but it worked. We had Pons Aelli.

SEVENTY-SEVEN

The Brits defeated themselves. They executed a plan perfectly but imploded fearing its failure. The victorious Brit army from Luguvalium marched back to Pons Aelli. We besieged the fortress for days awaiting reinforcements not contemplating the Brits also had an army outside the walls. The soldiers cramped in the courtyard rushed out to assault Drest's shield wall after five thousand Brit soldiers appeared on the horizon. With Drest forced to turn to face the larger army, the waiting Brits charge from the fortress to assault his rear-guard.

They allowed us to breach the wall and enter the fortress planning to trap us inside the giant courtyard of the northern gate. After defeating Drest, the Brit army could return to the square and kill the remaining soldiers the Roman elite held confined. An innovative tactic generated by strategical masterminds. I hoped we remembered these lessons in the future.

The Brits slept all summer but it had been a planned hibernation allowing the bear to rest and plan. The plan would have worked except for the return of Ceretic. Ceretic appeared behind the Brits making the inexperienced Brit rear guard panic and fled south.

Muir led a charge to the corner platform on the rampart but held his shield wall there allowing the Welsh to remain in control of the winch mechanisms. They saw the fleeing Brits and fearing the battle was lost raised the southern gates, allowing the Brits inside the fortress to join the retreating force that fled south.

Scots rushed through the southern gates across the open meadows towards our panicking foe, racing into the peaceful plain unaware of the wild commotion resonating from the north. A large army charged directly toward us. To this day, I do not know why the fleeing Brits broke so easily because the frenzied soldiers outnumbered the entire Scot force, yet they ran. A Brit brigade of cavalry thundered past flicking up large tufts of mud and grass as their hoofs struck the softened ground. The Scot shield men stumbled in the newly created tufts. Panic flooded through my bones as the retreating army broke from battle as one unit and bolted directly toward us. My heart felt heavy as I watched a few stupid young Scots waste their lives challenging the fleeing panic-stricken warriors that bolted for safety. The frightened bear may flee but still have sharp claws and a mighty jaw with piercing teeth.

    I span on my heels as the first retreaters dashed past. My shoulders hunched up and I lowered my head for fear a Brit would recognise me, although unlikely. I forced my left leg to hobble to give a reason for falling behind in the fleeing unit. Excruciating pain ripped through my body in every direction as my head spun. I stumbled left to right rather than moving in a forward motion. The left side of my head throbbed as if it split in two and my brains cowered in the harsh sunlight. I tried shaking off the limp but the hobble had not been in pretence. Every stagger with my left leg sent a searing pain through my ankle as I felt bones crunch. My shoulders ached from sheer exhaustion of battle. My left ankle faltered and I fell to the ground face first struggling to keep my heavy eyelids open. My body was too exhausted to hold my hands out to steady my fall. I do not remember colliding with the ground. My battle was over before then.

SEVENTY-EIGHT

My cousin Ailean was the last man I expected to see as I opened my eyes. My back rested against a steep bank keeping me in a seated position. A small drainage ditch flowed at the bottom of the embankment that separated two meadows. Ailean the younger knelt in the gentle stream swilling out some sort of red cloth. I watched as he dropped the cloths into the water and a wave of deep crimson ebbed away spreading down the river. Rich crimson invaded the crisp clear water. My head spun as the nauseating realisation that it was my blood sprang into my mind. Ailean looked up and smiled when he saw my eyes open.

This was the first time I saw my dearest cousin since that fateful day I left with my father for my first raid. Everything changed. It felt like a lifetime ago that we sat by the hearth in my father's hall drinking our first wines together only it was last winter solstice. Only months passed but we were different men now. He wore simple but elegant metal armour indicating he was a warrior too. His father had usurped me as Ealdorman of Dun Phris and plotted to kill me. Ailean was the brother that Bruce refused to be.

He tried to stand up to Bruce the younger for me once, that ended up in us both black and bruised. My brother was a brute and a bully but he was my brother. A sharp stab of regret pierced the middle of my heart. Now my best friend waded through ankle deep water washing away the blood that ebbed from my wounds. Another person sat slightly above me on the embankment and just out of my peripheral vision. Daghda smiled as I turned my head and winced in pain.

'What have you done to yourself? You silly boy!' exclaimed Daghda affectionately. He spoke quietly and muffled but the sound reverberated as if echoing from close buildings despite sitting in the middle of an open plain.

'I don't think he did much of that,' remarked Ailean with a smirk on his chiselled face. 'He wouldn't have done such a great job. Can he even hear us?'
I frowned, which answered his question. He had never been the cleverest boy in the family. I stopped playing latrones with him a few winters ago. It was no longer a challenge and stopped being entertaining for either of us. He was better at dice. Daghda answered my questions soon enough. He clambered next to me and put a reassuring hand on my shoulder.

'Can you hear us clearly Calum?' he asked in a muffled tone.

'Well if you spoke loud and clear I would be able to hear you well. Stop fooling,' I responded sharper than intended. My entire body throbbed and I felt nauseous.

'You broke your foot, lost an ear and gained several nicely stitched wounds along your body. Somehow you survived despite dripping blood throughout Pons Aelli.' His response was not short but I could tell my tone had rifled him. I disrespected Daghda on more than one occasion and our blossoming relationship had hit a wall. I need Daghda for the future and know I need to reign in my short temper. 'Others need tending. You need to rest.' He got to his feet by pushing gently on my shoulder. I winced as a pain shot down my arm.

His words did not sink in. I looked around me realising the embankment was crowded and I was not the only soldier being treated. Ailean approached me and passed me the wet cloth. I allowed the water to flow through my fingers unsure where to place it. My ear burned, my shoulder throbbed, my chin ached and my ankle stung. Ailean took my hand and gently pressed it against my left ear. I lost an ear, not the sort of thing you drop out of your kit pack during a long march.

I felt invincible during that battle as the bloodlust flowed through my body with intensity. I was oblivious of the severity of my injuries until my body gave way in the meadow. Ailean sighed deeply lying down beside me. I turned my gaze to the sky above and noticed the sun had moved east. The sky was bright blue in patches but the fluffy white clouds dominated the skyline.

'How long was I out for?' I asked.
'Two nights, nothing much happened over the past few days, so you've not missed much. The wounded are tended and the dead piled in a pyre to be lit tomorrow night, I think.'
I nodded in response not knowing what I agreed to. We laid in silence for a few moments before Ailean spoke again

'You've made a formidable reputation, the Cur,' he mocked.

'Behave,' I responded.

'You've always had ambition.' It was a statement but I could sense the hundred hidden question lying deep within.

'I have no desire for Dun Phris at the moment Ailean.' I turned to face him, knowing what he was asking, 'but I cannot deny a desire to regain my rightful place.' I spoke truthfully but the words caught in my throat. My uncle tried to kill me for the same reason my cousin discussed this now. My felt heavy as I wondered we he spoke of such matters. 'Is your father ok?' I asked dreading the answer.

Ailean chuckled. 'The Ealdorman is safe and well. He missed the majority of the fighting like me. But he is getting old Cal, and I am his heir apparent.' He spoke in a seriousness that I rarely heard from my light-hearted cousin. I knew his desires but that was a problem for another day.

'Now,' he continued with his usual jovial tone 'you are requested for this afternoons proceeding. Let's get hobbling into town.' He chuckled childishly. He handed me a long thick branch and hooked an arm across my back. Daghda told him I needed to use the crutch and rest my left leg but I ignored this advice and continued to walk normally despite the agony that seared through my body.

Shaun Green

    I was requested. Today's war council would debrief the battle events. Occasionally senior captains received invited but rarely a young divisional master. I could not help but fear the worst as I struggled toward the walled town.

SEVENTY-NINE

I instantly noticed six chairs perched on the large dais at the furthest end of the crowded white hall opposite the southern gates. The long steps led to the raised dark wood plinth. The simple plain backed chairs had wooden arms either side. The silk ribbons dangling from the arms and the plush cushions in the seat made them appear majestic. The green and purple chairs took pride of place in the centre of the platform.

Two regal figures stood behind them casting dark shadows into the crowd. Eochaid and Eoppa sat on the blue and red silk decorated chairs either side. The chairs decorated in white and yellow sat empty. I struggled to associate the rightful lords for these chairs. Nechtan normally stood with the council upon the dais, as did Ceretic's two sons.

I hobbled in the hall with the aid of Ailean. We shuffled to the left of the large majestic door that was propped wide open before he lowered me to the ground with my back against the cold white wall. The crowd of standing commanders blocked my view but standing during a meeting likely to last into the night was not an option for me in my condition.

The gentle din of talk that filled the crowded hall came to an abrupt end. Ceretic and Drest stepped forward from their positions behind their thrones. The masterful voice that boomed across the hall was expected but the words spoken took my back.

'King Talorc of Rheged... King Aengus of Elmet...' Drest bellowed the unfamiliar titles with a pause between them. He introduced the new kings to the senior warriors of the Scot alliance. The simple display had a ceremonial feel to it despite being a very simple crowning. Aengus was an Ealdorman of Dal Riada and King Eochaid's eldest brother. A respectful pause held throughout the hall whilst the kings walked up the steps to take their seats. Drest cleared his throat before beginning an uncharacteristically lengthy speech. He usually spoke few words allowing actions to speak for him. The speech had been born from the mind of Ceretic, who favoured detailed briefings for his followers. I remembered sitting at a table during winter solstice a few years ago with my father. The deliciously aromatic banquet in front of us was stone cold before Ceretic finished his welcoming speech.

Drest thanked us for the selfless acts of bravery committed this campaign, definitely Ceretic's style. He promised abundant rewards as the invasion continued deep into Rheged and Elmet. The hall erupted into laughter when Drest made a joke about every man having a duty to sire as many future warriors as possible this winter.

Optimistic enthusiasm stitched together a serious tension that hung heavy in the air. Merit alone led to promotions of new kings, lords and captains. He implored us to support the movement of men across the kingdoms' borders. We were one people and needed to accept this.

Drest stopped speaking as Ceretic stepped forward. Drest's long speech had been enlightening enough. I feared darkness would fall before this council ended and my bottom was already numb sat upon the clammy cold stone.

'I will remain brief,' bellowed Ceretic in a jovial tone.

Laughter erupted once again from within the hall. Ceretic's lengthy speeches were legendary amongst these men.

'Our campaign this summer is to end.' The laughter extinguished instantly. An eerie silence filled the great hall.

'Commands will be filtered down regarding the location where your unit will winter. These are orders. You are not to return home. Families may join you in your designated garrisons. The conquest has just begun. Remain vigilant through this time of recuperation.'

He paused and cleared his throat. His speech, like Drest's, had been completely out of character. The Lords game of politics was heavily involved in this display.

'I will not be returning to these lands in conquest.' Gasps of shock and deep guttural sighs erupted and hung in the air as Ceretic cleared his throat again. These words stuck in his throat revealing they were words chosen by another.

'I am king of Stratha Cluith and will remain so until my timely death. My sons will lead my army next campaign.' There was another uncharacteristic pause.

'We have made progress this campaign gaining new strongholds and taking control of the wall.' I felt embarrassed. I made a substantial oversight during this campaign. The wall housed a stronghold mainly controlled by Roman allegiance Brits every few leagues. They were hotbeds for espionage and treason with no one's allegiance steadfast. To leave these uncontrolled would put a resilient complication in the middle of our newly conquered lands.

'My final contribution this campaign is an urge for clarity. As stated in Luguvalium, we are different kingdoms but one people. We need to support each other, not just as allies but friends and kin. The kingdoms remain separate!' He boomed that sentence like a command.

'But we are one army. We need a figurehead capable and able to make the tough calls, even in the face of hostility and resistance. I ask you all to support King Drest and the other kings as we move forward. We are on a path to exceed the great Roman Empire. Domination is our destiny.' He cleared his throat again as his words got harder to cough up the more he spoke. Ceretic was not an overly emotional man but I could sense the turmoil in him now.

'In Drest we trust!'

EIGHTY

'In Drest we Trust,' echoed through the Roman great hall. Ceretic and Drest slowly walked down the long wooden steps together. The council was over, as was this seasons fighting. Some men quickly scuttled out of the hall with heads low and their hearts heavy. Others frolicked through the door with a skip in their step. The summer battles were over unless the Brits decided to retaliate which was unlikely considering how they crumbled. They will rally against us again, but needed time to recuperate and winter would be here before then.

An eerie tension hung in the air like the stale stench that followed every army. I stayed sat down with my back pressed against the cold wall whilst the hall emptied. Some men were overjoyed with anticipation for next year's conquest. Others seemed anxious about the obvious shift in power. Good warriors gave their lives to prevent a Drest dominant coalition, Men mourned fallen comrades from days past with survivor's guilt etched on their faces as they ambled through the hall with shoulders slouched.

An uneasy sensation festered in the pit of my stomach but I was unaware of the cause. Anticipation and excitement are set deep within an army marching forward or preparing to defend but that mood dissipated before the hall was empty. Men deal with winter in different ways. I loved winter as a child because my father came home. He hosted plenty of feasts and our religious celebrations were wondrous. I was no longer the son of the Ealdorman of Dun Phris or a man of Stratha Cluith. This winter would be very different. A Bryneich soldier I conversed with whilst on watch a few weeks ago was one of the last to amble out of the hall.

His forlorn look on his face was evident he was in distress. He stared at me but glanced away quickly when our eyes locked. Winter was a time of rest for soldiers, a time for peace and celebration with loved ones. For those who had lost, it was a time of remembrance.

My father was always quieter at the beginning of winter. By the time mid-winters solstice arrived, he was as bubbly as ever. Leading the proceedings with vigour and his joy would last until springs end. A long-buried memory I had not dwelled upon for so long shot back into my mind.

EIGHTY-ONE

My mother died when I was a small boy, maybe five or six summers. The bitter autumn winds blew the darkening leaves from the trees. My uncle Ailean arranged for her ceremony and the pyre lit just two days after she passed. I stood in the bitter cold as a young Pefen lit the pitch soaked thatch. The warmth that erupted filled my aching heart with an immoral glow.

The flames of my mother's funeral pyre raged high into the deep dark starless sky. I shuffled closer to my bigger brother. He looked down at me with anger in his watery eyes. He sniggered as he walked to stand the other side of our nursemaid. I felt a reassuring hand on my little shoulder and turned to see my uncle Ailean with a sombre smile on his strong face.

He did not speak and watched the flames dance as they took my mother's body to the after-word. The gates crashed open with urgency. I heard horses gallop hard and fast as my father appeared on a majestic black horse. He galloped toward the burning pyre. Ailean let go of me and raced toward my father. The rest of my father's entourage stopped at the gates except one other rider. Murdoch. The horse did not slow. She suddenly reared up onto her hind legs as the realisation of my father's intent filled her with fear.

My father half leapt and half fell from the saddle landing unceremoniously a few paces from the base of the raging pyre. He clambered to his feet, his face bright red, his eyes bright with agony, tears flooding down his face. He screamed my mother's name as he stumbled toward the flames in his frightful state. Murdoch grabbed him by the shoulders trying to pull him away but my father was too strong. He pulled loose with apparent ease and scowled at Murdoch. Ailean dashed forward grabbing him by the waist, dragging him down to the ground.

The searing heat must have blistered their skin. Only a pace of dry muddy courtyard separated the clump of men and the raging flames that billowed smoke into the night sky. My two other uncles, Iacob and Filib, leapt from their horses. They dashed toward the disturbing scene and jumped onto the other men forcing my father to the ground. They lay on top of my father pinning him down as he sobbed and cried for his lost love. He screamed my mother's name and vowed to kill every man stopping him from reaching her.

My mother was no longer there, only charcoal remains of flesh and bones, her soul long departed. I took a quick glance at my brother. He was roughly nine summers old but already bigger than most boys three summers his senior. His fists clenched and his teeth gritted. I lost my mother that day, but my father and brother were never the same again either.

EIGHTY-TWO

I blinked a few times when I realised my thoughts drifted my attention again. A few stragglers remained in the hall discussing whatever needed discussing. Someone sat beside me. It annoyed me I allowed my mind to drift away and allow someone to approach without being aware but I knew who was there without looking. I laughed as the fleeting thought passed through my mind. The first act he committed as a newly announced King was to sit in the dirt with me.

'Glad you are alive, Cal,' Talorc spoke casually.

'Me too,' I replied, bursting into a fit of laughter. We sat back against the cold stonewall laughing loudly. A few stragglers talking in the great hall glanced over at us but we continued to laugh. A sense of emptiness engulfed me. The conquest paused despite achieving a fraction of our potential. Our intent was clear. We desired total domination.

Talorc thrust his hand into a little pocket in his tunic and pulled out another arm ring.

'Next campaign we will take every part of Rheged,' he spoke matter-of-factly with true belief in his tone. 'You will be by my side and become the hero of my army. Then we will challenge King Ceretic's decision about Dun Phris.' He paused as he handed me the glistening bronze ring. The pattern etched inside showed the triquetra symbol used by the sons of Erb. Talorc kept his father's emblem. Not fighting under my father's emblem of yellow crossed swords upon a black backing irked me but the symbol belonged to the ealdorman of Dun Phris. I took the arm ring expecting him tell me to choose wisely before I promoted a troop leader to form my cavalry unit. A full division was great reward for my endeavours.

'My Royal House Guard needs forming. Do you want to keep all your men Captain?' He stared at me with unusual seriousness causing me to pause whilst I took in what he said.

'Yes,' I replied eventually 'I will be honoured, my King.'

'Good. It was not a request.' He spoke whilst he stood up holding out his hand to assist me back onto my feet. 'Now the hard work begins. We march at first light. A lot of reshuffling is required. I have two divisional masters in mind but you may promote the other two from within. Everyone stays at Luguvalium during winter. Let us get these orders out.'

He yanked hard, practically pulling me clear off the ground. I landed heavy on my broken foot and winced instinctively. I leant heavier on my crutch more than I had on the way here.

The afternoon sky darkened although it was mid-afternoon. The dark foreboding clouds swept across the sky casting a gloomy shadow throughout the fragmented town. The townsfolk of Pons Aelli either fled or kept their distance from the invaders. They were more loyal than the people of Luguvalium were. I wondered if we would be as welcome in Luguvalium when we returned for winter. The town lit up as if a blaze had erupted from the fires of Formoria through the ground beneath our feet before the ear-splitting thunder rolled through the small streets. Dark storm clouds opened lashing heavy autumn rain down with vengeance.

I saw none of my men after I crept along the parapet during the assault. It irked me that I had not thought about their well-being until I saw Tamhas trudging through the drenched mud path.

'You fool.' His aggressive tone was unexpected. His shoulders were tense, eyes reddened and his cheery spark had vanished. A deep despairing void left behind. 'If he doesn't wake up, I will kill you!' He was screaming at me with his fists clenched. He thrust his left arm forward to strike me in the face. In no fit state to defend myself, I flinched and closed my eyes instinctively.

I quickly opened them again when there was no contact to see Tamhas' fist an inch from my nose. Talorc's mighty hand gripped around his wrist. Talorc shifted forward striking Tamhas behind the knee with his foot forcing him to slump to the ground. No spite was in the kick, just enough to get him to fall to one knee. Tamhas crumbled into a disarrayed heap with his chest heaving heavily as he sobbed. He looked up at me with darkness in his eyes.

'He tried to catch me and it's your fault.' He quickly sprang to his feet moving back out of striking distance from Talorc. He and his twin were both small men but with a hidden strength, both very agile and knew how to look after themselves. I rarely saw one twin without the other.

'Just because men will follow you into the fires of Formoria don't mean you should lead them there before running off on some mindless crusade.' He spat as he spoke. Flecks of spittle landed on my hand that rested on the top of my crutch. He shook his head as he stood before me. I wanted to reply but my wits deserted me. It pained me to see one of my closest companions in such distress. He spat at the floor as he turned and trudged away. My mouth flapped like a freshly caught salmon as I turned to Talorc. Talorc put a hand on my shoulder as he stepped back beside me.

'When you jumped from the ladder you unbalanced the weight. Tamhas could not make the leap. His brother tried to catch him as he fell.' He was speaking clearly but nothing made sense. 'Tamhas is fine. Sti is unconscious and the Druids are concerned.' He took a step forward. I began my hard hobble back toward my men. As he spoke, my heart ached with deep irresponsible regret.

'Crushed by your own twin. What a way die.'

EIGHTY-THREE

Heavy rain and gusting winds slowed our return to Luguvalium. Tension amongst the men was high as we marched back toward a home that was not our own. Every Rheged man fit and capable of duty returned to Luguvalium for the winter. Their families were to join them there. The only exception I was aware of was Tamhas. He returned to Cathures with Ceretic to help tend to his brother.

Moods began to lift as the high walls appeared on the horizon. Mine did anyway. It felt like I was going home with every stride I took. I led the vanguard on horseback the entire journey. My divisions rotated but the only men I allowed in front of me were our cavalry scouts. Talorc appeared beside me expectantly.

'Captain, let us ride in as if we rule the place,' he wore a jovial smile on his face. Five riders sped down that hillside galloping toward the foot of the hill that Luguvalium crowned. The King, a Druid, two Lords and I galloped across that sodden ground splashing through the swampy meadow. The portcullis gates were already open upon our approach.

Murdoch stood in front of a disciplined division of his garrison. The reports of his death were inaccurate. I smiled when I spotted him but did not stop. The other side of the entrance stood a precision of townsfolk awaiting our arrival. I kicked my heels into the flank of the horse and steered toward the very end of the line, peeling away from the other riders. I was only interested in one person stood in front of that town.

My heart fluttered and my stomach flipped as I leapt from the saddle and raced toward the beautiful Gazella, overcome with joy at her elegant beauty. Lost in those beautiful, warming, emerald green eyes, it did not occur to me she did not feel the same way. She wore no smile. I stepped within striking distance before I saw the small brass skillet in her right hand. The cold wet metal was surprisingly refreshing as it smashed into the left side of my face, where my ear was missing. The blow was not hard enough to cause injury but I slipped in the boggy mud and fell backwards.

'You owe my father a tab,' she growled.

'I know,' I said smiling back at her. 'I will pay.' This woman was beautiful, smart, and could take care of herself. My feelings for Acair will always remain strong but as I gazed at this feisty red-haired beauty I realised I was in love. She carefully placed both her hands upon her belly and said those sweet words that still fill me with delight.

'...and a dowry.'

We married three weeks later with a smaller affair than most weddings I have attended. For sweet, modest Gazella it was the grandest event of her life. Two Kings and half a great hall of lords watched her stroll down the aisle clinging onto the arm of a smartly dressed Lenis, the tavern keeper. All I cared about was the gorgeous woman who carried my child and our future.

Despite my protests, we married in the church before Daghda performed the right ceremony in the great hall. Gazella is Christian but practices very seldom of the scripture. The feast after rivalled anything my father hosted with lords and ealdorman from across the Scottish kingdoms. No Brit lords attended but that was not surprised me. The Brit romans segregated the townsfolk with stone and water. The isolation made our succession easier. I hope the rest of Rheged is just as disgruntled.

Most of my uncles and cousins attended. They avoided me during the summer campaign believing I was responsible for my father and brother's death. Ailean the younger stayed until after the winter solstice. His desires of Dun Phris will be a problem to address in future but that matter remained unspoken. My Uncle Ailean saw the ceremony but Acair had not travelled.

She was due to give birth and Ailean had travelled back the next day.

Murdoch becomes more of a nervous wreck with every passing moment. He fills his time dealing with every little detail of Luguvalium. He was lord of Luguvalium but with a resident king. Murdoch appointed Daghda as resident Druid, which was no surprise. Nechtan and Drest kept eyes and ears on both Luguvalium and Rheged's young King.

His appointment of a Christian priest, Yaalon, as administrator was surprising. The Briton's priest demanded to see Murdoch the very day after the Scot armies departed during the summer. Talorc was pleased with his choice on his return. He is astute. He wants as many Rheged men to support his claim to the throne as possible. Considering how poorly the Roman Brits seemed to treat the common-folk, it is probably a smart move. Most of Rheged's people follow the crucified God and Yaalon is young and ambitious. I will keep a close eye on this strange creature but he appears a great help to Murdoch and Talorc.

Murdoch has not appointed a garrison captain yet so those duties fall onto me. It must be awkward for Murdoch to have a resident king in a fortress he holds command over. The entire Scottish Kingdom of Rheged is in one walled town, although it is the largest fortress in the Kingdom.

The winter days grow longer and the bitter winds weaken. Spring is upon the horizon and orders are expected. The conquest of Rheged has only just begun. It will not be long before my sword is slick with Brit blood once again.

EIGHTY-FOUR

The busy summer ended quickly. The busy winter rapidly approaches its end. I am unsure why have spent my time writing this account but it gave an excuse for solitude that has been greatly needed these few months.

I kept my original division and been given three more. Fert returned to the services of his father in the new kingdom of Elmet but his cohort remains in Talorc's service. Roinn is his successor. The annoying divisional master is even more arrogant as a cohort captain. Muir and Ruadh are two of my divisional masters having proven capable more than once last campaign. Sti woke, yet he will never fight another battle. The force of his brother's fall damaged his spine and he has lost the use of his legs. I sent my condolences and doubled his wages with my messenger. Tamhas has not shown for training despite orders for his return.

Ailbeart returned to Gwynedd. I sent three messengers in the hope he would come back but all returned with no response. I have spoken with Talorc about the information leaks. The evidence is indisputable and a spy hides within our ranks somewhere. Ailbeart? I still doubt that very much. The crumbs lead to just five men, my men, but crumbs can be misplaced. I will be vigilant in the future.

Most of the new recruits are young boys and men. Some drafted from the Scottish kingdoms but a surprising amount from Luguvalium and the surrounding area of Rheged. My heart is heavy with the idea spies are amongst them but if we want to challenge Coelhan, the Brit king of Rheged, we need soldiers.

I stopped writing to wipe the hairs hiding sweet Gazella's

angelic face. She lies on the bed with her head resting on my lap. She sleeps more each day but Daghda says it is normal during pregnancy. Her belly swells with each passing moment and her beautiful face glimmers ever more.

I train my men, ensure they fulfil their duties, and write. Murdoch has ventured to Cathures to meet his Grandson. My heart leapt with both joy and annoyance as I heard his name. Bruce map Ailean Dun Phris. It is an honour that they have named their son after my father. He will share the name with my second son.

Last summer began a new era of a Scot empire. In Drest we trust, and we trust him to lead us to domination. A single campaign does not create an empire but true optimism spreads across all Scot kingdoms and deep into Rheged and Elmet. Therefore, I write to record our mighty futures humble beginnings.

My father always said the written word has unparalleled power and I am beginning to understand the type of man he truly was. I miss him, and Bruce. I am a man in my own right now. I am a soldier of Rheged and royal guard captain to King Talorc. The tale of Calum the Cur, usurped Ealdorman of Dun Phris, the Scot scoundrel, raider of Fortresses has only just begun...

...And it will be a glorious story to be told.

HISTORICAL NOTES

The Scots marched south, under the command of King Drest I, after the Romans abandoned Britannia. Calum's existence and the general storyline is a work of fiction. The historical accuracy of this book is very limited with artistic licence applied freely.

The cities and towns are all places recorded in history during this period. The place names are localised using the relevant language for that area. The Welsh cities are Welsh, the Scot locations are Scottish Gaelic and Briton fortresses are Latin. No location is geographically accurate. The rivers are referred by historical names, although these may not be time accurate. Their courses are not geographically accurate either.

The Kingdom names are from historical sources. Kingdoms are omitted whilst others are enlarged to allow better literary flow. Their locations are not geographically accurate, nor are their times of existence. Some Kingdoms were yet to be whilst neighbouring kingdoms had already swallowed others. Literary licence was used heavily throughout.

The kingdoms have been divided into the nation states that we know today, Briton (England), Scotland, Wales and Ireland. The notion that they would see each other as kin is unsupported in historical sources. Common folk living in this time would differentiate each other in a local manner. Drest and Ceretic are military leaders who lived around this period, both viewed as successful conquerors. Drest is most associated with the conquest that is the subject of this book. A power struggle would have occurred at the start of any large-scale coalition. Ceretic provided a suitable adversary to be in overall command.

Dawn of Dark Days

The Romans left decades before this tale begins, rather than the suggested period of years. The Romans took all the diplomats and soldiers, leaving Briton defenceless. There is no historical evidence of a coalition created by Constantine II, although history suggests he held the title of high king or Pendragon. He is the alleged grandfather of the mythical King Arthur. All conflict, battles and sieges created have no historical support.

Military units, ranks and uniforms have been generalised. There is no accuracy in attire, building materials, or ways of life. This story is not a supported representation of life and events during this period, just a fictionalised view of events.

Printed in Poland
by Amazon Fulfillment
Poland Sp. z o.o., Wrocław